I0731387

Food for Thought
(Gifts of the Heart)

by Lea Carter

Chapter 1

Danny patiently led Genevieve, a beautiful one-year-old German Shepherd, through the obstacle course for the third time that morning. She hesitated briefly at the tunnel challenge, then cleared it.

She stopped and looked up at him with wide, intelligent eyes.

Chuckling, he patted her lightly. "Good girl, Genevieve. Now, come on, you have to finish the whole course to get a reward."

"I never would've believed it." Chuck, Danny's right-hand man, clapped enthusiastically as Genevieve completed the entire course without a fumble.

Feeling her tugging at the leash, Danny unclipped it and let her run over to Chuck for some well-deserved love.

"Good girl," Chuck crooned, scratching under her chin while his other hand stroked her back, only marginally impeded by her harness. "You fooled me, didn't ya, girl?" Looking up at Danny, he shook his head. "From the day she was born, she was as silly as a goose and twice as flighty. Now, I'm starting to think she might actually make it as a hunting dog."

"Let's take her inside with the others." Danny watched his breath form into a white cloud, then dissipate.

"Think it's going to snow tonight?" Chuck asked, rising and signaling for Genevieve to follow.

She barked instead.

"What's gotten into you?" Chuck frowned as she lowered her chest toward the ground, raised her tail, and barked again.

"She wants her reward." Danny dug the rubber bone out with frozen fingers and whistled. Genevieve scampered over and daintily accepted it from his fingers.

"Smart girl." This time when Chuck signaled, she bounded ahead of them, past the other outbuildings, heading straight for the kennel. "And I almost sold her as a family pet. How'd you know?" He turned curious eyes to his boss.

"You could've been right." Danny smiled. There was no way to be sure with a dog, but training dogs was more than a livelihood to him. It was a passion. He loved watching each dog grow from a nervous pup into a strong, confident animal that performed tasks with ease.

He unzipped his vest as they entered the kennel. Half of the enclosures were empty, same as always this close to the holidays. The last class of service animals for the year graduated a few weeks ago in September and Genevieve's class of hunting dogs would be ready soon.

He took special orders from police departments around the four-states. His service animals were the first recommendations for many physicians in the area. Service dogs, hunting dogs, cattle dogs, detection dogs, he trained them all.

His eyes were drawn to one corner of the kennel, where a handful of middle-aged dogs quietly observed the indoor play area. Quite a few ex-military dogs were adopted by their handlers or near family, but there were always a few that went begging. Danny took as many as he could, and not because, as his accountant gleefully pointed out, 'it was a great tax write off.'

These dogs needed his help, the re-training that he hoped to give them. Life was serious business for a military dog. A slip-up could mean death for them, their handlers, and who knew how many others. And a lot of them needed help with the transition back to civilian life.

Squatting beside a kennel marked 'Caesar,' Danny held out his hand for the dog to sniff. The Belgian Shepherd raised his eyebrows and whined, but didn't lift his head from his paws.

"If he doesn't start eating," Chuck observed the still-full food bowl sadly, "he's going to get his wish."

Danny scowled. Caesar's handler died overseas. Caesar nearly died and now sported scars that no amount of grooming could fully conceal. And, though he hated to admit it, the wounds on Caesar's soul might never heal.

"I'm going to sleep out here tonight," he decided abruptly.

"What?" Chuck stared at him like he'd lost his mind.

"You heard me." Danny stomped off toward the main house, leaving Chuck to secure Genevieve and the dogs in the play area.

He was back shortly, toting a sleeping bag. Chuck was smart enough not to say anything else as Danny set up near Caesar's kennel.

He lay there, wide awake after lights' out, barely hearing the yips and barks coming from all around him. He'd lined up new owners for most of Caesar's 'classmates,' but this dog needed something special. *Someone* special.

His dad? Rolling onto his stomach, Danny stared at Caesar's dark kennel while he mulled the idea over.

Alec Fitzsimmons was the foreman at the Rockin' R, a relatively large working ranch in southwest Missouri. Caesar would have enough room there. Might learn a new job like herding the eccentric owner's prize dwarf something-or-others.

Running a hand over his face, Danny had to admit that there was plenty of space for an active dog here at his training center. Jobs, too. Everything from teaching pups how to be dogs on up to keeping him and Chuck company while they ran errands. But no, that wouldn't work. Danny didn't have the time that a dog like Caesar required. Couldn't lavish the love on him that just might restore his will to live.

Maybe his dad didn't, either, come to think of it. On the other hand, his dad was the very definition of alone. It had just been the two of them ever since Danny's mom died. Unless—a dog was just what he needed?

Well. Next week was Halloween. Nobody from Fireclay, the nearest town, would come out this far to trick-or-treat, but he usually participated in the trunk-or-treat at church. He'd have to wait until after that to drive out and talk with his dad about this. Friday would probably be best, since his dad usually let someone else handle everything but emergencies on the weekend.

Somewhat comforted that he at least had a plan now, Danny pillowed his head on his arms and finally fell asleep.

Meanwhile in Cadmia, four friends were wrapping up a movie night. Petite, honey-blond Noella was the youngest of the group and a fairly recent transplant from Prince Edward Island. Willowy Grace was the friend of a lifetime, and the most easy-going member of the group, in direct contradiction to her fiery red hair. Vivacious Harmony, running so hard to keep up with herself that few people could keep up with her; luckily for their little group, she also happened to be a die-hard silver screen fan. And Merry, a somewhat aloof ginger brunette who'd surprised them all by starting the movie nights a year ago.

"Alright, well," Merry nodded at the clock on the wall, the red glints in her gorgeous brown hair catching the light with her movement, "if I don't get home on time, I'll miss my appointment with the sandman."

"Mmm, the sandman." Harmony grinned, stretched by arching her back like a cat, then bounced up off the couch. "Y'know, he's never once gotten my order right?"

"Never?" Noella grinned as she positioned herself to hug her friends as they left. "No dreams about handsome, single billionaires for you?" They all laughed at that.

Hugs and well-wishes later, Noella stood at her door and waved as her friends walked to their cars. She'd hosted another successful movie night, the last for October. Which meant she had less than an hour to get ready for her business meeting. Because ten at night in Cadmia, Missouri was 1 PM in Australia. The next day.

Tonight they would be working for Netherland Transport. The company had built itself a solid base, but had bold plans for a merger. Before they could get things finalized, however, the management of both companies insisted on a complete digital security check—which was where she and her partner came in.

She mentally reviewed everything she knew about the company while she loaded the dishwasher and hurried through washing the large pot she'd used to fry in.

Her phone went off and she popped in her Bluetooth earpiece.

"Hé, alles goed?" She greeted her partner in Dutch. "Almost ready."

"Knowing you, you were ready yesterday," Peter snorted in his awesome Australian accent.

Noella grinned and wiped her hands. "Here I come." Tapping the power button on her laptop, she took her seat. "Did you decide where to start?"

"The weakest link is always the employees."

"Which means you have…" A new email alert popped up and she clicked on it.

"Passwords."

Noella shook her head at the satisfaction in Peter's voice. But he wasn't wrong. Planting a program into an email that was then opened by an employee was an easy way to circumvent even the securest program.

"I can't believe this many people fell for your phishing email." She was *still* scrolling down his list.

"The real question," a faint slurping sound came through, "is how many of these people have useful security levels."

She nodded even though Peter couldn't see her. "Race you."

Peter hooted. "Loser has to post a video of themselves singing a parody on their employee page."

"The usual stakes, then." Noella brought up

the target website. Started a screen recording. "Ready?" She flexed her fingers.

"Go!"

For the next hour, Noella dug into the site, exploiting every weakness she found. Occasionally, she heard Peter mutter in exasperation as he hit dead-ends with one after another of the stolen access points. Lucking into a coding error that gave her employee-only access, Noella bluffed her way past the last few roadblocks.

"I'm in."

"What?!" A thudding noise came through loud and clear, as if he'd hit his desk. "Unbelievable!"

"Believe it." Noella sent a screenshot. "I have complete access."

"You win," he huffed.

A notification came that he'd ended his recording and she shut hers off as well. "I can't wait to hear you singing 'The Ugly Bug Ball'."

"Ah, no. I don't recall saying anything about the winner getting to choose the song."

"True." Noella's fingers danced over the keys as she wrote up her report. "Next time."

"You're on. Next time, I'm going to win."

"Of course you will." She politely refrained from reminding him he hadn't won since she'd lost her internet connection months ago. It had taken her two months after that and a lot of prayers to find a better provider here in Smalltown, USA.

"Right." Even he didn't sound like he believed it. "Well, we should get paid soon. Fifteen hundred dollars isn't bad for a few hour's work." They weren't splitting it, either. Netherland Transport agreed to their price because they were the best.

"Hmm, yeah." Noella sighed and rolled her neck to loosen the muscles that had automatically tensed while she worked.

After moving to Cadmia and making friends with some women from church, she'd been thrilled at the invitation to their weekly movie nights. What worried her now was that she couldn't remember the last time she'd had to decide *not* to go on a date so she could make the movie night.

"Hey, are you okay?"

"Sure." Noella massaged the bridge of her nose. "Just tired."

"Let me guess." Another slurp came over the line, longer this time. "You've got a relaxing hour or so of translation scheduled after this? Or maybe you're just completely redoing your entire meal planning website?"

She must've hesitated too long because he snickered knowingly.

"I'm not redoing it," she protested. "I just have to schedule some content uploads so they…"

"So they go in on time next week. You have an obligation to your subscribers. I know, I know."

The sound of paper crinkling told her he had finished his lunch and was disposing of the trash.

"Then you know I take it seriously." *Lame.*

"Yeah." Again, Pete's voice lacked conviction. "Ever considered selling it?"

"Huh?" Noella finished typing and attached her report to an email along with her copy of the recording.

"Your meal planning site."

"Sell Calendrier de Cuisine? What? Why?" A small part of her rebelled at the idea. She might not enjoy it anymore, but that site was her first official online success.

"Uh… People usually sell things to make money."

Rolling her eyes, she began switching programs. "I make money because of the site."

"Except you're past done with this one. I mean, even I can tell that."

"You got my workup?"

"Yeah, yeah, I got it. Looks good. And don't worry, I'm done telling you how to run your life." In her mind's eye she could see a grin on his face that matched the one in his voice. "Later." And he was gone.

Noella blew out a breath. Tapped her fingers on the desk while she stared at the screen.

She loved cooking. She loved recipes. Sharing them, trying out new ones. Pairing dishes, creating holiday menus. Helping her subscribers solve their problems.

And yet… If that were true, scrounging up the motivation tonight shouldn't be this hard.

The clock rolled over to eleven while she struggled with herself.

Ugh. Clearing her throat, she turned on some music. Got the job done. Because that's what it was. She had an obligation to her paying subscribers. Keeping the free content fresh would pull in new potential subscribers, which…which would make it easier to sell the site.

She wiped a tear as she shut her computer down and headed off to brush her teeth.

She didn't feel much better about it the next morning, but after praying about it and sleeping on it, at least the decision was made. Before breakfast, she sent out a handful of emails.

And regretted it all through her scripture time.

"Good grief." She put her phone on 'don't disturb' so she could focus on Thessalonians. "First, matters of the soul. *Then* matters of the bank account."

Chuckling, she finished her study, underlining several verses, and was about to set her books aside when the gold lettering caught her eye. She'd read the title a thousand times over the years, and still a wave of awe rushed through her as she read the words, The Book of Mormon: Another Testament of Jesus Christ. Ah, if only everyone had the blessing of this second witness of Christ's divinity!

Patting the book, almost in promise that she would do all she could to share it, she reluctantly rose and turned her attention to the business of the day.

She found that the emails fell into three basic categories: those who couldn't believe she would even consider selling it; those who would pass the information along; and yes, two solid maybes.

She sent the maybes a high level review of her financials for the last two months, then responded politely to the others.

By the time she'd bundled up to go shopping, she was confident that she'd made the right decision.

Shivering a little as she climbed in her car, Noella started the engine. Tugged her handmade scarf, a parting gift from her mother, up over her nose. Missouri wasn't exactly colder than Prince Edward Island. Browner, perhaps. Even last year when everything was under a foot of snow, it somehow still looked brown to her.

Better than an ice storm, of course.

Carefully she drove through slushy streets to Stock's, the town's only grocery store.

"Watch your step, there." Gideon, the store owner, paused in his work to offer his hand as she went to push the door open. "Blasted gutter has a leak and in these temps, the water freezes 'most as soon as it hits the sidewalk."

"Thank you!" Noella smiled as she entered, wiping her feet thoroughly on the matting before stepping onto the ancient gray linoleum. Armed with an only slightly wonky shopping cart, she started down her list.

"Miss Noella." Arlene Garello, Gideon's wife, looked up from the display she was rearranging. Premixed pie fillings might be all the rage in the cities, but as she'd tried to warn Gideon, folks in Cadmia still preferred to add their own seasonings! "Land sakes. Are you feeding an army?"

Laughing, Noella stopped for the obligatory chat. "No, no. Just the sister missionaries. I have signed up to feed them tomorrow." She was growing accustomed to the slightly worried expression everyone got when she mentioned anything remotely religious. As usual, she did her best to ignore it. "I thought a hot meal." She held up her gloves to remind the woman how cold it was outside. "And then I thought, how? I will be gone all day. Fortunately," she winked saucily, "I have the crock pot."

The crease in Arlene's forehead smoothed right out. She didn't want anything to do with Mormonism. Food, on the other hand, was her passion.

"You can make a lotta nice things in a crock pot," she agreed.

"Perhaps, even your minestrone soup?" Noella allowed herself a slow grin. Arlene made all the soups and sandwiches sold in Stock's miniature deli, and Noella had been trying to wheedle the recipe out of her since the first time she'd tasted it.

"Could be." Finished with the display, Arlene got up and dusted her knees off. "I'll have to try makin' it in a crock pot someday."

Noella laughed at the woman's cagey answer. "Will that be the same someday that you share your recipe with me?"

Arlene shrugged noncommittally, but her eyes sparkled with good humor. "Most likely." Now that she had a better angle, she surveyed the cart's contents with undisguised interest. "I don't know what you do with all the food you cook." Eyeing the younger woman's slender waist, she mentally added, *You can't possibly eat it.*

"Ah, oui." Noella lifted both eyebrows and cocked her head to one side as she studied the mound of food. Bags, cans, and boxes of it! "For me, the solution is the food kitchen. I make the test of new recipes on Monday, then take as much as I can to Father Tom."

Arlene blinked. Noella was a kind-hearted person so why her announcement came as a shock, she didn't know. Unless, perhaps, it was because she hadn't realized Mormons mixed with other religions. Even to do good!

"That's…nice of you."

Noella shrugged. "Who has not been hungry?" Sensing that Arlene's attention had shifted to something else, she held up her list. "A few things more to get, still."

"Let me know if you need help findin' stuff," Arlene offered automatically. A little silly, really. They never changed the layout of the store, not in the last fifteen years. Her gaze drifted over to the deli counter. Specifically, to the pile of papers where she'd stashed the card Noella gave her the first time she came to the store.

She'd never call the number on the back to get a free copy of the Book of Mormon, but she admired the picture on the front, a depiction of the Savior all in white, with folks looking up at Him adoringly. She'd never seen the like of it and couldn't bring herself to throw it away.

"Leave anythin' on the shelves?" teased Miss Birdie as she started passing items over the old-fashioned scanner.

"It is possible I may have missed something," Noella returned cheekily. They'd become friends while volunteering at the food kitchen and Miss Birdie may or may not have gotten some subscription-only recipes free just for being the darling that she was.

Chapter 2

"I hope you're makin' more of that meat pie." Miss Birdie's wrinkled, leathery hands moved the goods along with stunning efficiency as she spoke. "I know Sterling couldn't get enough of it."

Noella looked up from where she was arranging bags in her cart. "Is there any compliment better than to be asked for seconds?" Touching her heart, she took a moment to appreciate the information. "But of course I will make more. Oh." Abruptly, she frowned.

"Something wrong, hon?" Miss Birdie hit the "total" button and handed out the last bag.

"Wrong?" Noella swiped her card, then stood there pensively, turning the flat piece of hard plastic over and over in her hand. "I decided to sell my site, Miss Birdie. The one for the recipes."

"That don't sound like a good idea." Miss Birdie tore off the receipt. "You still gonna cook?"

"Always, I am a cook." Noella shrugged expressively. She simply hadn't considered that she wouldn't be able to write off her groceries as a business expense any longer. American taxes were confusing enough without changing the way she did them. Thank goodness her friend, Harmony, had recommended such an excellent accountant!

"Whatcha gonna do for an income?" Miss Birdie was in the habit of asking impertinent questions, especially of people she cared about. "You figured that out?"

"Yes, Miss Birdie." Noella had to smile. "The internet has many opportunities."

"Well. Alright. If yer sure?"

"Do not worry, Miss Birdie, I am sure."

Noella graciously accepted Gideon's help with transferring her groceries to her car, then headed home. The four lane road dwindled to two, then to an unmarked side street where two large vans couldn't have passed comfortably. Weaving expertly around the parked cars, Noella finally reached her rental and backed slowly into the driveway.

"Hi Noella!" Hailey, the oldest girl from the house next door, waved cheerily as she joined her. "Need some help?"

Noella did her best to hide a smile as she pretended to have to think about it. "That would be very nice, but of course, you cannot work for free." This was a game they'd begun to play that summer. Popping her trunk, she let Hailey get a good look at how full it was. "Ah! Perhaps you would like some gingerbread?" Those were their usual terms.

Once the bags were all inside, Noella set two generously sized gingerbread cookies on a plate and poured her guest a glass of cold milk.

"You make the best gingerbread." Hailey

sighed as she bit into an iced snowman.

"Not better than your mother!" Noella protested, still busy putting her groceries away. "She has tried the new recipe, yes?"

Hailey dropped her eyes. "Hasn't had time."

The disappointment in her voice hurt Noella's heart. But what could she do? Kirsten, Hailey's mom, worked hard to support two young girls. If that left no time for baking, Kirsten did what she must.

"Here." Noella lidded the old ice cream bucket and slid it toward Hailey. "I think there is enough to share with your sister."

Hailey stared at the bucket without moving. "Don't need charity," she mumbled.

Noella's heart positively broke at that.

"I do."

Hailey looked up, eyes wide in astonishment.

"Everyone does, ma petite," Noella added softly. "Charity, it is not to…to pity someone. It is the pure love of Christ."

"That's not what Mama says." Hailey's voice sounded very small.

"I do not pity you, Hailey." Noella held her gaze. "If I offer you the gingerbread, it is because I like to share. And you," she nudged the bucket closer to the girl, "like to eat it."

Hailey's mouth quirked up in a guilty smile. "It's real good."

"Then you take it, yes? This way, I can make more." Honestly, Noella wasn't completely happy with the recipe yet.

"Okay." Bouncing to her feet, Hailey hugged her fiercely. "Thanks!" Ice cream bucket in hand, she dashed home.

Noella whispered a prayer for the little family next door as she finished tidying up. If only there was more she could do. But, when she offered them a copy of the Book of Mormon, Kirsten had made it quite clear that the Bible was all the scripture she was interested in.

Her growling stomach reminded her that it was past time for lunch, so she made a simple chicken salad and sat down to her computer. Clicking through a few emails from Calendrier de Cuisine, she answered the recipe questions and forwarded one particularly unique food disaster story on to her two potential buyers.

"I find," she whispered as she typed, "some of my best ideas for articles in the lives of my subscribers."

Opening a different folder, she was happy to see an email from a long-time client, a popular Dutch mystery writer.

"At last," she muttered in Dutch as she set up to transcribe the audio files. "I've been dying to find out how Erica got out of the locked attic room."

Time flew while she transferred the story to text and soon she found herself sitting in a pool of weak light from her laptop, surrounded by shadows.

Squinting at the clock, she yawned. Her back released a series of satisfied pops when she stretched.

"If I hurry, I can eat supper before it is bedtime."

It was so late when she finished her meal that she only needed a glass of milk for breakfast the next morning.

She hung her coat on the rack in the back foyer of the church, gave it one last, longing look, then hurried through the chilly halls to the chapel. She was almost there when she noticed her friend, Merry, and a handsome, dark-haired man as they entered the building.

Hmm. Merry didn't look happy, though Noella had no idea why. She certainly wouldn't be annoyed to have such a handsome man talking with her. She might prefer someone a little closer to her own age, but really, in this area, she would just be glad to find a single man who was also active at church.

He said something and left, so Noella impishly stole forward.

"Wow." Noella liked English slang and she'd never had a better opportunity to use this word than to describe Merry's attractive new friend. Linking her arm through Merry's surprisingly stiff limb, she asked, "Who was that?" Naturally, she switched to French to thwart any potential eavesdroppers. People were alike the world around, she'd decided. Some were good, some were bad, and most were inherently curious.

"I am so glad to see you!" Merry gripped her hand like it was a life preserver. "Can you give me a ride home after church today?"

Startled, Noella opened her mouth to ask what had happened to Merry's truck, but the other woman rushed on.

"I couldn't drive myself this morning because I…didn't have enough gas." Merry stumbled a little over the explanation. "I got a ride in, but I could *really* use a lift."

"I wish I could." Noella frowned unhappily. If Merry needed rescuing, she would certainly help. However… "I have agreed to take the sister missionaries out on appointments for the rest of the afternoon. Of course," she half-shrugged and started leading Merry into the chapel, "I am sure you would be most welcome to come along?"

Merry's face fell. "I'd love to. Unfortunately, if I go out with you, I'll miss supper at my parents' this evening."

"Oh, yes!" Noelle nodded. "I forgot about that."

"It's ok." Merry smiled bravely. "I'll just ride with one of my sisters."

"Ah, but you have not forgotten about the meeting on Tuesday?" Noella spoke quickly, softly. "You will help with the set design?"

After listening to several people complain about how bored they were with the annual charity Christmas play—the exact same play every year for the last five years—she planned to present the community theater group with a new play at their next meeting. They hadn't taken any of her suggestions as yet, so this time she was coming prepared to volunteer her friends.

"Yes, of course." Merry gave her first genuine smile of their conversation. "I'll be there."

Relieved, Noella gave her hand a friendly squeeze and went quietly to her usual seat. She liked to sit where she could watch for unfamiliar faces, so she could smile and welcome them.

People continued to trickle in well after the prelude music started and she made sure to wave at the Petersons. When they came to join her, she greeted each of their two-year-old triplets with a smile and a forehead kiss.

It worked out quite well, really. Sister Peterson sat on one end of the row, with a triplet to her left. Brother Peterson came next, with a triplet on *his* left. Next came Noella, who was proud to be trusted with the third triplet, an adorable yet feisty little boy.

Noella loved helping him hold the hymnal during the opening hymn, "High on the Mountain Top," and holding his hand during the opening prayer.

After the sacrament was passed and the young men had rejoined their families, an older couple stood up to speak. Her arms full of a happily coloring toddler, Noella did her best to listen as they testified that Heavenly Father hears and answers prayers.

"We're used to things happening right away," the brother stated with a chuckle. "Frozen pizza. Instant messaging. Things like that. Well, prayer doesn't always work that way. It can take a little time and effort on our part. Sometimes more than we figured on. Maybe a whole lot more."

Noella was still pondering on that while the Petersons collected their crayons and books and trotted off to deliver the triplets to their nursery class.

Perhaps she was too impatient. For example, almost as soon as she'd thought of moving, she'd taken matters into her own hands. She'd chosen her general destination based on a one hundred-year-old theater ticket from her grandmother's journal. Glibly assured her parents that she wouldn't need much more than her laptop and a toothbrush.

And now… Now she was here, but was that all? Had she simply traded her boring life at home for a boring life somewhere else?

These thoughts occupied her mind throughout most of Sunday school, so that she was startled to hear the teacher offering his testimony in closing.

Rising slowly after the prayer, she saw the sister missionaries heading straight for her.

"Sister Cormier!" Sister Miller greeted her

enthusiastically. "Thank you so much for volunteering to go out with us today! Are you ready for our first appointment?"

"Yes, of course." Belatedly remembering Merry and her stated predicament, Noella was relieved to see her talking with her parents and that handsome new man. Confident that Merry would get a ride home from one of them, Noella gave her full attention to the sisters. "Shall we go?"

Noella chatted happily with the missionaries all the way to the edges of the ward boundaries, where they directed her to turn down a long, snowy driveway.

"I am not sure the car will make it!" She laughed, but mindful of the prayer Sister Hudson had offered before they left the church, she pushed cautiously ahead.

Once they had cleared the initial snowbank, the driveway proved quite passable, even for Noella's little four-door. As they came around the final curve, Noella's jaw dropped.

Snow-laden pine trees surrounded a clearing, looking for all the world like soldiers in white uniforms. A charming stone house stood in the center of the clearing, obviously their object of trust.

The front door was protected by an arch that led them through a short entryway to where they were able to ring the doorbell. After what felt like a long wait, the emerald green door slowly swung inward.

A thin, sweet voice invited them in and Noella half-expected to find herself in an enchanted kingdom as she stepped through the door.

A white-haired woman, as thin as her voice, closed the door behind them. "You girls shouldn't have come out in such weather," she scolded kindly. "But now that you have," she patted Sister Miller's arm kindly, "you better come in by the fire and warm yourselves."

Enthralled, Noella followed her hostess, a fairy queen in a threadbare gray cardigan and fuzzy slippers, into the next room.

"Ah." The queen settled into her throne, a padded wooden rocking chair, and extended tiny, weathered hands to the fireplace. "You must be Noella."

Stunned at being spoken to in French, Noella dropped onto the ancient couch between the sisters.

"I am."

"And I am Jane Bassett." Jane picked up a pile of wool that had knitting needles poking out of it. "Welcome to Maison Pour la Vie."

Home for life. Noella glanced about the tidy but comfortable sitting room. Pictured the pine sentinels standing just outside.

"Thank you," she agreed softly.

"We wanted to tell you that she speaks French," explained Sister Hudson in the following conversational lull, "but she made us promise not to."

"No, no, it is…delightful. A delightful surprise." Noella met the twinkling eyes of the older woman and had the strangest feeling of coming home. As if she'd found an old, old friend. Here, halfway across a continent from where she'd been born.

Jane's knitting needles flashed in the firelight as the sisters shared the lesson they'd prepared, and she asked several pointed questions regarding the doctrine of baptism. She nodded with satisfaction each time they answered her with scriptures, though she often wore a thoughtful expression when those scriptures came from the Book of Mormon.

"So, even though I was born and raised in a Latter-day Saint family," Sister Miller finished, "I had to pray and get my own testimony of these things. Just like we all have to."

Jane nodded. "Do you truly believe what they are teaching about this priesthood authority?" she asked Noella in French.

Noella took a deep breath. She'd done her best to support the sisters' lesson without interrupting, but had known deep down that something like this was coming.

"I do. The Savior himself traveled for miles out of his way to find John the Baptist because he had power and authority from God to baptize. Today, this authority has been restored to the earth as the sisters have taught you."

Again, Jane nodded, her beautifully coiffed white hair waving slightly with the motion. "Thank you for coming." She addressed them all in English. Looking at Noella, she invited, "Will you please offer a prayer before you leave?"

A weight settled on Noella's shoulders as she rose to pray. Half a dozen pictures smiled at her from the mantle above the fireplace, yet there was no evidence of recent visits from the sturdy, handsome young men and women. No overflowing wood box. No laughter from the other rooms. No pile of shoes by the front door or mittens dropped at random by careless grandchildren.

The snow outside—much like the silence in the home once she'd left with the missionaries—had remained unbroken from the storm two days ago until their arrival.

Bowing her head, she offered a simple prayer of thanks and asked for blessings of safety.

"Thank you, my dear." Jane's eyes were misty at the end of the prayer.

Noella sprang to help her when Jane began to stand, but the woman waved her away.

"I'm not as spry as I once was," Jane chuckled, "but I still manage."

"There must be some way we can help you," Noella burst out. "At least…at least let us fill your wood box."

"You?" Jane looked skeptically at their church clothes. "You will get dirty!"

"We've been dirty before," Sister Hudson announced matter-of-factly. They'd made the same offer on their last visit, and the one before. Jane always declined, but this time she seemed to be faltering.

"We'll be done in two shakes," promised Sister Miller, speaking so eagerly that Jane smiled.

"Well…"

"Wonderful." Noella didn't let her finish the sentence. "Where is the wood?"

Jane's smile wavered. "It's in the box outside the kitchen door," she said at last.

Noella and the others only had to see the inside of the box to understand her reluctance.

"What, this is it?" Sister Miller muttered under her breath.

"There can't be more than a couple of armfuls in here." Sister Hudson frowned unhappily.

"Come." Noella began loading up. "We will bring in what there is."

"Right." Sister Miller held the door and asked softly, "But what about when she runs out?"

"Come," Noella commanded. Re-entering the house, she stacked her armful of wood neatly in the box by the fireplace. Knelt by Jane's chair.

A slow flush crept up Jane's face as she sat, ramrod straight, in her rocker. "You needn't worry about me," she snapped. "I get along fine."

"I do worry about you," Noella fired back, taking them both by surprise. Closing her eyes, she took a deep breath. "Are we not sisters in Christ?"

A tear trickled down Jane's face. "I…" She shook her head.

"Jane." Noella took her hands. "We have this Saturday a project to cut wood. To bring good wood to homes that need it."

"Mormon homes," Jane asserted, but her tone revealed her uncertainty.

"Any home that will accept it," Noella corrected gently. Pulling a clean tissue from her pocket, she offered it to Jane, who had begun crying openly. "Let us help you, Jane. Let us live up to our covenants."

Nodding, Jane embraced her. "Thank you." She embraced both of the sisters and walked them to the door.

"I will come back tomorrow?" Noella suggested.

"I'd like that."

"Good." Noella hugged her again. "I will bring chicken and rolls and potatoes and…"

"I don't eat as much as I used to," Jane warned her, a twinkle back in her eyes.

Noella laughed. "We will eat only as much as we wish, and we will have the long talk."

"Wonderful." Jane beamed at her.

Noella didn't want to leave, but the missionaries looked so cold standing by her car that she gave in.

"I hope you two are hungry," she teased as she started the engine.

"Starving!" They chorused.

Noella joined in the laughter of the evening, but her heart was still in the doorway of Maison Pour la Vie, wrapped around a forlorn-looking little woman.

"Thank you so much," Sister Miller gushed when they arrived back at their apartment later.

"No kidding." Sister Hudson juggled containers of food as she unbuckled herself and got out. "This is enough food for a week!"

"Good!" Noella grinned at them. "You work hard, so you must eat well!"

"We sure will!" Sister Miller hesitated. "Thanks for coming with us to Jane's, too."

"I am glad I went. I think she needs a friend."

"Hey, Sister Miller? Can you...?" Sister Hudson grunted as she caught a sliding container with her chin. "I, um..."

"Coming!"

Noella watched, a little worried, until they were safely inside with the food, then drove slowly back to her home. Scowled at the clock, which flatly declared that it was too late to call her mother.

Grumbling, she took a hot shower and climbed into crisp, clean pajamas. Knelt by her bed and poured her heart out to her Father in

Heaven, apologizing for not making her move a matter of prayer and thanking Him for blessing her to meet Jane.

"Please also bless me," she whispered, "to be the friend she needs."

Knowing she would have a hard time falling asleep, Noella turned on the last general conference. Listened as she lay on one side, trying not to think too hard, even about Jane.

Chapter 3

Forty minutes away in Fireclay, Danny Fitzsimmons was also getting ready for bed. More or less.

"Hey." His best friend, Chuck, came into the kennel to make a final check before lights out. "Man, you haven't used that sleeping bag this much since you built your house."

Danny laughed and straightened the bag on the inflatable pad he was trying tonight.

"You're just lucky I already had the staff cabin built when I hired you," he joked. "Toni would never have agreed to camp out for weeks in the dead of summer while the construction crew built it."

"You've got that right." Chuck rolled his eyes at the thought of his wife trying to survive without central air conditioning. Jiggled a latch to be sure it was secure. "And you know what? I wouldn't have enjoyed it, either!" He snapped his fingers as something occurred to him. "Before I forget again, you have got to get someone out to take a look at the heater on the other kennel. It has started making noises again."

"I've heard it, too." Danny raked his fingers through his hair as he immediately thought of all the reasons why this was a bad time for an extra expense. A big one was that though they didn't exactly shut down during the winter, they didn't have any extra income, either. Instead of training and taking on new clients, he used the lousy weather to catch up on his paperwork, then had downtime for the holidays.

But he tried not to worry about business on the Sabbath. That wasn't what it was made for. So he dug up a grin and cracked a joke.

"It sounds like a cross between a screech owl and a wheat grinder."

Chuck snickered. "You *did* hear it!" Coming closer to where Danny was setting up by Caesar's enclosure, Chuck's smile faded at the sight of Caesar's food bowl.

"He didn't eat much today." Danny knew he was understating the problem. He'd seen canaries that ate more than this Belgian Shepherd was at the moment. On top of that, when they'd taken the dogs outside a few at a time to play earlier, Caesar had refused to leave his kennel.

"He's just wasting away." Chuck bit his lip. "I don't know. Might be kinder to…" He cut himself short when he met Danny's eyes.

Danny lifted his chin to stretch out his tight throat, then shrugged. "At least let me talk to my dad this weekend, okay? He'll help me figure this out."

"Your dad? Hey, he's awesome." Chuck nodded, glad for an excuse to wait.

"Yeah." Danny struggled not to sound defensive, but apparently he couldn't help it.

"I don't want to do it, either." Chuck understood perfectly. Patting Danny on the shoulder, he headed for the door. "Toni and I will be praying."

"Me, too."

"Ready for the lights?" He smiled when Danny pulled a small, powerful flashlight out of his pocket. There were certain perks to growing up in tornado alley, like always keeping an alternate light source handy. "Night."

"Good night."

Danny's mood slipped still further as he knelt on the concrete to pray. Halfway through the prayer, he shifted onto the sleeping bag and pad for his knees' sake. It helped, a little.

Unzipping his sleeping bag, Danny crawled into it. He started out on his side, but even with the inch-thick pad underneath him the concrete was pushing back against his joints. In fact, no matter which way he repositioned himself, tonight the concrete won. Defeated, he lay on his back, his head on his pillow.

"I think I'm getting old." His lips twitched, but he was only half kidding. He'd turned twenty-eight that summer and somehow his brain kept skipping twenty-nine to go straight to thirty.

"What's next, fella? What's the next milestone?" he asked an unresponsive Caesar. "Let's see. I got my driver's license at sixteen. Graduated high school *and* started voting at eighteen. I don't drink, so for me being able to rent a car at twenty-five came after that."

Caesar whined. Tilting his head back and squinting so he could see in the faint illumination of the single security light, Danny was surprised to realize that the dog had come up to the front of the enclosure.

"Hey." He rolled onto his stomach and folded his arms on his pillow. "Must be even worse for you, huh? You're…six years old? That's—" He paused to do the math from dog years to human years. "Whoa, man. You're forty-two! Compared to you, I'm just a kid."

Caesar didn't say a word.

"Guess you're way past kid thinking." The joke fell flat and Danny put his chin on his arms. "Don't give up, Caesar. I know it's hard, but," he swallowed the tears crowding his throat, "We'll find you a new home, my friend." He stroked the dog's head. "My dad'll think of something. He's really smart. In the meantime, though, would it really be so terrible to enjoy it here? Your home away from home?"

Caesar sighed and put his head on his paws.

"Shut up and go to sleep." He mock saluted the dog. "Got it." When he finally slept, troubled dreams took him to Cadmia, where he wandered from house to house like a traveling peddler, trying to find Caesar a new home.

In one home in Cadmia, Monday morning arrived slowly. Or it seemed to for Noella, who hadn't set an alarm. Rolling over, she stretched and yawned.

Mmmm, she loved working for herself!

This time, she wisely avoided her cell phone until after her scripture study, which included 1st Timothy 4:12, part of which read, "be thou an example of the believers, in word, in conversation, in charity, in spirit, in faith, in purity."

Offering a silent prayer that she would be such an example, Noella reluctantly closed her scriptures.

"Voila. The best part of my day is over." Then, she remembered Jane, and her lips curved upward. "But I can look forward to the second best part!"

Taking her laptop to her couch, she relocated her Halloween costume to the closet, then got comfortable under a blanket. Time to start her work day!

Much to her surprise, she found a firm email offer for her website! She spent the next hour with the potential buyer, ironing out details and turning the website inside out for them in a final review. Documents and images flew back and forth between them via email in addition to the video chat.

"Calendrier de Cuisine has, up to now, focused mainly on providing entire menus, but I have also had great success using the extensive recipe section to turn casual visitors into paying customers."

"And how often do you add new recipes?" They discussed the point briefly, then the other woman nodded, satisfied.

"I'm ready to sign if you are."

"Excellent!" She felt only a twinge of regret as she electronically signed the necessary documents and arranged to receive payment through a trusted third-party company. "After the funds are deposited, I will provide full access and post an article explaining the sale."

She maintained a professional tone until they ended the phone call, then let out a whoop of relief!

Jumping off the couch, she step danced into the kitchen, dialing her mother's number as she traveled. The dear woman answered on the second ring.

"Mama! You will not believe what has happened!"

"I'm fine, dear, so sweet of you to call to ask," Abigail responded dryly.

"Oh, I'm so sorry!" Noella covered her eyes with her hand. "I wanted to call before."

"Now, now." Abigail interrupted gently.

"I work too hard," Noella finished with her. They laughed. "But how are you really?"

Abigail answered as only mothers do, talking not about herself but around herself. "Ahhh, your brother came yesterday and…" Then, "And your father, last night he made the most delicious…"

Noella hugged herself with delight as she listened to news from home. She could've listened all day, her own news forgotten, if her phone hadn't started buzzing.

Her mother interrupted herself to ask, "Noella, what is that noise?"

"Nothing." She double-checked. "A call from Peter. I will call him back."

"Peter? Your business partner?"

Ooops. "Yesss, but…"

"Take the call, ma chérie," Abigail admonished. "We can talk again this evening."

"I have an appointment for supper this evening," Noella inserted quickly. "Tomorrow morning?"

"Yes, perfect. I love you!"

"I love you, too!" Grumbling, Noella pulled up her missed calls and dialed Peter. "Is this important?"

"Finally!" Peter ignored her opening jab. "Have you checked your email today?"

"Yes, a few of them." She pointed at her laptop, preparing to tell him about the sale of her website, but she didn't get the chance.

"Well read the rest of them, will you? And hurry!"

Opening her laptop again, Noella scrolled down to a cluster of emails from Peter. "This is important?" she persisted. "Wait." She squinted in the direction of her phone. It was in the middle of the night in Australia. "Why aren't you asleep?"

"Because I got a phone call from someone in Europe who has never heard of time zones." His brief rant ended with an emphatic yawn.

"Uh-huh." Her suspicions aroused, she returned to the emails. "You are much too happy for having your sleep dist…" The word broke off in the middle and she gave her full attention to what she was reading.

"You found it, didn't you?" Peter gloated.

"This is real?" she asked sharply. If it was, she could understand his not minding having his sleep interrupted.

"It'd be a rotten joke," he retorted.

"But this…" Words failed her. Netherland Transport wanted to hire them to test their online security. And they were offering a *lot of money*.

"Is the offer of a lifetime," he finished for her. "Six weeks' contract, at least."

"Perhaps." She opened the next email. "We should not underestimate their security team."

"Okay, so they'll bring in a good team. But we're better," he asserted smugly.

Laughing, she leaned back. "You have told them yes?"

"Before asking you? What kind of partner do you think I am?" His best attempt at sounding wounded didn't fool her for a second.

She snickered. "Then you made a counteroffer asking for more money."

He coughed. "I may have pointed out that their entire plans for expansion depend on satisfying the bank's demand for improved security."

"You are such a haggler. I love it!"

"So you're in?"

"Of course! So long as," she hastened to add, "we do not—"

"Work on Sunday," he finished with her. "Don't worry, I know that's not an option for you. We call the shots so long as we keep them on the defensive."

"And we do this by defeating their security."

"Exactly." The sound of keys clicking filled a short pause. "They estimate they'll have their upgrade finished by Wednesday at midnight, their time. I say we hit them right after."

"It sounds perfect." She couldn't help chuckling. She'd be sitting down to supper and he'd be cleaning up after breakfast—or "brekkie," as they called it down under.

"If we come up cactus, we just don't tell them."

"I thought you said we were better than they were?" she teased after translating his Australian slang for 'fail.'

"We are," he insisted. "Still, no point in advertising a temporary failure, is there?"

She bobbed her head from left to right, admitting to herself that he had a point. "I will plan on it."

"Fantastic. Fill out your half of the contract and send it back to me, alright? I'll finish negotiating our fee, then make the deal."

"I am nearly done with it. But Peter, please."

She clicked *send.* "Don't push too hard. Their first offer is very generous."

"Sure it's generous." He slurped on something. "What we have to remember is that we get a lump payment this time. If we go in ten times, twenty times, we get the same amount per week. Now, I get what you're saying. I'll be careful. I only want to make sure we're getting paid for all the work we're going to put into it."

They ended the call with a final agreement to tackle the new security system on—Wednesday at 5 PM for her, Thursday at 9 AM for him.

Her mind spinning with recent events, she mixed up some dough for the rolls and set it to rise, the familiar actions settling her somewhat.

Even so, she made four false starts before she eventually muddled through a first draft of her article explaining why she had decided to sell Calendrier de Cuisine. It was terrible, but she knew from past experience that she needed a break, so she closed her laptop and massaged tired eyes.

Getting up, she went into the kitchen and began gathering what she would need to make supper at Jane's. Baked chicken and mashed potatoes with green beans and rolls. Simple fare, which she hoped would not trouble the older woman's digestion. Her own grandparents ate plain food and lived well into their nineties.

Her thoughts drifted to her great-grandmother's violin. She'd dusted the case last week and the memory sent guilt cascading over her. That she should have to *dust* it, of all things. Violins were not meant to sit in a corner while the leftovers of life settled on them. Especially not violins such as this.

Making a spur-of-the-moment decision, she added the violin to what she took out to her car. Jane might enjoy a song after supper.

She had no trouble finding the little home again and was happy to return Jane's hug.

"I made snickerdoodles for dessert," Jane told her in French, watching eagerly as Noella unloaded her box on the kitchen counter.

"Oh, not really?" Noella opened her hands wide. "I love those!" She loved desserts entirely too much, and took great care to avoid them where possible. But tonight of course she would make an exception.

Lifting the chicken out first, she set it on the counter. It took three strides for her to carry her now mostly empty box over to a chair, where she put it so it would be out of the way. Four strides from there to the oven, which she opened first out of habit.

"My goodness." Confident now that the oven was completely empty, Noella gently closed the door and set it to preheat. "You have such a lovely oven."

Jane glowed as she explained the history of her entire kitchen, which she'd designed herself when her husband had the house built for them to retire in.

"The spices?" She paused to answer Noella's question. "They're in the cupboard to the right of the oven, dear."

Opening the cupboard, Noella selected two or three familiar spices, and, confident that they would be to Jane's liking, used them to season the chicken. Meanwhile, she listened in rapt attention as Jane told what was obviously, to her, the world's sweetest love story.

"He brought the carpenter back twice, mind you, *twice*, just to get the cupboards hung exactly the way I wanted."

Noella oohed and aahed sincerely as the story continued, conscientiously returning every borrowed item to exactly where she'd found it. She was glad there was a dishwasher, too, which she loaded after putting the chicken in to bake.

"I feel awful about making you do all the work." Jane pouted.

"Oui, bon!" Noella showed her the bowl of dough. "Then you will make the rolls while I prepare the potatoes?"

In answer, Jane lit up like a Christmas tree and eagerly joined her at the counter.

Noella felt perfectly at home by the time they sat down to their meal. Her cheeks colored when Jane thanked Heavenly Father not just for the food, but for her company.

"I must confess," Jane sighed as she buttered a piping hot roll, "I do get a little lonely sometimes."

"I understand." Noella nodded. "I also live alone."

Jane slanted a look at her. "A pretty girl like you must have a boyfriend to keep her company."

Laughing, Noella set a piece of chicken first on Jane's plate, then one on her own. "There aren't many single men my age around here. At least," she amended, "not many who also go to church." And most of those that she'd met were content simply to date—no strings, no desire to advance a relationship beyond casual companionship. To 'hang out,' as they called it. She'd had enough of that to last a lifetime.

"Hmm." Jane sighed a tad sorrowfully as she dug a hole in her mashed potatoes and poured in a generous helping of steaming brown gravy. "Mmm." She inhaled deeply. "I used to make meals like this three times a week. Had to feed my boys." A fond smile played across her face.

Remembering the pictures on the mantle, Noella coaxed Jane to talk about her family. As they ate all they could hold, she gradually came to feel as though she knew each of Jane's three children personally.

"We wanted more," Jane acknowledged. "Andy used to say he wanted enough for a football team of his own. But, that wasn't the good Lord's plan for us."

"It can be so hard," Noella murmured without thinking. In the back of her mind, her thoughts from the day before stirred uneasily. As sad as she was for Jane's unfulfilled dreams—temporarily, anyway; who knew what blessings eternity held for her?—Noella couldn't help wishing that she could see the Lord's plan for her own life so clearly.

"And you, my dear." Jane leaned toward her. "For you, the Lord's plan is that you belong to this Church of Jesus Christ of..." She hesitated. It was such a long name that she had trouble remembering it.

"The Church of Jesus Christ of Latter-day Saints," Noella supplied. "Yes, that is right."

"And," Jane raised her eyebrows, "this is His plan for me, as well?"

Noella exhaled slowly. "I know the sisters have taught you about the restoration." She waited until Jane nodded. "And I can tell you that I know for myself the Lord speaks to prophets today. He also speaks to us, answering our prayers. Have you prayed to know for yourself if what you're being taught is true? To know what He would have you do?"

"If I did, how would I know when I got an answer?" Jane lifted one hand. "I can pray for the sick. I can pray for my children. My grandchildren. With those prayers, I can see the answers as they come."

"This is true," Noella agreed. "But do you always see the answers you were hoping for?"

Slowly, Jane shook her head. "I prayed many times for us to be blessed with more children." A tear glistened on her cheek. "The answer was not what I hoped."

"Did you ever feel the Lord comforting you?"

Jane tilted her head to one side as she thought back. "Yes. Yes, I remember times when He did."

"It is the same with praying to know for yourself if you are to join the Church of Jesus Christ of Latter-day Saints." Noella spoke earnestly. "You ask Heavenly Father in the name of Jesus Christ, and He will tell you."

Jane raised an eyebrow. "But you will not?"

"I cannot." Noella spread her hands. "I could tell you everything I know and have come to know. However, my testimony will never be enough for you to make your decision."

A satisfied expression settled over Jane's face. "You speak wisely for one so young."

Smiling, Noella rose and started clearing the table. "It is a lesson every child should learn before they decide to be baptized at eight."

That led them to a discussion about the different auxiliaries in the church, from the primary organization to the missionary program. Noella admitted her ignorance whenever Jane asked a question she couldn't answer, which only seemed to intrigue the woman more.

Chapter 4

"So much to learn." Jane filled a glass of milk for each of them and set a plate of cookies between their places. "Now. We've spent the entire evening talking about me. Tell me about yourself." She waited politely—if a little impatiently—for her guest to take the first cookie.

Noella finished stowing her things before coming over to retake her seat at the table. "There is so little to tell!" The snickerdoodle she chose gave slightly under her fingers, but when she took a bite it was perfectly cooked. "Mmmm." Her eyes drifted closed. "I need this recipe."

"Don't change the subject." Jane shook a finger at her in mock chastisement, though she positively glowed at the compliment. Selecting a cookie for herself, she broke it in half and ate a bite with a sip of milk. "Where are you from? And why on earth did you move to a tiny town like Cadmia?" She'd visited the island many years ago and would've stayed there if she could've.

"I was born in Prince County on Prince Edward Island." Between bites of delectable cookie and sips of milk, Noella shared her short history. "I learned to swim and to fish in Bedeque Bay. My mother taught me to cook, and my grandmother taught me to play the violin."

Jane clapped her hands. "Yes, I saw the violin case. I was hoping you would play for me?" She was as eager as a child.

"And I," Noella dusted cinnamon-sugar off her hands, "was hoping you would let me!"

They laughed and tidied up the kitchen quickly, then moved into the living room, where Noella stoked the fire. Jane had revealed that the same man who took care of her lawn during the summer also delivered firewood during the winter, but Noella was beginning to get the feeling that it must be an expensive service. A dozen little things had caught her eye that needed to be repaired or replaced, and those which she discreetly mentioned to Jane were casually dismissed as having 'a few more miles left in them.'

Tuning her violin expertly, Noella drew her bow across the strings. Paused to savor the shiver of pleasure the familiar action brought. In a snug house with a friend, supper barely finished and a fire crackling cheerfully, it was almost like being back home.

Music flowed from her. Reels. Jigs. A few of her favorite classical pieces. She played for the sheer joy of playing, until her aching arms couldn't stand anymore. Breathing heavily, she lowered her instrument. She was *really* out of shape!

"That was marvelous! I've never heard such playing!" Jane applauded vigorously. "I felt as though you transported me off to some magical place where the fairies go to dance.”

“Ah.” Noella dragged in a deep breath, her cheeks rosy at the praise. “I only wish you could have heard my grandmother.” Setting the violin almost reverently in its case, she sighed. “For her, each note was a symphony.”

“I would have liked to have known her.” Jane spoke gently, realizing that her grandmother must have passed away.

“Thank you.” Noella wiped away an errant tear and managed a small laugh. “But look at the time! Oh, I have kept you up so late!”

Jane waved a hand and scoffed. “Don’t worry about me, my dear. If I’m tired, I will simply sleep in.” Then she frowned at the darkened windows. The sun started setting around five-thirty on a winter’s night, as she well knew, yet she had forgotten that the temperature dropped with each passing hour. “You be careful going home, now,” she admonished. “Mind you keep an eye out for deer, too. They can be bad this time of year.”

“I promise.” Noella hugged her warmly, slipped on her coat and hat, then darted across the snow to her car. She’d persuaded Jane to take all of the leftovers by telling a slightly embellished story about her own over-loaded fridge, so all she had to carry in when she arrived home was a box with her favorite potato peeler and her violin.

Chilled toes found their way into thick socks,

but memories of her evening with Jane warmed her heart and her dreams, so that she was still smiling the next morning.

After scripture study and a wonderful phone call with her mother, she grumbled her way through another revision of the article for her— no, *their* website.

Needing to relax, she got out flour, shortening, and set water to chill in the freezer. Once she'd lined a few pie tins with crusts, she started on the filling. Potatoes, carrots, beef, herbs, and spices all went into a giant saucepan, then into the crusts.

While the pies cooked for the food kitchen, she organized and cleaned her workspace.

Stretched up, up, onto her toes and almost touched the low ceiling with her fingers. It would soon be time to go to the community theater meeting. Bending to place her palms flat on the floor, she exhaled slowly.

This would not be her first time suggesting a play. Mid side-stretch, her controlled exhalation turned into a sigh. Nor was it likely that it would be the last time she got outvoted. She was, after all, still an outsider.

Raised in a small town in Prince Edward Island, she certainly understood the mentality she faced. She simply wasn't accustomed to being on *this* side of it.

Laughing at herself, she turned on music for a jig and step danced a few songs until she'd worked off some of her nerves. Stretching again for her cool-down, she hurried through a shower and dressed in jeans and a tee, Cadmia's unofficial uniform.

Leaving the pies on the counter to cool, she paused for prayer before heading out.

It wasn't a long drive to the community center, a plain-looking brick building just off the town's square. On the other side of the park sat the much grander courthouse, which still looked rather awful thanks to all the drab, dead grass surrounding it. She wished it would hurry up and snow.

Snow, like frosting, covered a multitude of defects!

Patting her bag with its precious cargo of ten scripts, she entered the community center. Where, to her delight, Merry was one of the first people she saw when she walked into the tiny auditorium.

Tucking her arm through Merry's, she started to regale the other woman with her battle plan for today's meeting, finishing with, "This time they will listen, I am sure of it! Yes?"

"You've got my vote." Merry smiled. She trusted Noella's experience. Noticing that the other committee members had begun forming up around the table at the front of the room she urged, "Hurry, go get a seat."

Determination in her stride, Noella joined the others in the ugly gray, metal chairs. Waited impatiently through the first ten minutes of the meeting, which covered old business and strayed into a dull argument.

"I only bought the chartreuse crepe because someone, who shall remain nameless," the speaker glared at the woman seated opposite, "said we could use it to make vines when we did *The Jungle Book* two years ago!"

Mrs. Arnold, the chairwoman, rapped her gavel sharply, ending the squabble. "I believe it's time for new business. Namely, this year's charity play." Her nostrils flared slightly at Noella's instantly raised hand. "The chair recognizes Ms. Cormier."

Noella couldn't understand why the woman refused to use her first name, especially given that she'd made a point of inviting her to, but she tried to ignore the implied slight. Rising, she smiled at each of the committee members in turn as she began her presentation.

"The Christmas play is a most important event." She started with a compliment. "Each year, the funds that are raised by selling tickets go to local charities, who use the money to help our fellow citizens."

"Thank you for your summary, Ms. Cormier." Mrs. Arnold glanced over those seated at the table with her as regally as any queen might've surveyed her court. "And this year, we intend to raise an additional thirty percent over last year. It will take a lot of hard work from everyone. Now…"

"Wait, wait." Noella hastily cut her off, then

shrank back a bit at the woman's icy stare. "I was just beginning."

"Well. Carry on." Mrs. Arnold narrowly avoided pointing her gavel at the impudent young woman. "But don't take too long, my dear. We only have so much time today."

"Oui. Um." She groaned internally. "Yes, of course." She proceeded to sketch the story of a busy modern family and how one Christmas changed their lives for the better. Encouraged by the questions and general engagement from the others, she took the chance. "Though *No Time Like the Present* is a small play, it teaches a big lesson. And I would like to propose that we put it on for the Christmas play this year."

From the corner of her eye, she thought she saw Mrs. Arnold's smile slip, but the woman's face was the picture of serenity by the time she'd turned to face her.

"All in favor of Ms. Cormier taking the lead on this project?" Mrs. Arnold asked, her tone a little too sweet. Every hand went up. "Motion carried."

The gavel descended. Chairs scraped and normal conversation resumed as the committee members walked away.

Thoroughly confused, Noella turned to Mrs. Arnold to ask her to call them back. They hadn't assigned the stage crew or discussed props or…

"Good luck," smirked the chairwoman, tucking her gavel into her oversized purse. "You'll need it," she fairly hissed.

Noella's smile faltered. She looked at the now-empty table. Turned back to ask the chairwoman what she meant. And found her sauntering away.

"Hey." Merry's hand settled lightly on her shoulder. "Let's take a walk, okay?"

"What just happened?" Noella inquired in French. She was too shocked to think in English. It couldn't be what it seemed. There was no reason for such rudeness.

"I think you got set up." Slipping an arm around Noella's shoulder, Merry led her away from prying eyes. As they left the building she asked, "How many times did you say you've been outvoted on what play to do?"

"Every time." Noella shrugged. That hadn't bothered her. Much. "Last time, I thought they were considering it, but it was late and the chairwoman, she closed the meeting before we could vote."

"Ah. And when they came back, they voted for the play she wanted. I'm sorry, kiddo." Merry's voice was sad. "I think you're on your own here." This was exactly the sort of thing she'd expect from Mrs. Arnold, but it blew her mind that the other committee members were going along with it! Was the pride of one petty woman really worth risking the charity play?

"But...but how?" Noella sputtered. The shock was wearing off and she was starting to get angry. And cold. As she put on her knit cap, she wondered where they were going. "They agreed to the play. They *all* agreed. You heard it!"

"I heard them agree that *you* were in charge of putting on the play," Merry corrected. "And, eh," she hesitated, probably mentally translating to French, "closed the meeting. Nobody agreed to do *the work*."

A teenager wearing hot pink earbuds wandered past them, singing along in a decent alto to a song Noella didn't recognize. There was something familiar about the overall pattern to the song, but she was still too flustered to pin down what it reminded her of.

She muttered to herself all the way to the Table Spoon Bakery, then threw up her hands. "Very well. If that is how they want to do things… Then I will show them how it is done!"

"Oh, hey, Alice." Merry stepped aside for a woman and her service dog, a pretty tan and white Jack Russell Terrier named Dinah. "How's she working out for you?" Alice suffered from seizures, so the day she got her specially trained medical alert dog was a day the whole town celebrated.

"I can't tell you how much I love my girl." Alice's broad smile took in Merry and Noella. "I've only had her a few months and she's already saved me so much grief." She nodded at her dog, who was staring intently at them. "Yes, we're talking about you, sweetheart."

"May I pet her?" Noella looked at the gorgeous dog with interest. She'd heard about Dinah, but never met her.

"Yes, and thank you so much for asking! Our trainers warned us about people who would just walk up and try to treat our dogs like pets." Alice smiled as Noella bent to pet Dinah. "Under her chin is her favorite spot."

Merry made a face. "That's sort of like trying to talk to a bodyguard about the football game while they need to focus, isn't it?"

"Exactly!" Alice frowned. "And sometimes worse. One of the other students in my class when I took my training with Dinah had PTSD. Her dog was trained to help with things like going out in public and it was so hard watching her endure our group exercises."

"I can imagine," Merry agreed quietly.

"Where did you get this amazing dog?" Noella regretfully straightened away from Dinah.

"Over in Fireclay." Alice pointed in the general direction of the town out of habit. "There's the most amazing dog training center over there, you wouldn't believe me if I told you!"

"If you tell me, I will believe!" Noella shrugged with her hands and they all laughed.

"Oh!" Alice looked around as her name was called. "Looks like my order's ready. Nice seeing you guys!"

Noella smiled as she watched them go. She'd grown up with dogs and they always calmed her.

"What'll you have?" Merry asked, bringing her attention back to the menu that stretched from one wall to the other.

She scanned it quickly. *More desserts. No, it is only desserts! I am going to gain so much weight!* And yet, she could always use it as another excuse to step dance.

"Sugar cookies, please."

Over fresh cookies and hot chocolate, Noella drafted her battle plan. She took courage from Merry's ready reassurance that she would handle set design and construction.

Eventually, she would put up flyers advertising auditions. Then she would try to persuade everyone who came to try out to help with the production in some way or other. No job was unimportant, after all. A bare or poorly lit stage would wreck a play the same way that bad acting did!

She was still pondering where to get the rest of what she needed for the play when she pulled up to the food kitchen for the supper shift later that afternoon.

"There she is." Father Tom shrugged into his coat as he stepped outside to see if she needed help carrying anything. She usually did. "Our most faithful volunteer." She opened the door just then and he got a whiff of what she'd brought. "I'm not sure we can use those." He did his best to keep a straight face.

"What? But, why not?" She looked from him

to the pies, trying to understand what was wrong with them. "I made them myself!"

Hearing the near-wail in her voice, he hastily unbent. "I'm kidding." He held up both hands, palms out. "Totally kidding."

She blew out a breath. Nodded.

"I guess it wasn't very funny," he apologized, worried eyes studying her face.

"It has been a long day." She did her best to smile. "Here." Giving him two pies, she carried the third into the kitchen herself, where she nearly choked on the ever-present scent of industrial-strength cleanser.

Somewhere she'd heard that the building used to be a restaurant of some sort, which would explain a lot. The walk-in freezer was, sadly, mostly empty. A huge fridge shared a different wall with twin stoves, while the center of the room was either counter space above floor cupboards or electric ranges. Her favorite part was probably the dishwasher in the far corner. Every single pot and pan and dish they would use tonight could be whisked through it in a fraction of the time it took to get them dirty.

"Here we go." Father Tom placed her meat pies on the serving area, behind the metal roll-up window. In another thirty minutes, they would open the window and supper would begin.

Rolling up her sleeves, she joined Father Tom and the other volunteers—most of whom were there for the meal, as well—in preparing giant pots of hot vegetables, trays of biscuits, etc., for their six o'clock opening time. She used to get there earlier, until Father Tom explained how important it was to for his guests to feel they had earned their suppers.

Tonight she got to dish out green beans and she smiled at everyone, making short conversation with those who had spoken to her in the past. As always, Noella's problems paled into obscurity as she served.

"Sterling! It's so good to see you!" She watched the older man's face brighten. "Now, I've waited an entire week to hear more about your cat, so please wait and have dessert with me." She wasn't really sure if he'd adopted the stray or if it had adopted him, but it was one thing he was always comfortable talking about.

Sterling nodded shyly and shuffled off to a table, his baggy jeans and jacket making him look remarkably like an underfed cat himself.

"Go ahead." Father Tom had arrived with a fresh pot of beans in time to hear her. "I'll take care of this, you go talk with Sterling."

"Are you sure?" She glanced around at the beehive of activity behind her. Soon the cleanup crew would finish their supper and relieve the set up crew, but she didn't want to shirk her job.

"I'm positive." He made a discreet shooing motion. "Sterling's one of the few truly homeless people in Cadmia. He needs fellowship as much as he needs food."

Understanding now, Noella joined Sterling and coaxed him to tell her about Found, as he'd named the stray. She couldn't help noticing that those nearest them stopped talking to listen, though they took care not to intrude.

Father Tom must've noticed, too, because when he handed her the stack of freshly washed pie tins he murmured, "Well done."

She rode the glow from her time at the food kitchen back home, where she polished off several smaller projects before tumbling into bed, exhausted.

Chapter 5

By lunch the next day Noella had finished designing flyers advertising auditions for the play. Pleased with her work, she sent it off to the nearest print shop and headed into town.

Halfway there, she remembered that she hadn't scheduled the community center for the date of the auditions! Slamming her palm against her forehead, she hastily dialed the facility manager, a Mr. Abe Tuttle.

"H'lo?" A gruff voice answered on the fifth ring.

"Good afternoon, Mr. Tuttle! I am Noella…" She stopped, frowning at the dial tone that filled her car. A quick check of her phone showed that reception was good, so she tried again.

"H'lo!" The voice was almost angry this time.

"Mr. Tuttle, I'm sorry to bother you, but I am told you have the keys to the community center?" she ventured timidly.

"Who is this?" Ordinary gruffness was back, paired with curiosity.

"Noella Cormier." She waited. "I need to schedule the building for November twenty-first, please?"

"Hang on." Mr. Tuttle's grumblings came through as he rattled papers and dropped things, perhaps while looking for his sign-out sheet.

"What organization?"

"Community theater. We're having auditions that day." She was all set to launch into her pitch for him to come try out when he snorted.

"Huh. Miz Arnold us'lly makes the appointments fer the community theater. Don't tell me the old gal's losing her grip on y'all's noses?"

Noella blinked, startled by his…frankness.

"What time?" he asked.

"I…beg your pardon?" Her mind was still reeling from his previous statement.

"What time are you holding the auditions?"

"Oh!" She told him the time and the estimated length of the activity.

"Got it."

"And the keys?" She interjected hastily, afraid he'd hang up on her again.

"They'll be in the usual place. That bein' behind the sign in front of the buildin'." He chuckled as if he found the whole thing highly amusing. "Under a rock."

Noella hadn't quite recovered from the odd experience by the time she reached the print shop, but she nevertheless hopped out and went inside.

"Hello! Max." She read the nametag of the young man behind the counter.

"Howdy. How kin I hep you?" He started drumming his fingers on the counter nervously when she asked for her order. "You wanted that fer today?"

"Yes, please." Somehow, she maintained a friendly smile.

"Well." He looked around the otherwise idle business. "I'll get right on it, then."

"Thank you." She said a little prayer for patience while he meandered back and forth, wearing a path between basically the same two points. The big printer balked and he smacked it with the heel of his palm, nodding to himself when it chugged to life.

"Won't be a minute," he called to her. Snapped his fingers. "Paper!"

Fifteen minutes and a great deal of printer-smacking later, Max chewed his gum noisily while he boxed up the flyers he'd just printed.

"Yer sure goin' all out," he observed. "Color'n'…everythin'." Sliding the box across the counter to her, he waited for the credit card machine to communicate a prompt to his monitor. "Miz Arnold us'lly ain't so fancy."

Noella smiled broadly. "I have been asked to manage the Christmas play this year." Accepting her receipt, she gestured toward his display window. "Will your business be the first to display the audition flyer?"

"Huh?" He stared at her for a couple of heartbeats, then sniffed and wiped his nose on the cuff of his sleeve. "Sure, go ahead." As an afterthought, he shoved a tape dispenser in her direction.

"Merci."

She got basically the same careless response in every store on the tiny town square, until she started to forget why she was excited. The Christmas play was old news. Everybody she asked said they planned to attend, but judging by their attitudes she might as well have asked if they were planning to wash their dishes.

She started for home, discouraged and hungry, as the sun started to set. Since tonight was the trunk-or-treat, she changed into her costume before packing up her crock pot of chili and going over to the church.

Among the first to arrive, she pitched in to help set up tables, chairs, and so forth in the cultural hall. Pausing long enough to straighten her straw hat and its twin, red braids, she spied her friend, Grace—in a *very* eye-catching catsuit costume.

Black with blue piping and silver sequins, it reminded Noella a lot of the costumes some professional step dancers wore. But for Grace, perhaps she wore it because she was a veterinarian? So, a 'cat' suit?

Noella wrinkled her nose at the terrible pun and greeted her friend with a smile.

"Wow!" Catching Grace's hands, she held her arms out from her body. Spun her, noting her graceful, fluid motions. In French, she announced, "I love your outfit! It's spectacular!!"

"Thank you!" Grace's eyes flicked anxiously

over the small crowd of people making their way through the foyer.

"Are you a dancer?" Noella understood stage fright. She'd overcome it many times to perform at local ceilidhs in front of family and friends. Once even at a semi-professional event, though she'd been sick all day beforehand.

"An…" Grace paused, her forehead wrinkling slightly. "An acrobat of the air?" she ventured uncertainly.

"Trapéziste?" Noella's jaw dropped. "Amazing!"

"And you." Grace's smile was puzzled. "Are you…dressed as Anne Shirley?"

"Oui, yes." Noella leaned closer and dropped her voice slightly. "I tell someone I am from Prince Edward Island and it is assumed I must love this character. So, I finally read the books." Laughing, she touched her wide-brim straw hat, under which she'd firmly secured and hidden her own, blond hair. "And tonight, I become her."

"Soooo…now you actually do like her?" Grace guiltily made a mental note to read the books. Up until now, she'd only seen the movies.

"Anne?" Noella shrugged. That could turn into a lengthy discussion. "I liked her better after she has grown into her love for Gilbert." Remembering Grace's explanation of her costume, Noella asked, "Do you still practice?"

"Oh, not really. Not enough, I mean." Grace bounced on her toes as if suddenly overcome with nervous energy. "C'mon." Linking arms with her, Grace steered them into the cultural hall.

"Grace, look!" Noella pointed at an adorable nine-year-old Mrs. Claus. "I must have the picture with her!"

She caught up with the little girl just in time to ask her mother—who had also dressed as Mrs. Claus—to take the picture. They chatted briefly, exchanged compliments, then parted ways as the little Mrs. Claus hauled her mother off toward a friend dressed as…a cartoon character? Yes, that was probably it.

Looking around for Grace, Noella spotted Merry. With the same man she'd ridden to church with on Sunday! *Hmm*. Although, if they were together tonight, Merry didn't seem to know what to do with him. Instead of chatting with him or smiling at the antics of the children, she stood rigidly to one side while he talked to whomever wandered past. Perhaps they did not know what to do with each other?

Rejoining Grace, Noella observed, "Mmm, I think that our Merry has a boyfriend."

Grace frowned. She took a step forward, a determined expression on her face.

"Wait." Noella gripped her arm. A sensitive person, she all but felt Merry's pain and discomfort in the noisy, chaotic environment. However… The man had turned to Merry and was gesturing at an empty table in the back. "See?

He's taking care of her."

Feeling Grace's arm relax under her hand, Noella was simultaneously glad that Merry had such a staunch friend in Grace and a little disappointed to still be single.

"Everyone!" At the front of the room, Brother Murdock clapped his hands. "May I have your attention, please? We're about ready to start the chili cook-off, so if you'll fold your arms, I've asked Sister Hixson to bless the food."

After the prayer, Noella squeezed Grace's arm. "I brought a pot. My mother's famous eight-bean chili!"

"Mmm." Grace squeezed her back. Whispered, "Does it have cinnamon?"

"Of course!" Noella immediately headed for the food line, Grace in tow.

"Naturally," Grace agreed promptly.

They each snagged foam bowls and plastic spoons, then made their way down the tables. Crock pots of all colors and shapes were arranged with small cards indicating that some were chicken or some were gluten-free, and so forth.

"This, it is Merry's mother's?" Noella asked, indicating Elaine McKinney's distinctive, chipped crock pot.

Grace smiled and nodded. They both wound up with two bowls, Noella making sure that Grace got some of the eight-bean chili she'd brought.

"We're holding up the line," Grace urged.

"Ah, yes." Noella chuckled. "Must leave some for the others." She winked conspiratorially.

They found seats at a table in the primary room, where Noella started to explain her mother's recipe. Which led her on to talking about her grandmother's recipe, then about chili in general. It really was amazing how the simple bean and meat dish had evolved over the years when one stopped and thought about it.

Not that Grace was listening. Noella knew the instant that Alec Fitzsimmons stepped into the room. She never said anything about it because she didn't want to embarrass Grace, but her friend clearly had feelings for the older man. Not *old*. Just...just old*er*. Which was to say that Alec was older than Grace, who was older than Noella, who gave up and focused on her chili.

"You know what?" Grace shoved her chair back, not an easy feat on the carpeted floor. "I've gotta go. I, um…"

Noella met her eyes while reaching out to stack the empty bowls. "Go," she said simply. Such things didn't need explanation between friends, but she appreciated the grateful smile Grace gave her before she slipped out the hallway door.

Sighing, Noella added her half-full bowl of chili to the stack and headed for the nearest trash can. She hated wasting food, but when it started to taste as bland as the tofu curds she'd once sampled for a recipe, well…what was the point?

The church's small kitchen was already full of helpers, so she walked past it to the table where they were stacking the clean dishes. Wiping the last of the water droplets off her crock pot, she took her things and ducked out one of the doors.

Thursday was a cold, gray day and matched her mood perfectly. Surprisingly, step dancing didn't chase away the hollow feeling in the pit of her stomach.

She didn't even get the usual rush from defeating the latest security upgrade at Netherland Transport. She responded politely to Peter's gloating, but begged off as quickly as she could and went to bed early.

Tomorrow was Friday, which meant movie night at Merry's. Burrowing deep under her covers, Noella told herself to look forward to that.

Unable to sleep, midnight found her up and in the kitchen, baking gingerbread.

She didn't usually mind being single. Somehow, though, seeing Merry and Grace at the trunk-or-treat had started her thinking.

Thinking…what?

Grumbling at herself, she shoved another cookie sheet into the oven. Picking up the bag of icing, she piped cheerful expressions onto the cookies she'd already cooled. Added snow to the limbs of chewy Christmas trees and pretty hemlines to the skirts of the gingerbread women.

While the activity did nothing to relieve her agitation, after a couple of hours she'd at least worn herself out. Covering the cookies, she turned off the oven and stumbled into bed, where her heavy eyes slammed shut.

She avoided the kitchen for most of the next morning, but eventually she had to acknowledge the mess.

By the time she'd finished decorating the cookies and cleaning the kitchen, she didn't care if she ever baked again. In fact, she'd had about enough of kitchens in general.

Maybe it was the sunlight that streamed through her windows. Maybe it was the new tube of lipstick. However it happened, Noella spent a few extra minutes on her makeup and hair after her shower.

Giggled at her reflection. "Who needs a date to feel good?" she asked it cheekily.

Tossing her purse strap over her shoulder, she closed the front door firmly behind her. Today, she would eat supper at Blinky's.

"Grace!" Spying her friend in the diner's far corner, Noella headed in that direction. "What a lovely surprise! Would you like some company?" She nearly tripped over her own feet when she realized that Grace not only *had* company, but was sitting with an extremely attractive *young*er man. She'd seen him somewhere before, if only she could remember… Ah, yes of course! This was the son of Alec Fitzsimmons. Drew? Or

Damen?

Danny, caught with a mouthful of burger, stared as a petite honey-blond woman rushed up to their booth. Words were coming out of her mouth a mile a minute, but high school French was a long time ago for him and he got absolutely nothing out of it. Grace, he noticed with some surprise, answered in French without missing a beat.

Suddenly terrified of Grace trying to introduce him to the pretty woman while his mouth was full, he began chewing as fast as they were talking. Swallowed. *Ow.* A semi-solid lump of food lodged in his throat, prompting him to take a gulp of his water. He choked when Grace motioned toward him.

"And this is my friend, Danny Fitzsimmons." Grace switched to English for Danny's sake. His face was an odd shade of purple and she studied him for a moment to make sure he was breathing semi-normally before she continued. "Danny, this is Noella Cormier, originally from Prince Edward Island."

"Hi." He started to stand and thwacked his thighs on the booth's table, nearly upsetting it.

Eyes wide with surprise, Grace automatically reached to steady things he'd set to rocking.

"Oops." Deciding to follow through with shaking her hand at least, he extended his arm. Aaand saw mayo on his fingers that he'd mysteriously collected in the last thirty seconds. "Um…"

Grace did her best to hide her amusement as she handed him a napkin. Shot Noella a sideward glance and was delighted to find that she was genuinely smiling.

"A pleasure to meet you," Noella said in her softly accented English.

"I'll bet." Since he couldn't sink through the floor, Danny scrubbed his hands with the napkin, then tried one last time. "Danny. Originally from Nebraska." He tagged that last on after belatedly remembering that Grace had already given his name.

"Ah, oui." Noella bravely put her fingers inside his massive hand. "I have never been to Nebraska." His massive, warm, gentle hand. And oh, his eyes. Gray, but not a plain gray. No, they were full of different shades of gray, like…like a stormy sky. "We are neighbors, yes?"

"Neighbors," he repeated, unable to think past the spark he'd felt when her hand touched his.

"That's right." Grace popped a couple more fries into her mouth, snagged her shake, and got up. "Now, why don't you be a good neighbor and buy the lady supper?" She dropped a wink on the side Noella couldn't see, then stepped back.

"I'd like that." He meant it.

Noella shrugged expressively, retrieved her hand with a small flutter of fingers, and glanced surreptitiously at Grace. The tiny nod she received in response spoke volumes. Yes, she would be perfectly safe with Danny. She looked at him through her lashes. Safe—all except where her heart was concerned.

Grace lifted her shake in a 'goodbye' salute and started to turn away, only to have Danny take a step after her.

"Grace." He touched her arm lightly. "Maybe this isn't such a good time for me to surprise Dad." He shrugged significantly. She'd explained about her date with his dad for the next evening, among other things, and he had no desire whatsoever to get in the way.

Noella made a point of not hearing the rest of their discussion, though she noted Grace's firm head shakes and wondered what she was saying no to. Whatever it was, Danny didn't seem too upset by it. Just the opposite, judging by his broad smile as he slid into the booth opposite her.

Danny could feel the goofy grin on his face. He just couldn't make it go away. "So." He rearranged what was left of his meal, wishing he hadn't eaten so fast. "What can I get you?"

Susan, Blinky's manager, came over, pen and order pad in hand.

"Noella, hi!" She made a point of assessing the younger woman. "Don't you look pretty today!" She gave Danny a sly glance, trying desperately to figure out which woman Danny was dating—Grace or Noella.

"Thank you." Noella caught on instantly. Blinky's wasn't busy yet, not for a Friday, and anybody could've taken her order. "A green salad, please, and the grilled chicken sandwich."

Susan hung around, pretending to write, but they were just smiling at each other, so she retreated with a soft huff.

"Poor Susan." Danny twisted a napkin without realizing he was doing it. "She's got a bad habit of trying to figure out what she thinks she sees and hears in here."

"Understandable." Noella rested her forearms on the table to make it easier for her to play with the salt shaker. "What is it like, Nebraska?"

"Hmm? Oh." Danny dropped the napkin. "I don't remember very much. We left there when I was eleven."

Noella observed a faint shadow cross his face. "It was a difficult move?"

Hearing the gentle note in her voice, Danny hesitated, then explained, "My mom died that year."

"I am sorry." She touched his hand to comfort him and felt something. Not a spark, exactly. Something deeper, like nothing she'd ever felt before.

His lips twisted in what might've been meant as a smile. "Worst year of my life." There was more to the story, but he stopped there. Telling about his parents' divorce or...or how his mom died in a one-car accident—that wasn't exactly first date material.

Chapter 6

Squaring his shoulders, Danny changed the subject. "What about you? What brought you to Missouri?" To his surprise, she opened her mouth. Closed it.

"I am not sure," she admitted with a light laugh. "I just. Came." She lifted her hands in a helpless gesture.

"Here's your salad." Susan set down a plate and a small squirt bottle of dressing. "Your sandwich will be right out." Again she hovered, but again was disappointed.

"I don't think I understand." Now that she had something to eat, Danny started nibbling on his fries. He wanted to finish his burger, too, if he could figure out how to do it without making a mess of himself. "How can you not know why you moved?"

"I must sound very silly." She shook her head as she picked the red onions off her salad and set them on the side of the plate. Why was it she could never remember to ask for them to be left off?

"No, it's not that." He paused, his eyebrows drawing in. "Exactly. I mean..." Her shoulders started to shake and he allowed himself to smile. "Maybe a little." He liked that she saw the humor in it, even though it was at her own expense.

"I think so, too," she admitted. "It just

happened so quickly." Swallowing a bite of salad, she sighed. "One day, I was at the market, buying groceries for my mother. Somewhere between the potatoes and canned soup, I suddenly realized I was bored."

He waited, but she stopped there for another bite of salad. "That's it? You were bored?" Perplexed, he sucked down some of his drink. "So you, what? Threw a dart at a map and hopped on a plane to Nowhere, USA?" He didn't have anything against the place, he could just think of a dozen other more interesting cities she might have chosen to move to. Hey, what was he saying? If she'd moved somewhere else, they'd never have met!

"Something like that." She grimaced. "I grew up with the ocean less than a day's drive in every direction. Somehow living far from the water seemed exciting."

"Exciting?" he echoed. Cadmia, Missouri hadn't made any lists lately that he knew of, but especially not the list of the top ten exciting places to live. Or top hundred, for that matter.

"My grandmother came once to visit the church history sites," she offered. "That is what brought this area to my attention. I have since had the pleasure of visiting many of them."

"Chicken sandwich?" asked a bored teenager.

"That's us." Danny motioned for him to put it in front of Noella and glanced over at where Susan was standing behind the counter, studiously ignoring them. "I don't think she's very happy with us," Danny observed in a stage whisper.

Noella laughed. "What shall we do about that?"

Danny took a bite of his sandwich. "Hmm. Let's think." Abandoning their discussion of why she'd moved there, he made one ridiculous suggestion after another until Noella was laughing so hard she could barely breathe.

"Ça suffit," she gasped. Realized she'd spoken in French and waved her hands for him to stop. "It is too funny!"

"Yeah, I guess you're right." Grinning, he sat back and let her finish eating her sandwich. "Besides, she's been watching us for the last ten minutes and is jumping to her own conclusions."

"Mmm, no doubt they are much more interesting than anything we, um, *I* could come up with." Her sides and cheeks ached. She hadn't laughed so much since her twin nieces discovered puns.

"Of course." He leaned in and gave her his most engaging smile. "If we left together, that would give her a lot more to imagine."

Flattered, Noella stalled for time by dabbing at her mouth with her napkin.

"I would love to."

His smile dimmed at her apologetic tone. "But?"

Her phone buzzed with a reminder and she held it up for him to see.

"Movie night." He perked up. "That sounds fun. Have you got room for one more?"

She quirked an eyebrow. "Eh, this cannot be." Opening to her calendar, she showed him the rest of the reminder.

"With the girls," he read. Cleared his throat. "Ohhh." Shifting, he flexed his arm muscles just enough to be funny. "I don't suppose I'd fit in."

"Thank you for supper." She resisted the temptation to just enjoy the sight he presented and slid to the edge of her bench instead.

His hand forced, he rose with her. "Tomorrow?" He caught her scarf as it slipped off her arm while she juggled her things. "I mean, what are you doing tomorrow?"

"In the morning, I will go to the ward wood cutting project."

"And after that?" He took a chance and carefully laid the scarf over her shoulders, releasing the ends before he came off as a creep.

"What did you have in mind?" Something deep within her responded to the warmth in his eyes and smile so that she felt like a fudgsicle on the fourth of July.

Danny couldn't help watching her mouth as she spoke. How was it possible that her lipstick was still perfect after eating a salad and an entire chicken sandwich? Because, much to his great satisfaction, she hadn't just nibbled around the edges, then claimed to be full. She hadn't batted an eye when he ordered a second burger, either.

Realizing she was waiting for him to answer her question, he cleared his throat. "There's this restaurant I've been meaning to go to, over in Fireclay where I live. We could start with dinner, then see what else the town has to offer." He spent most of his time on his small ranch, which was as far outside of Fireclay as was physically possible while still claiming the zip code. That didn't mean Fireclay didn't have things to do, just that he hadn't bothered to figure out what they were. One thing he knew for a fact was that Fireclay had more things to do than Cadmia had ever dreamed of.

"Fireclay?" she repeated, biting her lip. That was over forty minutes away. She hadn't counted on such a…time commitment. On such short notice, at least.

Sensing her withdrawal, Danny stammered, "Not that there's anything wrong with Blinky's." He winced as he caught sight of Susan's annoyed expression out of the corner of his eye. Hastily following Noella out the door, he tried to get his foot out of his mouth. "I didn't know if you'd want to eat out at the same place two nights in a row."

"I eat almost always at the same place." Noella chuckled even as she noted the way his hand cupped her elbow. Gallant. Hmm, she liked that. "My own kitchen."

Danny wisely kept his mouth shut while he tried to work out how he was meant to take that. She *might* be inviting him to join her for dinner, for example. Then again, she… He pasted on a smile to cover his confusion when she stopped by a car and looked up at him.

Keys in hand, Noella hesitated. While she felt drawn to this handsome stranger, she knew she would be tired after the wood cutting project. Yet Grace had given him the nod.

"I can see I'm failing to persuade you." He watched her face carefully while she unlocked her car. "I usually don't resort to begging, but I sort of need to be out of the way tomorrow evening. As a favor to Grace."

Noella blinked, simultaneously amused and terribly curious. If this was what they called "a line," it was a new one.

He cleared his throat again. Ugh, why did he keep doing that? He sounded like he was getting sick or something.

"Pick me up at five o'clock." She pressed a business card into his hand. "At this address." That wasn't how she usually arranged her dates, but right now she was running very late for the movie night. Thankfully, he didn't seem to mind.

"I'll be there." He tucked her card into a pocket and closed her door, taking care not to slam it.

His face was so close to hers as he waved goodbye that even with a window separating them her heart rate picked up speed.

Danny's heart sank as he watched the beautiful blond driving away from him. It seemed oddly foreboding, like she wasn't going to be in his life very long. Still… He tapped the pocket where he'd stowed her card and permitted himself a small smile.

Who knew what tomorrow would bring?

Hopping into his truck, he headed out to the Rockin' R. It was a lot later than he'd expected to arrive and he sort of hoped he'd find the trailer dark. No matter what they decided about Caesar, the dog's life would be exactly the same for the next forty-eight hours, so that could wait until tomorrow morning. Plus, he was still processing the bombshell Grace had dropped on him.

Turning onto the main highway, he ran his fingers through his hair. He'd never claim to be an expert on women, but he'd known for a long time about Grace's crush on his dad. Long enough to have accepted it as well as her honest friendship. If she didn't mind the sixteen year age gap, neither did Danny.

Now what, though? How would things change once she officially started dating his dad?

He blew out a breath, amused at the question. How *wouldn't* things change? Good grief, what if they got married? A mental image of himself standing in the receiving line at their reception sprang to mind. His thoughts continued traveling along that road to the day when he got the call that he was a big brother at twenty-nine or thirty years old. A really, *really* big brother.

Realizing he was approaching the Rockin' R's turnoff, he almost kept driving. Grace hadn't meant to tell him she loved his dad. It just sort of slipped out after he reassured her that he didn't mind the idea of his dad dating.

But what an awkward thing for him to know before his dad did!

Shaking his head ruefully, Danny signaled and took the turnoff. His dad was still his best hope for finding a home for Caesar and he couldn't let the big dog down. No, he was just going to have to guard his tongue the way he'd guarded peanut butter while serving his mission abroad.

Parking in front of the trailer where he'd grown up, he grabbed his duffel and entered without knocking.

"Danny?" Alec finished drying his hands and wrapped his son in a bear hug.

"Hey, Dad," Danny wheezed, unable to recapture the breath his dad had squeezed out of him. "How are you doing?"

Not three minutes later, he was seated at the kitchen table. "Dad, I just ate!"

"Oh?" Alec paused on his journey to the fridge, eyebrows thoughtfully drawn together. "Well. Can I get you...anything? Glass of water?"

"That'd be great." Danny shoved himself to the far inside of the bench so their knees wouldn't knock into each other when his dad sat down. Whoever designed this trailer couldn't have been more than five and a half feet tall, leaving a growing, teenage Dany to discover by sad experience that being over six feet tall had its disadvantages.

"How's Chuck doing these days?" Alec surprised him by plopping himself in the room's slightly-more-comfortable arm chair.

"Chuck? Oh, he's doing fine." Danny nodded enthusiastically. "I haven't told him yet, but next year I plan to have him take some of our training classes." With an appropriate raise, of course.

"Good idea," Alec approved. "He's been working with you for what, two years now? Giving him more responsibility is a great way to show how much you trust him." Alec winked. "Not to mention you'll be giving yourself some time to relax. Hey." He brightened. "Maybe we can finally go fishing."

Danny did his best to laugh while his conscience needled him. "I'd love to, Dad."

Alec lowered the glass of water he'd been about to drink from and looked at him steadily, obviously hearing a 'but' coming.

"And hopefully I can, in a couple of years." Danny spread his hands apologetically. "See, I figured we could double our capacity by having us both training at the same time. That way we increase our revenue while maintaining the smaller class sizes."

Alec nodded slowly. "Sure. Yeah, that's…"

He looked down at his glass. "That's good business."

Danny's self-reproach skipped a few gears and slammed into overdrive. "No reason we can't go fishing tomorrow," he suggested. The more he thought about it, the better he liked the idea. "We could go to Miller's Hole. Head out early, be there by dawn and stay till we catch our limit." That way, they'd be completely uninterrupted while he tried to sell his dad on the idea of Caesar.

"I'd like that." Alec didn't look like he knew whether to smile or frown. "Except there's the ward wood cutting project tomorrow morning and," he rubbed his palms on his jeans, "I've got a date tomorrow evening."

Danny swallowed. "A date?"

"With Grace."

"With Grace?"

Alec's eyes narrowed. "You're not surprised."

Danny laughed weakly. "Never could fool you." Caving under his dad's scrutiny, he ventured, "I bumped into her at Stock's. We went to Blinky's to catch up over a couple of burgers and she told me." He left off there before he said more than he should.

Alec tugged at his ear. "And...you're okay with it?"

"Yeah, sure, Dad." Danny gulped down the rest of his water. "I think it's a great idea. She's had a crush on you since I can remember." Alarm bells started going off in his head, but his dad interrupted just in time.

"You mean you knew, too?" Alec threw up his hands. "Why didn't you tell me?"

Danny snickered. "Riiiight." Clearing his throat, he channeled a typical after-school discussion from his teenage years, talking too rapidly to be interrupted this time. "I did pretty well on the math test, probably going to flunk English, but I really like track, and oh, by the way, Dad, my best friend likes you."

Their eyes met and Alec gave in with a laugh.

"Fair point." Grinning ruefully, Alec got up to take Danny's empty glass. "So, what brings you out here?"

Danny suddenly wished he had the empty glass back so he'd have something to do with his hands. "I, uh…"

"Don't tell me, let me guess. You've finally gotten a steady girlfriend?"

He blinked, his mind going back to his impromptu supper with Noella. He must've hesitated a tad too long, because his dad turned to face him.

"Really?"

"No." He shook his head. "No, not…" But he couldn't ignore the way he'd felt. "I, um, I do have a date."

"How about that?" Alec regarded him curiously as he returned to his chair. "When?"

"Tomorrow night."

"Oh." Alec's face fell. "I guess you won't be able to stay for the wood cutting, then."

"No, I'll go." Danny put up his hands to forestall the question he could see his dad was about to ask. "Let me start at the beginning, okay?"

Alec folded his hands in his lap and leaned back, eyebrows raised expectantly.

"So, I came out here to ask you about one of my dogs." Danny sighed and relaxed for the first time since Grace came up. "Caesar." Folding his arms, he rested his elbows on the table. "He's ex-military, a beautiful Belgian Shepherd."

"Retired?"

"Well…" Danny stared at a chip in the edge of the table. He'd probably dropped a butter knife there or something. "Medical discharge." Haltingly, he told what he knew of Caesar's story. "He walks pretty well now, but he'll never be able to go all-out like he used to."

Alec frowned sympathetically. "And that's in addition to his not wanting to eat?"

"Yeah. Makes finding him a home a little more challenging, y'know?"

"I'm sure."

"That's why I was wondering if you could take him." Danny had already mentally discarded the part of his argument about his Dad being alone. Now he planned to point out that Grace, as a veterinarian, would be the perfect co-owner.

"The Rockin' R would be big enough for a dog his size, plus you've got stock he could learn to guard and..." His voice trailed off as his dad started shaking his head.

"The Rockin' R isn't my place, son. It's Mr. Brooke's and he has guests in and out of here on a whim, sometimes with children. That's not counting the hired hands, who also sometimes come and go on a whim." Alec sighed. "And even if it were my place, I'm too busy to give him the care he needs." He gestured broadly. "The place is too busy, with too many strangers, too many other animals, and so forth. I'm afraid an animal like Caesar, with special training and subsequent special needs, wouldn't do well under the conditions here."

"I didn't think about the guests." If Caesar happened to bite someone, no matter how good his reason, some hotshot lawyer would almost certainly call for him to be put down. Pinching the bridge of his nose between his thumb and forefinger, he exhaled slowly. Good thing he hadn't brought Caesar with him, to help 'persuade' his dad.

"I'm sorry, Danny." Genuine regret filled his dad's voice. "I hope you find a place for him."

"Thanks." He drummed his fingers on the table. "I don't suppose you can think of anyone who could take him?"

"Not off-hand, sorry. I'll pray about it tonight, and let's sleep on it, alright?" Rising, his dad patted him affectionately on the shoulder. "We need to be at the Tomlinson's at eight."

A glance at the clock confirmed that it was getting late.

"Your room's ready for you." Alec winked as he turned to head down the hallway to the master bedroom. "And you can tell me about your date on the way over in the morning."

Danny rolled his eyes. Half-laughed, then grabbed his duffel and headed to bed.

Chapter 7

As Noella climbed into the Peterson's van after the wood cutting project, she glanced wistfully at the last few volunteers stacking wood in the Tomlinson's barn. She'd found herself elbow-deep in helping to make lunch without quite knowing how it happened. Not that she minded preparing food for the volunteers she could see through the foggy kitchen window. It just wasn't how she'd planned to serve that morning.

"You look so tired," Sister Peterson sympathized as she handed Noella her clean soup pot.

Just what I hoped to hear before my first date in weeks. Noella stifled a sigh.

Brother Peterson coughed loudly. "Honey, can you help John with his buckle?"

Sister Peterson jumped forward in time to catch John as he tried to escape the van. Groaned when he began howling indignantly.

"I guess one of us had fun!" Brother Peterson shouted over his son's protests. Smiling ruefully at Noella, he went around to help his wife.

That left Noella, who was seated between the girls in the back, to keep them preoccupied instead of chiming in. No stranger to naptime meltdowns, she started singing a favorite nursery song.

John had already begun calming down, but when he heard the song, he decided that being in the van wasn't the worst thing in his world and allowed himself to be buckled into his car seat.

Soft children's music began playing as soon as Brother Peterson turned the engine on and all three children were snoring peacefully when the van pulled up in front of Noella's.

"Take a hot shower and a nap," Sister Peterson suggested helpfully. "Then a really, really cold shower when you wake up. It'll help with…"

"Thanks," Brother Peterson interrupted hastily, "for all your help today."

Noella had to laugh as they drove away. Sister Peterson's window didn't get rolled up in time and she heard Brother Peterson starting to explain that not everyone wanted to be told when they didn't look their best.

She took the advice about the hot shower, mostly to ease the kinks in her shoulders. She hadn't done marathon peeling like that in ages. Carrots, potatoes, hard boiled eggs… Whew!

Tumbling into bed, she slept like one of the dozens of logs she'd seen sectioned, split, and stacked that day.

Danny wasn't so lucky. His dad had given him the shortest lecture of his life on their way back from the wood cutting project and his mind was still spinning.

"As my grandmother would say, you marry who you

date."

Sitting up in the bed where he'd been tossing and turning, Danny put his face in his hands. He wanted to take a run, to try to wear himself—and his nerves—down a bit, but he was too tired after working in the cold for most of the morning. Anyway, he hadn't packed enough clean clothes to shower twice today and still look presentable for his date tonight.

Maybe he could wear some of the stuff he'd left behind? Rising, he opened his top drawer. Shook out a tee and stared at the faded graphics. Cringed at the sweat ring around the collar. The two other shirts weren't any better. *Now* he remembered why he'd left them there. He just wished he'd thought of checking the drawer much earlier. A little dish soap before washing would take care of the worst of the damage he'd done to his good shirt that morning, but…

Shaking his head, he tried the tiny wall closet. Brightened at the slate gray button-up shirt he found inside—with sleeves that no amount of tugging would bring down to cover his wrists.

As he reached up to scrub his hands over his face, the worn fabric around his biceps split and something in the back of the shirt tore. Right. Back to Plan A it was.

Dropping the ruined shirt on his bed, he reached for his rolling suitcase. Lifted out the garden green button-up and shrugged into it.

As he brushed his teeth and hair, his father's

voice continued echoing in his mind.

"Dating with marriage in mind can keep you from wasting a lot of time that you'll wish you had back when you find the right one."

And, *"You have to know that there are blessings you're missing out on."*

Staring at his reflection, Danny tried to think it through logically. By the time he picked Noella up, they'd have known each other for roughly twenty-four hours. Aside from having a good time at supper last night, he'd seen her exactly once, when he stopped cutting wood long enough to have some hot soup at the Tomlinson's.

His heart swelled as he remembered seeing her standing at the sink, her cheeks flushed with the heat of the kitchen, an apron over her clothes and a smile on her face as she helped scrub dishes.

A scripture bolted into his mind like one of his dogs racing forward when they heard the rattle of their food dishes.

I will make him an help meet for him.

Drying his face and hands, Danny re-entered into his room and picked up his scriptures. It took him a minute to find the exact reference, he didn't read the Old Testament nearly as much as he should, but there it was—Genesis 2:18. "And the Lord God said, It is not good that the man should be alone; I will make him an help meet for him."

Massaging the back of his neck, Danny considered the term 'help meet.' He'd always thought that was a strange way to say 'wife' until his dad showed him the footnote that read, "a helper suited to, worthy of, or corresponding to him."

Now, what did that mean in his life? What did he *need* in a wife?

After a brief struggle, he blew out a breath. Was he supposed to be keeping some sort of list of…of qualities and traits that summed up his idea of the perfect woman? Did men do that?

The closest he could come to anything like that was knowing what kind of woman he chose to date. Smart. Funny. Kind.

His eyes fell on his mother's picture. He'd hung it himself the day they'd moved in. His gut twisted as he remembered the police officer standing in the doorway of their home in Nebraska.

Sir, I'm sorry to inform you that your ex-wife has been in a fatal car accident.

Only eleven years old, he'd struggled to understand how his mother could've been in a one-car drunk driving accident. A 'drunk driving accident' meant that one car hit another, didn't it?

Groaning, he knelt beside his bed. His toes were jammed up against the wall, but he didn't care. Tonight suddenly felt like the most important first date of his life, and he needed Heavenly Father's help.

At length, a peace settled over him. He knew next to nothing about Noella, and felt that he should keep an open mind and heart.

Alec was waiting in the front room-kitchen when he stepped into the hallway. Danny had never felt taller than he did as he met his father's measuring look with the quiet confidence that came from earnest prayer.

"Are you all ready for tonight?" Alec asked around the lump in his throat. He'd spent most of his life watching his son grow up and doggone it if every time he thought his boy was a man he didn't get impressed all over again by Danny's growth.

"Yes." Seeing a suspiciously watery look in his dad's eyes, Danny cleared his throat. "Yeah, absolutely. We're going to Taste of Tuscany in Fireclay."

Alec nodded. Cleared his own throat. "I'm taking Grace to Little Persia."

"Nice." Danny wished he'd thought of it. Little Persia had the best Middle Eastern food in a day's drive of Cadmia. Except…no, bad idea. Going on a first date was rough enough without sharing a table with his dad who was on *his* first date in over a decade.

"So." Alec slid his hand into his pocket and raised his eyebrows. "Got enough cash for tonight?"

Danny cracked up and came forward for a hug. "Who uses cash anymore?"

They swapped lighthearted jabs all the way out to their trucks, where they hugged again and parted ways.

Danny offered a prayer for his dad's date as he drove to Noella's, which turned out to be just across the street from where his best friend, Philip, used to live. Her door opened as he pulled up and a middle-aged woman stepped out, a thoughtful expression on her face.

Noella appeared in the front room window and watched the woman walk to the house next door, then spotted Danny. Smiling, she waved for him to come up.

"Here goes nothing." Exiting his truck, Danny went up the walk to her house. Finding her door slightly ajar, he knocked.

"Come in!" her voice called.

She was nowhere to be seen as he entered, but he liked what he did see. A single chocolate brown couch sat across the living room from a modestly sized TV. Floral pillows kept the couch's darker color from dominating the otherwise cheerful room, and a colorful rectangular throw rug beside the couch drew his eyes to the kitchen.

"I will be right with you!" Noella called from where she was repairing her makeup in the bathroom. Hailey's mother, Kristen, had just stopped in to talk about 'charity' with her and the conversation had prompted them both to shed a few tears.

"Take your time." Danny unzipped his coat partway and moved a little way further into the room. Curry, jalapeno, cinnamon, and a dozen other scents assailed his nose when he inhaled, driving his taste buds crazy. Underlying the hints of her impressive culinary repertoire came the clean smell of dish soap.

"I am ready." Noella hadn't spoken immediately. Upon re-entering the room after touching up her makeup, she was surprised to find him so seemingly engrossed in studying her kitchen that she'd taken a moment to study him. His green shirt and dark jeans accentuated his lean, muscular body, but what she loved most was the way the corners of his eyes crinkled when his mouth curved up in a smile. "You must spend a lot of time outside," she said without thinking.

Danny blinked. "That's right, I do." Curious, he picked up the coat she'd left draped over the back of a kitchen chair. "How'd you know?" He admired her hair as he held her coat for her. It looked like honey and felt like silk against the backs of his hands.

"I know." Smoothing her hair over her collar, she smiled. He smelled nice, like a wind-swept meadow after a goodly rain.

Nonplussed by her answer, Danny offered her his elbow and led her to the door.

Noella's smile slipped slightly as she walked out into the fading evening light. The weather prediction wasn't bad, but years of living on her island home had ingrained in her a respect for Mother Nature's fickle behavior.

Blissfully unaware of her concerns, Danny solicitously opened her door for her before moving around to climb in on his side.

"It's kind of a long drive." Flashing a smile, he handed her his phone with the music app already open. "I don't have a lot of music, but scroll through. We can listen to whatever you want." This was almost a survival tactic for him, because he hated it when all the small talk got used up on the drive.

Intrigued, Noella did as he suggested. She could tell a lot about a man by what he listened to. The names that she recognized at first were all country music stars. There were a handful of jazz artists, what she thought might be a religious group, and then…

Opening the folder marked classical, she found several composers she was familiar with.

Danny shot her a startled look when a violin concerto started playing. *That's a first.* He had a theory about women and music. He'd never made it to a second date with the ones who picked an artist at random just to get some noise going. Or with those who complained about his taste in music and insisted on their own because he would 'love' it—or else.

His best experiences came from the times where his date either picked an artist that they liked, too, or were at least willing to try something new. But this was uncharted territory. Noella hadn't just broken the record for how long it took to pick a song, she'd zeroed in on his classical music.

Noella had a funny feeling that she'd just passed a test when Danny reached over to turn the volume up. The exquisite violin music filled the cab, carrying them over the first half of their journey.

She surprised him again by switching to the Vocal Tones, an insanely talented acapella group he'd discovered after his mission.

"How do they even do these things with their voices?" Her eyes wide in amazement at their vocal antics, Noella added, "I must tell my brothers about them." Lifting her phone, she sent a text right then.

Danny broke a rule and turned the volume down to talking level. "How many brothers?"

"Two." She wrinkled her nose slightly while still smiling. "Marq, short for Marquard, and Tallon. They are both older than I am."

Danny could remember Mark easily enough, but he took a moment to repeat the second name to himself.

"Any sisters?"

"Oui, two of those." Her smile was in full force now. "Darcia, my older sister, and Elisette, the youngest."

"Pretty names." He'd never be able to remember them, though. He was terrible with names. "Must be nice to have a big family."

"I love it." Staring into her memories, she wondered how everyone must've changed since she'd left. Her nieces and nephews would be getting taller, learning new things.

"You must miss them." And cue the tears. He gripped the steering wheel, waiting for the waterworks and mentally berating himself. Both for making her homesick and for being stupid enough to put himself in such an awkward position.

"I do." Noella looked out the window and surreptitiously wiped at her eyes. "But enough about me. How many brothers and sisters do you have?" Watching his jaw go slack she wondered if she'd asked the wrong question. Odd. In her experience, men liked to talk about themselves. Some liked it too much.

"I'm…an only child." He'd been mentally calculating how many leftover fast food napkins he had stashed in his glove box and now it looked like he wouldn't be needing them.

Unsure of how to interpret his apparent reluctance to answer, Noella simply nodded and let the subject drop.

Only this time, the music wasn't enough of a filler. Danny could feel the silence tugging at him, clawing at him, searching for a chink in his armor through which to rip an ill-conceived…

"I'd like to have a big family," he blurted. "Y'know," he stumbled. "Someday."

Noella stared at him. What in the world could she say to that?

"Me, too."

Danny smiled weakly and pointed as the restaurant came into view. "Here we are."

"Oh, good." Noella clapped her hands. "I am starving."

He allowed himself a couple of deep breaths and another prayer as he walked around to open her door for her.

"So, I guess you like classical music."

"Yes, I do." Noella smiled brightly. "My grandfather could play a great many classical pieces by heart."

"That's incredible." He nodded when the hostess asked if they wanted a table for two and let the conversation lag while they were being seated. "What instrument did he play?"

"The violin mostly." Noella liked the way he smiled at their young waiter when he brought the menus.

"I'm Tim and I'll be your waiter tonight." He clasped his hands earnestly. "I'll give you a few minutes to look over the menus, then come back to take your order. Alright?"

"Thanks." Danny nodded and flipped to the menu's first page. "I'm glad you're hungry." He flicked a glance at a small mountain of pasta being served at a nearby table.

"I may still need the doggie bag." Noella had also noticed the enormous portions as she walked in. Something about Danny's chuckle caught her attention. "What?"

"Oh, nothing." Danny fiddled with his spoon. "I just train dogs, and that particular expression always makes me laugh."

"You do?" Noella shook her head as thoughts collided. "I mean, you train dogs?"

"Yeah, I have a kennel outside of Fireclay."

Noella opened her mouth to ask him more questions, but saw Tim coming back toward their table. And she had barely looked at the menu!

"We're not quite ready." Danny apologized. "I'm on the third page, though." He showed where his finger was on the menu.

"We do offer a lot of amazing dishes," Tim agreed. "I'd be happy to make a recommendation."

"That's alright." Danny moved on to the next page. "I finally found the steaks," he announced.

"Excellent choice. We have several wines that go well with…"

"We don't drink, actually." Danny gave him another friendly smile.

"Certainly, sir." Tim didn't miss a beat. "We also," he caught Noella's eye before opening to the last page of her menu for her, "have a number of delicious non-alcoholic drinks."

"Thank you." Noella turned back to the page

she'd been studying. "A few more minutes, please?"

"Take your time." With a slight bow, Tim hurried off to tend his other tables.

"Shouldn't take me too long to decide which of these steaks to have," Danny chuckled.

"I think," Noella took a quick peek at the steak prices for comparison, "I would like the beef ragù."

"Really?" Craning his neck to see the pictures on the page where she was, Danny turned back a page. "I've heard of that."

"But have you ever eaten it?" she teased.

"Can't say that I have." He consulted the menu. "Beef, vegetables, tomato sauce. Sounds sort of like an Italian pot roast."

Noella giggled, but was pleased when he ordered two beef ragù. They discussed his dog training business while they waited, then she had the pleasure of hearing him praise the food.

"I have to get the recipe for this." Danny sat up as tall as he could to look for Tim. "It'll probably push the limits of any cook I can find who'll work out in the middle of nowhere, but this is not a onetime dish." While he did his own cooking over the holidays, they offered meals and accommodations during their training camps.

"Oh, you don't want *this* recipe," Noella objected.

He sat back. "I don't?" Eyeing her nearly empty plate, he simultaneously wondered where she'd put all that food while he prepared to point out that she'd clearly enjoyed it as much as he had.

"My recipe is far superior." She frowned a little. She hadn't meant to sound arrogant.

He closed his half-open mouth, glad to not have the taste of work-boot in it. "You can make beef ragù?" he clarified.

"Yes, of course." Noella blushed a little under his admiring gaze. "I had a small menu planning and recipe website until just this past week." Turning her hands palms up, she concluded, "I made all the instruction videos myself."

"I see." Wiping his mouth on his napkin, Danny leaned toward her. "Have you ever considered working as a cook at a dog training facility?" Her lips twitched and he rushed to rephrase. "Okay, that came out wrong." Shifting in his chair, he tried again. "I run specialized training camps from spring to fall for service animals and their new owners. They all board on-campus and every year it's a battle to find a cook who can make more than grilled cheese sandwiches and barbecue."

Noella drew circles on the tablecloth with a fingertip. The offer was flattering, but foolish. Having a recipe meant nothing. Yet, did she dare…?

"You should never hire a cook without tasting their food first." Slowly, she lifted her eyes to his.

Danny swallowed. Was she inviting him to dinner? Or just flirting? Either way it was a good sign, right?

"If you return to Cadmia soon," she could tell his heart was with his business in Fireclay, which was perfectly understandable, "I would like to cook for you."

Definitely asking him out. "I'll be back."

Tim, in the middle of bringing them their bill, was caught off-guard enough by the firm statement to give them both an odd look.

They laughed and Danny slid his card into the portable payment station Tim placed on the table.

"C'mon." Stuffing his wallet and the receipt back into his pocket, Danny helped her into her jacket again. "I think you're going to love what I found to do next."

Filled with misgivings, Noella tried to ask her question casually. "Bowling?"

"Nope." He grinned. And kept grinning mysteriously until he pulled into the next parking lot.

"Ice skating!" Noella gave a happy cry.

Chapter 8

"This place is pretty busy during the summer," he explained as they walked, hand in hand, "but this time of year most people prefer their own pond or one of the nearby lakes."

"I learned to skate on a lake." Noella laughed at the memories.

"Me, too." Danny grinned, delighted. "It's a great way to collect bruises."

Noella groaned. "Yes, all over."

They swapped stories as they rented skates and in short order they stood at the entrance to the rink.

"I guess I've got you by a broken bone," Danny teased as he stepped onto the ice. Things were going better than he could've hoped.

"Oui, and I have you by the dunking." She shivered dramatically but joined him.

He shook his head. "That had to be terrifying." At least with his broken bone nobody had to chop him out from under the ice first.

She nodded and sidled closer to him even as they merged with the other skaters.

Putting an arm around her, he took her left hand in his and held her close for the first few circuits. It was awkward until they both relaxed and got their rhythm down.

She liked the steadying effect he had on her. It had been longer than she realized since her last foray onto the ice, which made her a little sad. She'd never decided to stop skating. She'd just forgotten about it.

He guided them a little further into the circle, to an invisible 'lane' where the skaters were going a bit more slowly.

Tipping her head back, she asked, "How did you get started training dogs?"

"It's sort of my dad's fault." He maneuvered them smoothly around a gaggle of shrieking teenage girls, none of whom looked like they were capable of staying up on their own. "His theory on raising a teen as a single dad was that busy was better than bored." He laughed with her. "So when his boss, Mr. Brooke, brought in a fancy dog trainer," for a pedigreed dog that the family tired of in less than a year, "he arranged for me to spend time with him. I liked it a lot and I learned a lot. The rest is history." He shrugged. "What about you? What do you do for a living?"

"A little of this, a little of that." She never quite knew how to answer that question.

"For example?" he coaxed when she didn't continue on her own.

"I type for others. And run my website."

"The one you just sold?" he clarified and she nodded. "Whoa!" He twisted them around to the right to avoid a hotshot skater and they wound up spinning crazily.

Noella braced herself against his chest, trying not to overreact and counteract what he was doing.

"Okay." He eased them to a stop near a wall. "Okay," he repeated, whether to reassure her or himself he couldn't be sure.

"That was fun." She rested her still spinning head against his shoulder.

"Yeah." Danny scanned the other skaters without success. The hotshot hadn't stuck around to watch.

"Better than bowling."

"Bowling?" That got his attention. It was the second time she'd mentioned that. "Do you like bowling?"

She opened one eye a crack. "I don't, but I thought you would." The dizziness had passed, leaving her with a pleasantly giddy awareness of his proximity.

"Not I." He shook his head firmly. "I'm terrible at bowling. Not to mention the number of times I've had bowling balls dropped on me." He made a point of studying the skaters to keep his mind off her soft-looking lips.

"By women?" Her eyes opened wide, then scrunched shut. "Pardonne-moi, I did not mean to ask that!" His answering chuckle rumbled through his chest, setting her pulse to skipping.

"C'mon, let's try this again." He made sure they worked together as they eased their way back into the circle, and this time he kept his eyes open for showoffs.

Needing some space after her blunder, Noella decided to skate beside him instead of with him.

Was it a coincidence that she'd never felt so cold?

"Want something from the concession stand?" He asked when skating around in circles grew tedious for him.

She perked up. "Yes, thank you!" She appreciated the way he shifted back and to the right so he was between her and 'oncoming traffic,' making it easier for her to reach the exit and step onto the waiting rubber mat.

"Think you'll want to skate some more?" Seeing a couple of teenage boys headed their way at breakneck speed, he caught her around the waist and lifted her to one side. The boys dashed past without apology and he bit back a reproach.

Gasping, she held onto him until she was able to fully realize what had happened.

"Get a room!" Someone jeered as they whipped past.

He didn't even waste a glance in the heckler's direction. It wasn't the first time that evening that he'd been tempted to kiss her, but he still gently set her down and stepped back.

"Sorry about that." His stomach flipped when her hands moved on his chest—almost as if she wanted to put her arms around his neck.

"No, no." Breathless, she waved his apology away. "I…I have always wanted to be swept off my feet."

He waited, and when she made no attempt to retract the statement, he began to wish he'd just kissed her.

Fortunately, a couple of families walked past just then with their hands full of a variety of goodies.

"Oooh. That looks good!" Noella smiled brightly.

Chuckling, he took her hand and started toward the concession stand. Remembered they were wearing skates. The whole area was padded and they could've easily walked right over, but muscles he'd forgotten he owned were already starting to protest.

"I'm so glad you thought of this," she told him as she veered in the general direction of the locker where they'd left their shoes.

"I'm glad you had fun." Relaxing, Danny followed her lead in removing his skates and putting on his street shoes.

Small talk filled the rest of the evening, punctuated with chocolate candies, popcorn, and a gooey banana-flavored dessert that she didn't recognize but enjoyed thoroughly. He bought them each a tall hot chocolate to fortify them against the frigid night air when the time came, and all too soon he was pulling into her driveway.

"I'll walk you to your door," he offered.

She opened her mouth to protest, but he'd already shut his truck off and was on his way around to open her door for her.

"You are mad," she laughed, tucking her arm through his as if to ward off the cold. "You could've stayed in your nice, warm truck."

"There are worse things than being cold." He winked. "And this way, I get to prolong our evening."

"Mmm." She unlocked her door. Hesitated, torn. First date kisses were rare for her, but tonight… All at once, his arms went around her in a bear hug that brought her feet up off the ground.

"Thanks for going out with me." He deposited her just inside her door. "I'll see you at church tomorrow?" Their gazes locked for a handful of heartbeats before she nodded.

"I'll be there."

"Great." Flashing her one more grin, he closed the door between them and strode back to his truck, whistling softly.

Moving to the window, Noella watched. Waved. And sank onto her couch.

Was she relieved or miffed that he hadn't tried to kiss her? Most of the dates she'd gone on since moving here ended either with an awkward handshake or a too soon kiss attempt.

Her lips curved up as she admitted to herself that she rather liked how Danny handled it.

The next day was the first Sunday of the month, traditionally a day to fast for others. She used the time she usually would've spent making and eating breakfast to go back over her favorite parts of that week's lesson before church. She'd called Jane earlier in the week and made plans to have supper there again this evening, the perfect way to break her two-meal fast.

That didn't leave much, if any, time for Danny, but she didn't yet know what to expect where he was concerned anyway.

Kneeling by her couch, she said a prayer reviewing the people and things she was remembering in her fast, then drove to church.

Danny caught her the moment she entered the door and lead her to one side. "Morning."

"Bonjour," she answered, trying to ignore the goosebumps rushing up her arm from the hand he held.

"I wanted to…" He paused to smile and wave at someone he hadn't seen in a while, then had to shake someone else's hand. "Fine, thanks. Yourself? Great."

Noella disguised her impatience behind a friendly smile and was glad when Danny turned back to her.

"I have to head back after church today, but I wanted to ask if you'd like to come over this Friday." Realizing he'd left out key details, he tried again. "I mean, would you like to come visit my training center? I could give you the grand tour and you'd have an entire six-person cabin to yourself. Then on Saturday we could go out for breakfast, just sort of do whatever we wanted." His voice trailed off as she bit her lip.

"Noella." Alec chose that moment to interrupt. "How're you this morning?"

She shook his warm, calloused hand, so much

like his son's, and did her best to smile. Much to her surprise, he didn't give her a chance to answer.

"Does Chuck know you're inviting company over?" Alec asked Danny. "As I recall, he and Toni don't care for surprises." Briefly he related an exaggerated account of the one time he'd spontaneously decided to spend the weekend.

"I haven't told them yet," Danny admitted, wondering what his dad was up to. "Chuck and Toni have their own cabin, and I wouldn't expect her to cook for a guest anyway."

Noella's apprehensions vanished at their words. A weekend alone with Danny wasn't going to happen. But a weekend with Danny and the associate he'd spoken so highly of, as well as his wife? Yes, that would be alright.

"Ah, I hear prelude music." Smiling broadly, Alec tipped his head to Noella and vanished as abruptly as he'd arrived.

"We…should probably go in." Danny's smile felt forced.

"Danny." She touched his arm lightly. Smiled and slipped her hand into the crook of his elbow. "I cannot come Friday, but if work will permit, I will come Saturday." His face softened and his eyes lit up, making her glad she'd agreed.

They sat next to each other during fast and testimony meeting, then Sunday school, where she enjoyed his quiet comments immensely.

All too soon the meetings were over and they were walking toward the door.

"I'll come pick you up on Saturday," he promised.

"Mmm, that is very kind of you but I should drive myself." She wasn't anticipating trouble, she just didn't want to be stuck without a way out.

His forehead creased. "Are you sure? I mean, it's no trouble for me to come get you, if that's worrying you."

She shrugged. "If I must return early, I would feel better to have my own car." She smiled and left it there.

He seemed about to try to argue the point, then rubbed the back of his neck and nodded. "I guess I'd feel the same way."

He gave her a little warning this time before engulfing her in a hug.

"Who taught you this?" she asked, her cheek pressed firmly against his.

"Grace." Reluctantly, he straightened away. There were plenty of eyes on them, but they had a small corner of the foyer to themselves, so he went on, albeit in a lowered tone of voice. "She said hugs were safer than kisses and," he brushed a strand of hair from her face, his fingers lingering on her cheek, "she always knew what she was talking about."

"Oh." It was all she could do to find enough air for the small word as his eyes dropped to her mouth. She really appreciated that he didn't immediately—automatically—try for a kiss.

Taking a long step back, he handed her something, winked, and walked away.

Belatedly noticing the whispers from others exiting the chapel, Noella got in her car before checking to see what he'd given her.

Her lips curved up in a smile as she turned over the business card in her hand, revealing an address on one side and a pair of dog paws cradling a heart on the other.

She showed it to Jane later that evening and naturally had to tell her all about their first dates, both the unofficial and official. Then she listened as Jane reminisced about skating parties in her youth and they rounded the evening off by singing a few hymns.

She met with Jane and the sisters again on Wednesday for a wonderful discussion about the commandments, but spent most of her week clearing her workload.

One happy, unexpected result was a grateful email from her two favorite authors, both of whom promised to recommend her to everyone they knew.

Suddenly, it was Friday, and movie night at Harmony's. The delicious, piping hot empanadas that Harmony served were an amusing contradiction to the extravagant sets of *The King and I*, which they all enjoyed thoroughly.

"You're sure it's okay if we sing along?" Merry

asked for the third time as Deborah Kerr's character abruptly lowered the telescope.

"If you don't, I'm gonna solo and nobody wants that." Harmony snickered, wondering what her vocal teacher would think if she could hear her say that.

Noella liked the music so much that she bought the soundtrack and sang along with it while she drove the next day. It helped keep her from thinking too hard about the butterflies swooping around in her stomach.

They flopped to the metaphorical ground in disappointment when she reached her destination. It turned out to be a plain brick building with a small parking lot, a short sidewalk, and a nicely manicured lawn.

Pushing her sunglasses up on her forehead, Noella looked around in confusion. Where were the twin kennels? The obstacle courses Danny'd spoken of with such pride? The forest sloping off into the distance?

She was double-checking her location on her GPS when the sound of a motor slowly invaded her perception.

"Hello!" A young woman with short, straight black hair waved enthusiastically from her seat on a motorized, two-passenger cart.

Noella lifted a hand in return, sort of recognizing her from Danny's description. Pocketing her phone, she climbed out of her car.

"Noella?" Toni parked and slid out. Her

insulated coveralls bore the business name on the bib and sported shiny knees, as if they'd seen a lot of action. "Noella Cormier?"

"Oui. Um, yes." Was she ever going to start thinking in English? Noella stuck out her hand. "You must be Toni."

"That's right." Black eyes watched her warily from a tan face as Toni shook her hand firmly. "The boys got caught up in a minor emergency and I'm the replacement welcome wagon."

"Oh, I see." Noella managed a smile. The 'boys' had to include Danny, which meant she'd see him soon.

"Did you bring any luggage?" Toni prompted.

"Ah." Smiling apologetically, she popped her trunk. "Yes, of course."

"One bag?" Toni arched a perfect eyebrow and reached for the rolling bag. "I like a girl that travels light."

"Well, and this." Noella lifted her laptop bag out of the trunk as well.

"Uh-oh." Toni shook her head. "Brought your work along, huh?"

Smoothing her hair back, Noella frowned. She wasn't thrilled either, but somehow Toni's innocent remark rubbed her the wrong way.

"Do your best to act interested when Danny gives you the tour, okay?" Toni didn't look up from where she was strapping the first bag on the back of the cart. "Hop on."

As they drove past the office building, Noella

was finally able to see the brass plate that quietly proclaimed the business as the Working Dog Training Center.

Toni gave her the short tour on their way to the guest quarters, a row of five cabins.

"Chuck and I stay in the cabin at the far end." Toni pointed at the largest cabin. "And that's Danny's cottage."

They passed within a hundred yards of a small stone building with a chimney in the center and what looked like a solid wood door. Bare hedges formed a wall off one side of the cottage and Noella could just barely see lawn furniture beyond it. If she squinted ever so slightly, she could've convinced herself she was in a Jane Austen novel.

"You should see this place in the spring." Toni whistled softly. "Danny's got a flower garden you won't believe."

"A flower garden?" Noella hadn't meant to sound quite so surprised.

"Yup." Toni eased the cart onto a pavement pad by the first cabin. "Scratch his surface and you'll get a floral bouquet." She held up a hand when Noella started to get out. "I'm just going to drop off your bags. The boys are over there in Building A."

Noella handed her laptop bag over to the efficient woman, then twisted in her seat to get a better view of the buildings Toni was pointing at. She could've walked the distance just as easily, but did as Toni asked.

"Here's the key to the cabin." Returning, Toni dropped the cabin key into her palm. "I hope you don't need the internet for anything."

That got Noella's attention. "Pardon?"

"The internet." Toni waved in the general direction of everywhere. "We're too far out to get a cell signal. The front office, where I picked you up, and employee housing have it, but none of the cabins do."

"Oh." Noella squeezed the key tightly. It shouldn't be too much of a problem, unless Peter needed to get in touch with her. Or her mother, or…

"Everything okay?" Toni squinted at her in response to her sigh.

"Yes, of course." Noella got the impression that she hadn't fooled Toni at all. But it would be fine.

"Here we are."

Noella clenched her teeth as they stopped with a bit of a jerk. Thankfully, she'd automatically braced herself when she sat down, a habit from a dozen summers of riding on her uncle's tractor.

"C'mon in." Toni lazily slid down and headed for the door.

She allowed herself a deep, calming breath, then followed Toni into the building. The barking she'd heard as they drove up intensified as they walked further in, but wooden walls absorbed some of the noise.

"Hey!" Danny jogged over and wrapped her in a hug. "You made it."

Something about the way he said it made her want to snuggle against his chest and stay there for the rest of her life.

Chapter 9

"Alright, I see how it is," a man's voice called out. "You think just because you own the place you get to ditch the work for a pretty girl."

Noella was laughing before she even saw the man the voice belonged to. "You must be Chuck." She shook his hand, liking his wide smile and friendly eyes at once.

"Charles Darius Taylor, at your service." Taking his hand back, he draped his arm around Toni and kissed her cheek affectionately. "You've already met my better half."

And she doesn't seem to like me. Noella couldn't explain the other woman's cool reception. Every signal Toni gave off as she stood in Chuck's half-embrace shouted that she was right where she wanted to be, which ruled out jealousy. Thank goodness. But then…what was wrong?

"Um, boss?" Chuck raised his eyebrows. "The work?"

Noella's eyes followed Danny's fingers as he raked them through his hair.

"Right. So." He brought both hands up in a 'here's how it is' gesture. "The heat pump in our other kennel died a horrible death at oh-dark-thirty this morning."

"And we've been moving dogs ever since," Chuck inserted, stretching his arm muscles.

"Yeah. Called the repairman and he can't get

out here before Monday." Danny shrugged, rubbed tired eyes. "I thought we'd have things squared away in here a lot sooner."

Noella unzipped the coat that was starting to stifle her. "What can I do?" From the corner of her eye, she saw Toni quirk a disbelieving eyebrow. And right in front of her, Danny watching her with knitted brows.

"We just finished transferring pups a few minutes ago." Chuck scratched his chin. "Maybe you could help Toni keep them corralled while we haul over the last of the equipment?"

"That'd be great," Danny agreed, brightening. "Fifteen, possibly twenty minutes? Then I can show you around?"

"Perfect." Noella turned to Toni as the 'boys' hurried out into the cold.

Toni started for the far corner and Noella fell in step beside her.

"These kennels weren't designed to hold anything smaller than a six-month-old pup, so we need to monitor them pretty closely until they finish setting things up." Toni spoke in a crisp, business-like tone.

Noella put her hands to her mouth as six adorable puppies swarmed the side of a large cage.

"Their mothers do the best they can," Toni's voice had softened, "but we don't want to take any chances."

Noella located the dam, half-hidden in the

shadows. "Is she friendly?"

"Maid Marian?" Toni all but cooed the name, causing the dog's ears to perk up. "She's the sweetest dog on the place."

Noella had met four more dams by the time the boys returned, lugging in bags of food and equipment. While the others arranged and rearranged things to their satisfaction, Noella kept an eye on the puppies.

"You're pretty good at this." Toni offered her a water bottle.

"Puppies are escape artists everywhere." Noella shrugged off the compliment and was pleased to see faint approval in Toni's eyes.

"You've ruined your good jeans." Toni took a swig of her water.

She chuckled as she examined the small snag she'd gotten from one of the hastily constructed cages. "It is nothing." Actually, she might enjoy embroidering something over it. She hadn't done needlework in forever.

"You're not what I expected." Toni leaned against the wall. Looked her up and down. "The way Danny talked about you and your online business, I figured you'd be full of yourself."

Noella blinked. "Pardon?" Toni started to frown and she held up her hand. "I know the words, but I do not think I understand what you mean."

"Full of yourself." Toni hesitated, then tried again. "Y'know." Her hands started to circle aimlessly. "Like you think you're super important."

"Ah, I see." Noella worked hard to keep a straight face. "No, I am not filled with myself. To work online is not something special."

Toni coughed. Cleared her throat, then coughed again.

Suspicious, Noella asked, "Did I say it wrong?"

Danny got there in time to hear Noella practicing the expression and cocked an eyebrow at Toni, who excused herself with a laugh.

"Glad you two are having a good time," he teased, taking Toni's spot against the wall. When she didn't answer, he glanced over the cages, automatically accounting for each puppy. "Listen, about the tour that I promised you. I'm kind of a mess," he gestured at his coveralls, "but Chuck's volunteered to finish in here, so if you're not starving I can show you around."

"Yes, I'd like that." The butterflies soared in her stomach in response to his warm smile.

"Wonderful." Danny straightened, then hesitated. "Toni mentioned you brought your laptop with you. We can stop by the cabin and get it, then you can get caught up?"

"That is alright." She slipped on her jacket and stepped outside, where the cold made her catch her breath. "I will check the messages on my phone, but I am not expecting anything very important right now."

"Okay." A slow smile spread across his face. "Let's go."

She waited in the entryway of his cottage while he hastily changed, concentrating on her phone as she sorted through her communications, downloading two transcription files in case she got a chance to work on them later at the cabin.

"Ready?" Danny reappeared as she was finishing up.

"Perfect timing."

His arm around her waist kept her warm as they started out. The tour took them from the obstacle courses at the back of cleared property to the equipment shed and around the cabins.

"We use the forest sometimes for search training and that sort of thing, but the most important work is usually done…" He talked on and on, painting a picture not just of the business as it was, but as he hoped it would one day become. "I'm tempted to buy some of the property to our south. It's just a matter of time until 'progress' catches up to us and then we'll really need the buffer. Now, over here…"

They got so caught up talking that Noella didn't realize she was cold until she started shivering.

"Uh-oh." Danny scowled. "Come on, let's get you inside." He rubbed her arms to try to warm her up while they walked, nearly tripping over himself in the process. "Some host I am."

"I'm f-f-fine," she lied.

"You will be soon. In here." He escorted her into the living room, where he exchanged her coat for a heavy blanket that he wrapped around her.

Again she got the impression that he wanted to kiss her, but instead he brought her back to the kitchen.

"Oh, before I forget, here's the internet password." He handed her the folded piece of paper Toni had slipped him as they headed out on their tour.

"Ah, yes. Thank you." She took a moment to program it into her phone, then joined him at the counter.

"Hot tomato soup now." He pulled things out of the cupboards as he spoke. "And a grilled cheese sandwich in a minute." Grimacing, he began opening a can. "Not exactly the meal I had planned."

"Tomato soup?" She tugged the blanket more tightly about herself and watched with interest as he poured a can of tomato sauce into a pot.

"Yeah." He filled the can with milk next and poured it into the pot as well. "It's one of a very few college concoctions that I still eat."

"Can I help?"

He hesitated, then handed her a whisk. "If you'll keep the milk from scalding, I'll get the sandwiches going."

She sensed his eyes on her as she moved the whisk through the tomato sauce. Something about wearing a blanket in his kitchen gave the whole setting an intimate feeling.

"Did you make the bread?" she asked as he worked.

"In a manner of speaking." He set aside the four pieces he'd just sliced and re-wrapped the loaf. Patted a white appliance to his right. "I put the ingredients in here and it did the rest."

"Very nice!"

"Really?" His hands continued assembling the sandwiches as he shot her a questioning glance. "You don't think it's cheating or…something?"

"No, not at all." She moved to one side so there was room for both of them in front of the stove as he began warming the frying pan. "I have a crock pot. A dishwasher. A washing machine."

"Point taken." He dropped both sandwiches into the pan and did a double-take at his guest. Was it legal to have hat hair that cute? The food forgotten, he toyed with the idea of replacing the blanket with his arms.

"The heat, it is too much." Noella resisted the urge to fan her cheeks, which had warmed readily under his appreciative gaze.

"What? Oh!" He turned the flame down and waved his hand over the pan, dissipating the smoke that had started to curl up from the overheating butter. "Glad you caught that. I hate it when the smoke alarm goes off."

Her eyebrows shot up. "That happens often?"

He deflected her tease easily and they fell into friendly banter while the food finished cooking. Almost too soon, they were seated at the table. Noella looked at him expectantly.

He offered her his hand and they bowed their heads in prayer.

A warmth coursed through her that no other source could mimic as the Holy Ghost touched her heart. After the amen, her eyes met Danny's.

Still holding her hand, he brushed his lips across hers.

They shared a smile that was ruined by a violent sneeze. The blanket, which had already begun to slip, drooped down around her arms while she smothered two subsequent sneezes in her napkin.

Tenderly, Danny lifted the blanket back into position. Handed her a spoon with a wink.

To her surprise, his 'concoction' was quite tasty. She hadn't thought she was still cold, but the soup drove out the last vestiges of her chill. Pity she'd sold her website. This was definitely a recipe her subscribers could use!

When he dipped his sandwich in the soup then took a bite of it, she nearly dropped her spoon. He was eating with his fingers?

Embarrassed, Danny wiped his mouth. "I…

um…" *I've been eating alone so long that I forgot how messy this is?*

Inspiration struck. Noella used a fork to cut a corner of her sandwich off, which she promptly dunked in the soup.

"Mmm, delicious!" She returned his wink from earlier.

Relieved, Danny followed suit. In just a few bites he came to the conclusion that it was a lot tidier that way.

"You will have to feed the dogs soon?"

"No, we hire that out. There's always someone from church who's looking to earn money for their missionary fund." The smile she gave him made him feel ten feet tall. Before his head could start to swell, he diverted his attention to mopping up the rest of his soup with the last of his sandwich.

He glanced up when her phone dinged. "Go ahead." Rising, he reached for her dishes. "Take your time."

Noella didn't try to hide her frown as she saw missed phone calls, then read the new email. And the next one. She worked as quickly as she could, but hadn't made it through half of her communication by the time he'd started the dishwasher and finished wiping down the stovetop.

"Everything alright?"

"Yes." Setting her phone aside with a sigh, she hand-shrugged. "My partner wanted to plan our next project. I have explained…” Her phone dinged again.

“Better take it.” He filled a teapot at the sink and set it on the stove.

“Sorry.” Embarrassed, she read one more email and answered it. “Peter can be very stubborn.”

“Sounds like Chuck.” Danny continued measuring ingredients into two blue, stoneware mugs. “Hope you like hot chocolate.”

“Yes, thank you.” She folded the blanket and draped it over the back of her chair. “But what are you adding?”

“Only good things,” he promised. “Dark chocolate shavings. A tiny bit of salt to help counteract the chocolate.”

“And the other container?” She tried in vain to see around him into the cupboard.

“Which container? The gray one with the white lid?” Scooping up everything he was done with, he hastily piled things into the cupboard and closed the door. Turned to face her. “That’s the secret ingredient.”

Amused, she tried to reach past him to open the cupboard and get a look, only to find herself held securely in his arms.

“The penalty for trying to figure out the key ingredient is one kiss.” The words escaped before he knew what he was saying—but he knew it was what he wanted. He watched her closely as he bent his head, ready to back off if that was what *she* wanted.

Her breath caught as his lips captured hers. They lingered, though not for quite as long as she would've liked. In a crazy moment, she considered going up on her toes as he straightened away. But no. If he wanted another kiss, he wouldn't be turning to tend the teapot, which had begun whistling.

Disappointment swirled through her, settling in her stomach. Hadn't he enjoyed it as much as she had?

Danny left an arm about her waist while he poured hot water into their mugs and handed one to her. He kissed her forehead, then guided her into the front room, where he seated her comfortably on the couch and took the recliner for himself. He needed the distance.

"Tell me about home," he invited.

She blew on the mug, surprised it wasn't steaming like crazy, and tentatively touched her lips to the rim. Found him grinning when she cast a puzzled glance his way.

"I fiddled with the teapot," he explained. "Changed it so that it whistles at a much lower temperature."

"That's brilliant!"

He rubbed the back of his neck, embarrassed. "I don't know about that. I just got tired of burning my mouth."

Laughing, she slipped off her shoes and tucked her feet up under her legs. "What do you want to know?"

"Everything." He meant it, too. She was rapidly becoming dear to him and he wanted to know everything about her. But they could start with her home. He'd heard Prince Edward Island was a beautiful place.

"Alright." She sipped her hot chocolate, savoring the rich flavor, then tilted her head to one side. "It isn't very large. Just eight rooms and an attic. Although," she held up a finger as if to correct herself, "when I was a young girl, the attic was my favorite place to sit and watch the boats sailing on the bay."

Danny stared at her, a slow smile spreading across his face as he wondered if she'd deliberately misunderstood him or not. Either way, he'd just learned a lot about her!

She told him all about the house where she'd grown up, including a particularly hilarious tale involving kittens, blueberries, and an ill-fated pie.

"Poor Mama." She wiped a stray tear, her stomach muscles aching from all the laughter. "I think she believed she would never again enter her kitchen without having to scrub blueberry pie filling from somewhere."

"I can imagine." Danny shuddered emphatically and related a story from his own youth. "To this day," he finished solemnly, "I still haven't figured out how the grape juice traveled clear from where I dropped the pitcher to under the fridge."

They laughed all the way into the kitchen, where he offered her a refill and she politely refused.

"It is late." A thought struck her. "What time is church tomorrow?"

"Starts at eight." Opening a tall, thin cupboard beside the fridge, he handed her some medicine bottles. "This is my favorite multivitamin. I take it at the first sign of a cold. And this…"

"I really do feel fine," she told him even as she accepted the three bottles.

"Right, but when was the last time you got so cold you were shivering?" Closing the cupboard, he shrugged into his jacket. "I'm not saying you have to take them, but humor me. Carry them to the cabin with you in case you change your mind." He ran his hands up and down her arms as he spoke. "Deal?"

She nodded. Waited until his back was turned, then rubbed her forearms to dispel the goosebumps his touch had caused.

Taking a flashlight from beside the door, Danny automatically flicked it on and off. "Ready?"

"Ready."

His porch security light winked on as they stepped out into the dark. In fact, there seemed to be light coming from everywhere, including two tall poles at either end of the row of cabins.

Catching her looking curiously at the flashlight,

he gestured at Building A, which had the working heater. "I'm going to check on things before I go to bed. If I turn on the main light, it'll set off some of the younger dogs, so." He twirled the flashlight.

"I will go with you," she volunteered.

Arching an eyebrow, he double-checked his watch. "Are you sure? I'll be a few minutes, assuming nothing's wrong."

"Yes, I'm sure." A minute later, she giggled softly as he opened the door to sounds of snoring.

Danny checked the cages and found that Chuck's adjustments were working perfectly. He'd be glad to get the dams and their litters back into their own accommodations, but at least he didn't have to lay awake worrying.

Satisfied, he started searching for Noella, taking great care not to let the light fall on any of the more excitable dogs.

He froze when he spotted her—kneeling on the floor in front of Caesar's cage! His muscles bunched in preparation for the sprint over there so he could pull her back to a safe distance... Except. Except she *was* safe. More than that, the one piece of Caesar that he could see was the tip of his wagging tail.

That was great, except an ex-military dog could be unpredictable at best.

Switching the flashlight off, he crept forward. Noella's voice drifted over to him, but he couldn't quite make out the words. Step by step, he edged closer, praying desperately that he wouldn't startle Caesar and make him strike.

Suddenly, he knew why he couldn't understand what she was saying. She wasn't speaking English!

As if she sensed his approach, Noella pulled back from the cage and got to her feet. "You can come over now, Danny," she called in a voice barely above a whisper.

"What do you think you are doing?" he hissed, coming abreast of her in two long strides. "Do you have any idea what kind of dog that is?" Caesar growled deep in his throat as Danny took her by the arm. "He's a military dog! He could've shredded," he looked at the secure cage, where Caesar's teeth glistened in the darkness, "whatever part of you got near enough for him to bite!"

Caesar erupted into a fury of barking when Danny pulled Noella away from the cage.

"He would not harm me," she protested. Her heart sank at the frustrated expression on Danny's face.

"Great. Just great." Danny scrubbed a hand over his face in irritation as a chorus of high-pitched yips started, followed by the baying of a hound that he'd agreed to re-school after a hunting fiasco.

In a matter of seconds, the entire kennel was in an uproar.

"What in the sam hill…" Chuck and Toni burst into the kennel and flipped on the light, adding to the chaos as the dogs barked at them, then at each other, then at shadows.

"What's going on?!" Toni yelled over the cacophony.

"Nothing!" Danny went to the nearest cage and spoke soothingly to the dogs.

Gradually, and with a great deal of effort, order was restored. Every dog on the property was wide awake and raring to go, but they had stopped barking at anything that moved.

Chapter 10

A frazzled Danny, Chuck, and Toni congregated near the door.

"So." Toni folded her arms across her chest. "What happened?"

"I…" Danny shook his head. "I don't even know." They both looked at him in disbelief, so he pointed at where Noella was standing by Caesar's cage. "Night check. I came in to do a night check, that's all. The next thing I knew, she was over there and…"

That was when he realized they weren't really listening anymore. Toni's shoulders had relaxed and Chuck's head was tilted to one side.

"How about that?" Chuck spoke first.

"How about what?" Confused, Danny tried to look at them and Noella at the same time, nearly pulling a muscle in the process.

"Caesar." Toni leaned against Chuck, honest admiration in her eyes and tone. "He's got a new friend."

"Oh no." Danny was adamant. "There is no way she can have Caesar."

Chuck glared at him. "Keep it down, man. We just got things settled in here."

Danny closed his eyes and took a deep breath. "She can't have Caesar."

"Why not?" Toni quirked an eyebrow at him. "He's as gentle as a lamb."

"Gentle as a…!" Once again Danny gestured in that general direction. "He snarled at me like he wanted to take my arm off!"

"Caesar?" Toni held up both hands in self-defense when Danny scowled at her. "I've been working with him for over a month and he's never been anything but a gentleman."

"Excuse me." Noella hesitated, a few feet from the edge of their small group. "I know why Caesar growled."

Danny's jaw dropped. "You do?"

"Oui. Ummm." She laughed nervously. "Yes."

"Awesome." Chuck gave a short hand wave, inviting her to continue.

"He was defending me," she said in a small voice.

"Defending you?" Danny felt like his head was going to explode. "From me?"

Toni punched Danny unceremoniously in the arm, eliciting a startled, "Hey!"

"You mean," she addressed Noella directly, "that big dog over there decided to protect you. Even from Danny." She added that last with a conciliatory glance in Danny's direction.

"Yes." Noella put her hands in her pockets. She didn't know what else to do with them.

A whine made them all turn to look. At Caesar's cage.

"Well, I'll be a peanut butter and jelly sandwich." Chuck rocked back on his heels with glee. "He's calling her."

Toni gave Chuck a meaningful look, then walked over to Noella. "Let's go talk to him."

It was a fearsome battle of wills, but in the end, Danny caved under the weight of Chuck's persuasion.

"Fine. Caesar can spend the night in her cabin." He glowered at all of them. "But Toni has to be there, too." He would have volunteered himself for the job except that was obviously out of the question.

"No problem." Toni promptly opened Caesar's cage and chuckled when he pranced over to Noella. "We're gonna have to change your name, big fella." She handed a collar and leash to Noella for her to put on the ecstatic dog. "Maybe she'll call you Galahad or something a little more respectable."

Noella looked at Danny from the corner of her eye, taking in his slumped shoulders. "You will need some things, yes?" she asked Toni, stroking the top of Caesar's head.

"Yeah." Toni shrugged dismissively. "A toothbrush, some pjs. I'll go get them." She paused on her way out to collect Chuck, who didn't seem to have gotten the hint that Noella wanted to talk with Danny.

"Will you walk me over?"

Danny stepped back a smidge and held out his hand for her to precede him.

She walked past, grateful that Caesar didn't

repeat his earlier aggression. They trudged along in silence until they were nearly at the cabin.

"I'll open the pet door for him," Danny announced glumly. That was as easy as removing the panel that kept out passing raccoons and other varmints while the cabins were unoccupied. "Leave that collar on him overnight, it's wired to shock him if he strays past the working area here." His vague gesture took in the cleared ground between the cabins and the security poles.

"Sure." She bit her lip, wondering how she could fix the tension between them. "Danny." She touched his arm as he turned to go.

He sighed. "Don't worry about it." Running his fingers through his hair, he blew out a breath. "I've had a long day and I'm being a grouch."

Impulsively, she hugged him.

He eyed Caesar warily as he lifted his arms to return the hug. For reasons he didn't understand, the dog just sat there, panting.

"Hey, you two!" Toni called cheerfully. "Are you trying to catch pneumonia or something?"

Noella got another rush of goosebumps when Danny's sigh stirred her hair.

"Or something," he told Toni, returning his hands to his pockets as he stepped back. "Have fun, but not too much. Breakfast at seven, then we start for church at seven-thirty." He sent Toni a final 'You'll be careful, right?' look, which she answered with a reassuring smile.

"And inside we go!" Toni took charge. "Every

cabin has doggie basics, water bowls and such, so let's get things set up for Caesar."

Her brisk efficiency accomplished that in a few minutes, during which time Noella watched Caesar investigate the cabin inch by inch. Apparently satisfied that it was safe, he came back to Noella and sat on her foot.

"Wow. He really likes you."

Smiling, Noella rested her hand on his head. "What can you tell me about him?"

"We only got the short version." Toni opened her toothpaste. "He lost his trainer when he got shot up overseas. They did the best they could to patch him up, but his limp is permanent."

Noella mulled things over as she got ready for bed. Felt a thrill of companionship when Caesar came to sit beside her while she prayed.

"Oh, no." Toni paused outside her door on her way to the kitchen for a glass of water. "No dogs on the bed." She stopped on her way back to stare in shock at Noella, who'd curled up on the floor, using Caesar for a pillow.

They all rode to church together the next morning. Everyone except Caesar, of course, who'd whined piteously but obeyed Noella's instructions to go into his kennel.

Chuck and Toni chatted quietly in the back, but Noella couldn't find any words to express what she was feeling. The deluge of curious onlookers at church didn't help, and she was just as tongue-tied on the ride back.

"Nice meeting you." A considerably warmed-up Toni gave her a hug, then headed for her cabin with Chuck, who waved.

In Danny's kitchen once again, she stood uselessly behind one of the chairs while he went over to the cupboards. Opened them. Closed them with a sigh.

"A dog is a big investment." Danny had been praying since the incident in the kennel last night and hoped he knew what he was doing. "Any dog, not just Caesar." He took her nod as encouragement to continue. "Belgian Shepherds live roughly fourteen years. Caesar's already six, which means you're looking at anywhere from four to eight years of owning a dog who already has health problems."

"That is not long enough to have a good friend."

"Noella, are you listening to me?" He groaned. "Yes, he'll be a friend, but he has baggage. A whole train car full of it. Now, I don't know what made him snap last night and I don't know what will make him snap the next time it happens, but I guarantee it can happen again."

She wilted visibly and he shoved aside the looming suspicion that he'd just won the 'monster of the year' award.

"It is a valid point." Noella sighed. "And yet, he is my dog." The simple conviction in her eyes and voice removed all argument.

Danny scrubbed his hands over his face, then crossed the room to pull her into a hug.

"What do I do?" Her words were muffled against his chest.

"We'll work it out." He kissed the top of her head and cradled her close. Took a deep breath and let it out. "Tell you what." Straightening away, he looked at her solemnly. "If you can come and stay for three days a week, we'll get you and Caesar trained to each other. It's not foolproof, but it should help prepare you both for what could go wrong."

"For how long?" She bit her lip. It wouldn't be easy. She'd have to change her day for volunteering at the food kitchen. Bring everything she would need so she could work from here. Ask her neighbor, Kirsten, to watch her house while she was gone. Keep the play on track—well, *get* the play on track, including auditions, rehearsals, finding a stage crew…

He scratched his chin, eyes focusing on an invisible spot on the ceiling while he did the mental calculations. "A couple of months, at least."

She frowned and paced away from him, then back. "Three days a week?"

"Or more." Instructor Danny asserted himself firmly.

At length, she lifted her hands helplessly. "If I must, I must."

She cried a little when it came time to say goodbye to Caesar, who seemed as distraught as she was.

"Now don't worry." Danny hugged her as he walked her to her car. "We'll take good care of him, you know that."

"Yes. Yes, I know."

He wanted to kiss her, but it felt awkward somehow, so he hugged her instead. Waved as she drove away, then went to commiserate with Caesar.

"This is not how I planned for things to go," he told the dog as he cautiously opened the kennel. Caesar ignored him. "She was supposed to focus on me, not you." Still no response. "She's coming back, you know."

"You tellin' him or yourself?" teased Chuck, who'd come in without his noticing.

Danny cleared his throat. "Hey."

"She really coming back?" Chuck nudged his shoulder.

"Yeah." He rubbed his hands on his thighs, then got up to start the feeding rounds. He gave his employees the Sabbath off from that, but the dogs still had to eat.

"Guess she must really like you."

Danny shot him a look, prepared to warn him off, but Chuck's expression told him his friend was serious.

"Jury's out." Smiling tightly, Danny let his mind drift a little as his hands performed the same chore they'd done thousands of times.

Noella was more than pretty. She had brains, plenty of spunk, a great sense of humor, and doggone it, being around her made him happy. *Most of the time.*

Chuck invaded his space intentionally as he started setting out bowls to fill. "So she doesn't like you, but she's coming back."

Rolling his eyes, Danny shoulder-shoved him to a more comfortable distance. "She wants to adopt Caesar."

If Chuck's eyebrows had gone any higher at that news, they would've had to apply for citizenship on his scalp.

"I'm not kidding." Danny picked up the bowls he'd prepared and went to serve them.

"Wow. I mean, I knew they took a shine to each other, but…" Chuck lapsed into a whistle.

Danny grunted. "She's agreed to spend three days a week here training with him." He turned back to find Chuck frowning at him.

"Will that be enough?"

"I told her it would take a couple of months at least." Chuck's frown deepened and Danny sighed. "I thought we could start by putting her through a crash course version of what a military dog handler goes through."

"Okay." Chuck's tone was that of someone patiently waiting.

"Then I thought we'd wing it from there."

"Wing it?" Chuck came back for more bowls. "That's the best you've got?"

"Look, I've got no idea what's going to come up over the next couple of weeks. Caesar…" He heard a bark as if in answer and was startled to realize that the dog had come over to join them.

"I think he wants to know what's going on." Chuck scratched behind the dog's ears.

"Smart dog." Danny smirked. Still no sign of aggression from Caesar, which was fortunate for Chuck's hand. "I was just telling Chuck here," he addressed the dog directly and was rewarded by Caesar's undivided attention, "that Noella is going to train with you. If you're a good dog, and if she doesn't flake out, she's going to adopt you."

Chuck punched his arm, none too gently. "If she doesn't flake out? Why you…"

"Hey!" Danny held up his hands, palms forward. "I just met the girl, alright? You can't expect me to vouch for her long-term."

"Hold on. I'm confused." Chuck leaned one fist on the counter. "You invited her to spend the weekend at the center. You can't take your eyes off her while she's here." He overrode Danny's halfhearted protest. "You agree to spend your downtime training her. And you're telling me you have no idea as to her character?"

Danny stood there, fuming at himself for not having a ready answer. "Just feed the dogs," he muttered.

"Yes, boss." Chuck slanted a look at Caesar and twirled a finger beside his head in the traditional 'he's crazy' motion.

Danny's mood didn't improve over the next two days despite praying for and receiving answers on how to train the strange pair.

So he couldn't figure out why his whole outlook improved the second he saw Noella's car pull into the drive.

"Don't get out." He waved for her to stay in the car and climbed in on the passenger's side. "Pull around to the left of the office building."

She followed his directions back to a two-car garage near his house. Hesitated, then parked inside it when he insisted.

"This is nice!" She exclaimed, looking around.

Larger tools hung neatly on one wall above a pair of tool cabinets, and a workbench lined the wall that the garage shared with the house. A bicycle hung from the ceiling between the car spaces. In short, there was wall-to-wall floor everywhere she looked.

"I don't think I have ever seen such a tidy garage."

"It's a matter of willpower, I guess." Opening the back door of her car, he hefted out a slightly larger rolling bag than she'd brought last time. "I've made up the spare bedroom for you."

"Danny." She shook her head. "I'm not sure that's a good idea."

"Ordinarily, I'd agree with you. However, we both know that you need the internet to do your job." He looked at her over the top of her car. It hadn't been an easy decision, but he couldn't keep asking Toni to do his job. "And, since you'll be chaperoned at all times by an overprotective, fifty-something pound Belgian Shepherd, I think everything will be fine."

Her mouth formed an 'o' of surprise. A sharp, joyous bark cut through the silence and she dropped to her knees to greet a wildly excited Caesar. All the adjustments she'd had to make to her schedule were worth it, even switching to Monday night at the food kitchen.

Toni watched from where she'd given up and released Caesar's leash before he broke it. Winked at Danny and walked away.

"Take your time," Danny called to Noella. "Right now we want to convince him that he's the most important thing in your life."

His bad mood nearly returned as he spoke the words he'd planned, but her whole-hearted enthusiasm for the idea made him smile despite himself. Carrying her bag into the guest room, he laid it on top of the foot locker at the end of the bed.

A flurry of clicks on the hardwood floors alerted him that they had come inside and he stuck his head into the hallway to call her.

For half an hour, he gave her what he called the "two cent tour" of the cottage, with a special emphasis on the dog-related aspects.

"Oh, and Toni told me what happened in the

cabin." He ticked the next two points off on his fingers. "No dogs in the bed. No humans on the floor."

"But Danny." She stroked Caesar's ears. "He needs to be near me."

Caesar whined pitifully and Danny felt his resolve weakening. After all, he'd spent a few nights on the kennel floor in a sleeping bag for the same reason, hadn't he?

"Nope, nothing doing." He put his hands in his pockets, striving for a stern yet casually-confident-that-he-knew-what-he-was-talking-about air. "I know you're okay with it now, but we're playing the long game here, remember? The next eight years or so. You have to think about your future husband. Your kids."

Their eyes met and the atmosphere in the room was suddenly charged with electricity. He couldn't even breathe.

"Yes, Danny." She dropped her eyes demurely and he sucked in a breath.

"So." His voice came out hoarse and he coughed to clear his throat. "A military dog handler goes through an intense training program. Today we're going to start you on a shorter version of that program. This'll help you get an idea of what Caesar did for a living and teach you why he does certain things. Ready?" Their eyes met again and his heart did a series of loop-de-loops that almost undid him.

"Ready." Not really, though. Would she ever

be ready to look up and find Danny staring at her with his heart in his eyes? How could he sound so professional and look so…personal, at the same time?

Hours later, she was wondering if she'd imagined it.

"We're not training Caesar today," he snapped when she failed to remember one of the dozen or more commands they'd gone over. "He knows these commands by heart and will obey all of them without question. We're training you."

"I know!" She couldn't help snapping back this time. Caesar bared his teeth and growled menacingly at Danny, bringing her up sharply. "I know," she repeated more quietly, and used a hand signal to command Caesar to lay down.

"Okay, that's enough for today." He'd had as much of playing the gruff instructor as he could stand. Besides, he could tell Caesar's growl just now had rattled her. "We'll have supper in thirty minutes. I suggest you spend that time playing with your dog, Miss Cormier."

She stared after him in disbelief as he walked away. *Miss Cormier?*

"What if this isn't such a good idea?" she asked Caesar with a sigh. Did she have to lose Danny to get Caesar? Caesar had proven over and over again that Danny was right. He was a working dog, trained in detection and capable of things that never would've crossed her mind.

"You busy?"

Noella looked up to find Toni standing halfway between her and the building they called the mother's lounge. A new heater had been installed yesterday, so it was back in use.

"I'm not sure," she admitted.

A strange smile flitted across Toni's face and she waved Noella over. "Give me a hand?"

Noella had taken a few steps toward her before she realized that Caesar wasn't beside her. Looking around for him, she groaned when she saw that he was still lying obediently where she'd left him.

"I don't think I can do this." Rather than helping Toni as she'd intended, Noella leaned against the wall inside the mother's lounge and rubbed tired eyes. Frowned when Toni snickered.

"You've got to hand it to Danny." Opening a gate, she let a pile of eager puppies spill into the room. "Okay guys, bath time!"

Noella's heart melted as she watched the clumsy puppies tumble over each other and their own paws as they happily followed Toni.

Chapter 11

"It's taken Danny a long time to get good at playing the tough guy." Toni carefully set each puppy into a tub of warm, shallow water.

"Tough guy?" Noella perked up. "Why would he do that?" Something brushed her hand and she looked down to find Caesar watching the puppies in fascination.

"Why wouldn't he do it?" Toni corrected. It was important for their dogs to be comfortable with water, so she let the pups play for a few minutes before selecting one to shampoo. "Caesar's already had his heart broken once. He might have a crush on you now, so to speak, but picture him six months in the future. It finally clicks in your head that he's not an ordinary overweight pooch content to sleep eighteen hours a day and whoa." Bringing a dripping hand almost to her heart, Toni twisted her face into an expression of fake horror. "You just can't cope!"

"And if I can't cope," Noella stroked Caesar's head, "he goes to a shelter." That was enough to stiffen her resolve, but what Toni went on to say made her ill.

"Where eventually he gets put down because they need the space." Toni didn't bother sugarcoating it. "Grab that towel, will you?"

Noella did as she was asked and was startled when Toni deposited a squirming puppy into her hands.

"Rub her down gently but thoroughly, then take her back to Athena, okay?" Toni had already started on the next pup.

Caesar stayed on her heels as Noella carried them one by one from tub to their dam. She let him sniff the pups to satisfy his curiosity and laughed at his comical expression.

"Do you think he knows they are dogs?" she asked Toni.

"Oh yeah, he knows." Toni got to her feet and stretched her back. She usually enjoyed bathing the puppies, but she could tell it was time to train one of their junior employees for the job. Her backache would only get worse.

"Look." She turned to Noella. "You made it through today. Hang onto that. And remember that once you get Caesar home, you'll be walking him twice a day, playing ball with him, or just chilling at your place. You definitely need to know what he's capable of, but that doesn't mean you'll be taking him out on patrol."

"That's right." Noella squinted at nothing in particular. "Yes, that is right."

"So no matter how tough tomorrow is," Toni didn't want to give anything away, "you'll handle it. Not because it's easy. Because you want to." She dropped the soggy towels into the washer. "And Danny'll put you through your paces because it's the only way he knows to keep the two of you safe."

Noella nodded thoughtfully, her memories of the day taking on a whole new light.

Danny, meanwhile, was in his weight room trying to work off some of his guilt doing bench presses. When that failed, he moved on to the dumbbells.

He was just starting to wonder where Noella and Caesar were when the doorbell rang.

"I'll get it!" Noella called as she walked through the kitchen door. She assumed Danny was somewhere in the cottage and would hear her, but couldn't really say for certain.

"Thanks for ordering from Fireclay Pizza, where your pizza is our business." Three pizza boxes were shoved unceremoniously in her face when she opened the door. "Have a good night!"

"Dinner's served," Danny said wryly, having arrived in time to see what happened. "Here." He took the boxes from her.

She hung back in the entryway, fingertips pressed to her mouth as she tried to look anywhere except at his retreating form. *Good grief.* She'd seen sweaty men before. Her father, her brothers, cousins, and more local boys than she could count, all stinky and sweaty after working in the garden or on the docks.

Oh, but this was nothing like that. Scrunching her eyes shut, she ordered herself to get a grip.

Catching Caesar watching her with a worried expression, she sternly whispered, "Don't you dare tell him.”

Danny chose that exact moment to pause in the doorway. “There you are.” Oblivious to the effect his post-workout state was having on her, he pointed at the kitchen with both hands. “Pizza’s on the counter. Plates are over the microwave. I’m going to take a quick shower, so don’t wait for me, okay?” He disappeared down the hallway.

She was befuddled enough to turn and walk into the wall. Stepped back and put both hands on her hips. Muttered to herself in French.

“Are…you okay?” Danny had come back to investigate the random thud he’d just heard.

“Mhmmm.” Noella nodded vigorously. “Yes, I…” She pointed toward the kitchen. “Pizza?”

“Right.”

“Right.” She walked briskly through the door, around the corner, and stopped at the pantry, where she silently mock-banged her head against the wall.

Danny blinked. Cocked an eyebrow at Caesar, who growled softly then followed his mistress. “Riiiight.” Something weird was going on. Well, whatever it was, it would keep until after he’d cleaned up.

He didn’t solve the mystery that night. He had barely re-entered the kitchen when Noella jumped to her feet, plead exhaustion, and disappeared into her room. With the door shut firmly behind her.

Nonplussed, he stared after her. Groaned. "Monster of the year. Yep, I should just have that carved onto my headboard." Appetite gone, he boxed up the pizza and stuffed it into the fridge. At least he wouldn't have to cook for a while. "Change the name of the business to Monster Training Center. Short. Pithy. Confidence-inspiring."

Things were still tense between them the next day. And the next. Of course, having her watch Chuck and Toni demonstrate a suspect-takedown with Caesar probably explained some of it. The dog suit and his training kept Chuck perfectly safe the whole time, but watching Caesar attack him left Noella ashen-faced.

"You did well out there today." Danny leaned against her doorjamb as he watched her finish packing.

"Thanks." She hadn't told him, but she'd sprained her ankle during the last drill and it was really starting to hurt.

"I think we've been working too hard, in fact." He smiled brightly. "Next week," he had his fingers crossed that she was coming back, "we'll only work a half day on Wednesday."

Surprised, she looked at him from the corner of her eye as she zipped her bag. She'd seen and done a lot more than just train with Caesar over the last three days. With a little effort, she'd even managed to coax Caesar to catch a Frisbee for her yesterday, though he'd been a bit put out at the indignity of it.

"Caesar's hip will probably always bother him." Was he rambling? It felt like he was rambling. "And an important part of re-training him for civilian life will be getting him used to spending time off-duty. While you watch a movie, for example." Oh, he was definitely rambling.

"Or while I work on my laptop for two to three hours at a time," she suggested helpfully. They generally took a few hours off in the middle of the day so she could catch up on her work and to give the other dogs a chance to use the clearing for exercise.

"Yeah, um, exactly." Not at all what he'd been angling for. He leapt to help when she started to take the heavy bag off her bed and found himself face to face with her. Close enough to smell her shampoo. To feel the heat radiating off her.

"Are you inviting me to watch a movie with you, Danny Fitzsimmons?"

Suddenly tongue-tied, he settled for nodding.

"Hmm." Leaving him holding the bag, she picked up her coat and started for the garage. "I will think about it."

Exhaling slowly, he pulled on the handle of her bag until it was fully extended. Did a double-take at Caesar, who seemed to be watching him with a pitying expression on his face.

"What're you looking at?" Chuckling, he strode out of the room.

Noella was true to her promise. She thought about the possibilities all the way back to Cadmia, where she made a gallant effort to forget it for the duration of movie night, laughing with the others at the cartoons Grace showed that evening.

But she consistently found herself looking for or reaching for Caesar, her ever-present shadow of the past three days. She also almost asked Grace for the recipe for her nachos, until she realized she wanted to make them for Danny. While she'd been respectful of his kitchen so far, she knew she'd only be able to hold out for so long before the itch to cook something overcame her.

Especially if he kept ordering enough pizza for her entire stay. Pepperoni, too. *All three of them.* Her stomach roiled at the memory. How much pepperoni could one man eat?

"Strawberry shortcake?" Harmony offered a dish of dessert to her abnormally distracted friend. Noella was usually the first one in the kitchen, whether to help make something or cleanup after something or whatever needed doing.

"Thank you." Noella accepted the dish eagerly. Her eyes closed as she savored the first bite and her thoughts ran straight back to Danny. What kind of dessert did he like?

Ugh. She was not a child with a crush. She could go more than five minutes without thinking about him.

Harmony's sudden coughing fit distracted her.

"Fine." Harmony cleared her throat emphatically and smiled at all of them. "Wrong pipe."

Noella frowned skeptically, but didn't want to push. Suddenly, the time showing on Grace's wall clock registered and she exclaimed, "Regardez l'heure!" Unwilling to waste even a bite of the dessert, she hastily scooped up the last of it. "I didn't realize it was so late!"

"It's barely nine," Merry responded in French.

"Oui, mais…" Remembering her manners, Noella took a calming breath and forced herself to think in English. "In the morning, I have an appointment."

"Oh, that's right," Harmony agreed quickly. She should've remembered. Hadn't Noella muttered to herself about the job for nearly the entire drive over? In Dutch, which meant Harmony only mostly understood her. The job was obviously important, though. "Hate to eat and run," she apologized to Grace.

"Don't worry about it. I actually have plans tomorrow, too." Grace waved the apology away.

Merry practically levitated off the couch. "Now you tell us!"

"Thank you for the evening!" Noella sighed when she came up for a goodbye hug.

She did her best to smile when Grace directed her to, "Have fun tomorrow."

Peter had outlined an attack designed to decimate Netherland's new security measures, and she wasn't sure if she hoped it would work or not. If it did work, they were guaranteed another month's employment. If it didn't, they would be sorting through small jobs again. That could be more interesting, but it was often also sporadic. She had some savings built up, and the generous fees from Netherland Transport would stretch a long way with careful budgeting.

Her mind darted back to—nope, not Danny this time. Well, not exactly. To Caesar. She bit her lip. She'd have to start pricing dog supplies. Food, a bed, um, other things?

Harmony looked over in time to see her rub her forehead. "Troubles?"

She sighed. "I'm adopting a dog."

Harmony whistled. "That's a big commitment."

"No kidding." She tried to laugh but all that came out was frustration.

Harmony grinned, tickled at Noella's choice of idiom. In so many ways, the young woman seemed younger than she really was. Not naïve, exactly. Just…sweet. A lot like her little sister, Lydia.

"When are you adopting it?"

"Him."   Noella wrinkled her nose apologetically. "It is a him."

Harmony grinned. "Keep talking."

It all came out in a rush, or as much of a rush as she could manage with Harmony constantly interrupting.

"Fitzsimmons?   Any relation to Brother Fitzsimmons from church? Is he as attractive as his dad?"

Why are all of her questions about Danny? Noella had a sneaking suspicion she was being teased, but she plowed ahead with her stories of the training.

"I nearly died when Toni sicced Caesar on Chuck."

"Well, he was wearing a dog suit, right?" Harmony focused on parking at Noella's.

"How did you know that?" Noella squinted uselessly at her friend. It was too dark to see anything.

"I had a friend in the military," Harmony answered vaguely.

"Oh." She unbuckled her seat belt. "Dogs trained like this, they really can become, eh, civilians?"

"Absolutely."   Harmony personally knew of several success stories. "You just have to get the hang of his quirks." She spent the next five minutes explaining the idiom *she* had chosen to use.

Reassured, Noella hugged her and went inside. She checked her phone and grumbled when she found that it had gone dead. How could she have forgotten to plug it in during her drive back?

She left it to charge on her nightstand while she got ready for bed. Returned to find the most peculiar text from Danny.

"Buy a teddy bear for Caesar?" She shrugged, yawned, and climbed under the covers. "Why not?"

She sent him a picture of a toy as large as the dog and was rewarded with several laughing emoji's, along with a link to a much smaller bear.

Too tired to shop around for the best price, she ordered the bear, using Danny's address for the destination, then crawled under the covers.

Luckily, when she looked at the bear again in the morning, she liked it immensely. Dogs couldn't see color, of course, but the caramel 'fur' and darker face reminded her of Caesar.

After she and Peter finished their probe of Netherland Transport's security, it was late enough—even for a Saturday—for her to do a chore she'd been putting off.

The flyers for the play had been up in town nearly two-and-a-half weeks, her contact information clearly listed, yet nobody had reached out to volunteer for the Christmas charity play. Not even the so-called 'regulars.'

She wasted a few minutes tidying her workspace. Stalled while she leafed through the list of community theater volunteers. Offered a short prayer, pasted on a smile, and started making phone calls.

Her smile slipped, then faded out altogether by the time she'd made it to the end of the list without a single commitment. Most responses were vaguely indifferent. Two of the more important volunteers—stage crew chief and refreshments—politely but firmly declined to have anything to do with the production at all. One had made plans to visit relatives in another state and the other would be busy hosting the relatives coming to visit her.

Frustrated, she slammed her phone down on her table. Groaned and peeked at the screen. Thankfully, it wasn't damaged.

Too upset to concentrate on other work, Noella turned on an exercise program. Some of her aggravation faded as she focused on something else.

She still had Merry's support, at least. Quickly, she composed and sent her friend a text to confirm their appointment next Thursday while she marched in place and hit 'send' just in time for the arm raises.

She didn't feel much better by the end of the program, but she'd had an idea. Showering and changing into her street clothes, Noella headed into town.

She had a headache and a pinch between her shoulder blades when she knocked on Jane's door later that evening.

"Oh, my dear." Jane stood back to let her in. "Are you well?"

Noella walked straight over to the couch and sat down with a huff.

"I am stumped." Taking off her knit cap, she slammed it onto the couch cushion beside her and ran cold fingers through messy hair. "How does one woman wrap the entire town around her finger?" She held up her own pinkie for emphasis. Turned to the fireplace, where she was happy to see a fire blazing cheerfully. Brother Murdock, the Young Men's president, had made a point of assuring her that they would keep Jane's wood boxes full.

"Well, I'm not sure." Jane eased herself into her overstuffed chair. "Why don't you start at the beginning?"

So, she did. The 'sandbagging' at the last community theater meeting. The flyers, the phone calls, no ticket sales, and her most recent failure—the local newspaper had rejected her ad.

"I find that difficult to believe." Jane was in earnest. Newspapers didn't get any smaller than the Cadmia Express, which hadn't had a local headline since the school's marching band won something somewhere else three years ago. "Are you sure they said they *wouldn't* take your ad? Not that they didn't have room for it today or…" Her voice trailed off as Noella sadly shook her head.

"The play happens every year like clockwork."

She mimicked the editor's bored voice. "Old news, Missy. Mighty old news."

Jane was twice as confused now. Noella had submitted an ad, not an article.

"I have the sinking feeling." Noella patted her stomach. "The play will never happen at this rate."

"That's no way to talk," Jane admonished her. "We'll think of something, you can count on it."

"We will?"

"You bet your boots we will." Jane got to her feet. "I always do my best thinking in the kitchen, so c'mon. Let's put on our thinking caps while we get supper ready."

As they prepared pork chops, green beans, mashed potatoes, and thick slices of freshly made bread, they discussed the problem.

"I think I'm beginning to see the woman behind the curtain." Jane finished setting the table just as Noella returned from the pantry with a dusty jar of apple butter.

"The what?" Noella blinked, confused.

"Mrs. Arnold." Jane leaned one fist on the table and nodded. "Sounds to me like little Tammy Nolan hasn't grown up as much as she'd like us all to think."

They sat down and said a prayer over the food, then Jane told her enough about 'little Tammy's escapades' for Noella to realize what she was up against.

"Regular queen bee." Jane took a bite of her

apple butter-smeared bread and let out a sigh.

"That is too bad." Noella took a moment to enjoy the delicious, home-canned green beans. "And I do not see how we can possibly make the play if she is so dead set," she wrinkled her nose at the new idiom, "on having her children perform the same old play."

"It doesn't look good." Jane cut a piece of pork chop and used it to scoop up a mouthful of fluffy potatoes, dripping with brown gravy. They ate in silence, then Jane mused, "She's been at this a long time. Knows how the people in this town tick, you might say." She shrugged. "I suppose you could bring someone in from outside. Someone who doesn't know Tammy or care what she thinks or…"

Noella was staring at her. "This is brilliant!"

"What is?" Laying down her fork, Jane reached for her glass.

"Your idea!" Noella pressed both palms flat against the table in an effort to suppress her excitement. "Someone from outside Cadmia. Of course!"

"Sakes, girl, I wasn't serious. You can't just…bus in an entire cast, crew," Jane gestured wildly, "*audience.*"

"No, no." She laughed. "One person. Or one group. One who will bring in the rest."

Understanding dawned and Jane grinned. "A big name. Or, at least, big for this area."

"Oui!" Noella stood up. Sat back down. "Who

"Who should we get?"

Their debate lasted clear through dessert, a lemon merengue pie Noella had taken her frustration out on earlier. She'd never made such firm, light merengue.

They finally narrowed it down to a reasonably local group.

"Mind now, I'm not sure they'd be my first choice." Jane closed the fridge on the leftovers. "But if they're as popular as you say, and *if* they're available in the middle of the holiday season, well." She shrugged her approval.

"Thank you, Jane." She hugged her friend enthusiastically. "This will work! I am sure of it."

She thought of two more names on her way home that night and emailed all of them before going to bed, all while praying fervently that one of them would be available.

Chapter 12

Tuesday was rapidly becoming his favorite day. Despite his best intentions, Danny felt a smile tugging at his lips as he watched Caesar and Noella's touching reunion.

She started to turn toward him and he hastily composed his face. And wished he hadn't as her mouth drooped.

"Aren't you glad to see me?"

Danny lifted his chin and rotated it like someone had cinched his tie too tight, then gave in.

"I sure am." Dropping the stern instructor face, he pulled her in for a kiss on the cheek and a warm hug. She leaned there, her face against his chest, like she needed his support to keep standing. "Rough week?"

Drawing back with a sigh, she lifted one shoulder noncommittally. "Lots going on."

"Yeah?" He patted her shoulder. "Let's get your things inside and we can talk about it over lunch."

"Lunch? We're not going right to work?"

Hauling her bag out of the trunk, he shook his head. "We've been working while you were gone and he's making great progress. So for the moment, I think it's more important to let him enjoy you."

Caesar chose that moment to plant himself on

her foot, making her laugh. "Get up, you big beast," she scolded. "Come inside. Come."

He bounded ahead of her and disappeared into her bedroom, then just as quickly was back at her side, holding something in his mouth.

"What's this?" Making sure they were out of Danny's way, she knelt by Caesar. Gasped. "Oh, look!! It's your teddy bear!"

Caesar's tail wagged like crazy as she oohed and aahed over his new prize.

Danny slipped an arm around her waist as he walked past and casually carried her, squealing and protesting, into the kitchen.

"Funny thing about that bear." He set her on the counter.

"What's that?" Her words came out as near gasps. She peeked around him at Caesar who, as it turned out, had gone to his bed in the far corner of the room. Apparently, he was getting used to them.

Her heart fluttered as she wondered if she was similarly growing accustomed to this time with Danny.

"It's my fault." He set bread and sandwich fixings on the counter beside her. "I meant to have you bring the teddy bear when you came today."

"Oh?" She hopped down and got a couple of paper plates. "But, why?"

"He misses you when you're gone." Gesturing for her to go first, he retrieved the milk and some glasses. "Having a toy that smelled like you would've been reassuring for him."

"I see." She frowned. "I'm sorry."

"Nah, it's not that bad. I actually have the strangest feeling he knows exactly where it came from." He nodded at her wide-eyed look of surprise. "I gave it to him on Saturday and he hasn't been without it since. Well." He reached past her for the peanut butter. "Except when we're training."

"You say he has made progress?"

"Plenty of it." Danny shared some of the highlights with her while they ate and pretended not to notice that she kept trying to coax Caesar over with a bit of her sandwich. Eventually, though, he had to tell her, "He, um, he won't take it."

She blinked innocently. "Who won't take what?"

Crumpling his napkin, he enunciated clearly, "Caesar won't take the piece of your sandwich that you've got under the table." Her answering blush was endearing as she dropped the scrap onto her plate.

"It was worth a try."

He laughed. "Not really. In the first place, he was trained not to eat human food. In the second, he couldn't possibly love you more than he already does." Somehow, his hand had reached across the table and was holding hers.

She felt her cheeks warming further. "Are

you sure you're speaking for Caesar?" She bit her lip, almost instantly regretting her tease.

"Honestly?" He'd spent more hours with her in the last two weeks than he usually did with an eligible woman over the span of two months. Still, he couldn't possibly be in love with her— could he? Not this soon? Except...

He took so long to answer that she playfully shoved his hand away from her.

"Because I think he would say it with a thick accent."

Danny's eyebrows rose. "Who?"

"Caesar. He is a *Belgian* Shepherd, no?"

He hooted and got to his feet. "Goofball. See if you can get him to follow you into the front room."

Alone in the front room with Caesar, Noella was drawn to the piano. Her fingers had itched to play it each day last week. If only she hadn't been so tired.

Hmm. She wasn't tired now.

Seating herself, she opened the lid and ran a scale. It was a little out of tune, as though it wasn't played often. She tried a few more test scales, then decided it would do.

She started playing a bouncy folk tune her grandmother loved. Transitioned into a slightly better-known sea shanty. Moved on to a lively classical piece. Paused to catch her breath.

"That's amazing." Danny stepped forward from where he'd been hovering a few paces away, afraid of distracting her. "I can barely pick out the top hand, and that's when I have music!"

"You must practice," she laughed. "Here, sit." Scooting over, she patted the spot to her left.

What could he do but accept? And so, instead of him training her, she taught him his scales.

"Whew." He flexed his fingers. "Okay, that's enough practice for one day."

"But you are making progress!"

"That's very kind of you." He cocked his head at her. "Notice anything else?"

Confused, she looked at him. At the piano. Her gaze continued traveling to her right until it settled on…

"Caesar!" He sat patiently staring up at her, a ball in his mouth. "Oh, you poor dear." Rising immediately, she headed for her coat. "Let's play!"

Danny allowed himself a smile as he watched them go. Yes, he decided, Noella would make a good dog owner. Once she had a little… He got to his feet and gently closed the piano lid. Once she had a little more practice.

Pulling an emergency casserole from the freezer, he popped it in the oven, then headed out to join them.

"Hey!" Noella glared at the snowball he'd plastered all over her shoulder.

Danny clapped for Caesar, who brought his ball over at the gallop. "Go get…" He tried to dodge her retaliatory snowball only to have it catch him square on the side of his face.

"Oh you are so on!"

Their impromptu fight was promptly crashed by Toni, Chuck, and, of course, Caesar, who couldn't resist chasing all of them as they raced around like crazy kids.

Noella zigged right into Danny's arms and they landed in a snowdrift that was at least two feet deep.

"Oh, you." She slapped Danny lightly on the chest. "Are we having a snowball fight or playing rugby?"

Danny started to respond only to realize he was precisely at eye level with Caesar. Was that fear or melting snow running icy fingers down his spine?

He'd never been so glad to be ignored in his life as he was at the moment that Caesar's approaching teeth bypassed his face and got a tentative grip on Noella's coat.

"Caesar?" She reached up to stroke the dog's ears and he let go to nuzzle her hand as he whined. "What are you doing, my good boy, hmm?"

Danny eased himself away from Noella, moving to the side of her where Caesar wasn't. "He's worried about you."

"Worried?" She sat up enough to hug Caesar. "Poor boy, did you think I was hurt? I'm okay. Yes, I'm okay! Ooof!" She suddenly had a lap full of Belgian Shepherd.

Danny cleared the laughter out of his throat with a cough behind one gloved hand. "That's not a behavior we want to encourage, Miss Cormier."

She stuck her tongue out at him and tried not to think about how handsome he looked with mischief sparkling in his eyes.

"Caesar, off." She reinforced the command with a firm push that walked him back off her lap and onto the snow. "Inside? Yeah?"

Caesar half-started to go, then stopped to whine and touch his nose to her cheek.

"What's that?" Noella struggled to her feet, nearly falling on Danny in the process. She shot him an apologetic look, then spoke to Caesar again. "You want me to come with you? Okay!" She injected as much enthusiasm into her words as she could, then raced off as a poor second even to Caesar's limping run.

A minute later Toni and Chuck jogged up to Danny from the other direction, laughing at something only they knew.

"Whew, boss." Chuck rubbed his hands together, his damp gloves doing less than nothing to keep his fingers warm. "We should train like that more often."

"You think so?" Danny's eyes—and mind— were on Noella.

"Absolutely." Toni winked at Chuck. "Especially with our non-paying clients."

Danny hid a smile. "It's okay with me if that's what you really want." His straight face slipped when he stuffed his hands in his pockets and found a micro-ton of snow from when he'd taken down Noella.

"I…" Chuck blinked. "What?"

Danny shot Toni an amused glance and was halfway to the house before he heard Chuck's extra loud, "Ohhhh."

Sheesh, what a ham, he thought as he kicked snow off his shoes before entering the kitchen.

The first thing he saw was Noella setting the table and he almost pinched himself to make sure he wasn't dreaming. She'd already changed out of her wet clothes. The teal sweater she had on now looked so soft he couldn't help reaching out to touch the sleeve.

"You better hurry and put on dry things." With an effort, she controlled her voice, if not the swirls of longing in her blood. "Supper's nearly ready."

He was so busy watching her over his shoulder that he ran into the fridge as he walked past it, and then the corner of the pantry. He still hadn't shaken the sight and sound of her humming as she worked in his kitchen by the time he'd pulled on clean socks and combed his hair.

"You've got it bad," he told his reflection seriously. Then, he touched the scripture he'd printed and taped to his mirror, where he'd see it every day.

"Nevertheless neither is the man without the woman, neither the woman without the man, in the Lord." 1ˢᵗ Corinthians 11:11

He'd completed a special fast on Sunday for help understanding his relationship with Noella. She wasn't a paying client, as Toni had mockingly reminded him. She was never going to be 'like a sister' to him, either.

"Danny!" Her voice floated down the hallway and he smiled at the faintly French pronunciation of his name.

Bounding into the kitchen, he threw a leg over the back of his chair and sat, grinning at her.

Startled, she froze halfway into her own seat, not sure what she was supposed to do. He hadn't been gone more than ten minutes, but the new light in his eyes—it was as if he was lit from within.

He put his hand on the table, palm up.

She finished taking her seat and put her hand in his, as they'd begun doing for prayers. Only this time, he studied their joined hands for a long moment before blessing the food.

"I think we've had enough fun outside for one day." He passed her the plate of bread and she slid the casserole closer to him. "Do you know what movie you want to watch?" He didn't have a huge collection, but he hoped they could agree on something. And if it came down to it, he could probably be persuaded to use one of those online rentals.

She shook her head. "I can't tonight. I got a huge transcription job from one of my regular clients, a popular European author, and she needs it back as soon as possible." Plus, waiting to find out who had stolen the antique vase from the baroness at the beginning of the story was driving her crazy! Naturally, she had her favorite suspect, but she had yet to outguess the crafty author.

"Oh." His appetite disappeared so fast a magician would've been proud of it.

"Possibly tomorrow?" She took a bite of the casserole and worked hard not to grimace. She'd seen the stash of casseroles in his freezer last week but it never crossed her mind that they could've been in there long enough to get freezer burn.

"Sure." He forked some casserole into his mouth. "Ugh. That's awful!"

She hid a smile behind her hand as he spat the food into his napkin.

"Don't eat…" He groaned when he saw her portion was already down substantially. "You could've said something!"

She stirred the remaining food briefly, then clasped her hands over her plate. "Maybe I should cook tomorrow?" She studied his face, detecting flickers of hope, then mild disappointment, both of which came and went so quickly she wondered if she had imagined them. But no. Her imagination wasn't that good, to see disappointment where she didn't expect it.

He shrugged. "That's okay. I'll just order some pizza." Rising, he took his plate to the sink to scrape the rest of his casserole into the disposal. Almost missed seeing her wrinkle her nose in obvious displeasure. What was that about? She'd eaten the pizza with him last week.

"I could..." Her chair scraped as she got up to join him. "I could make homemade pizza." *Just not pepperoni.* Her taste buds cowered at the thought.

He was even more confused. "You want to make pizza." It didn't come out as a question, exactly. Probably because he wasn't sure what it was.

"Yes." She smiled hopefully. "Or..." She stopped, realizing she didn't know what he had on hand. "Or something else."

He ran his fingers through his hair even as his stomach rumbled, unhappy about being teased with the bite of casserole.

"Want a sandwich?"

"Sure." She handed him her plate, then started collecting the sandwich 'fixings,' as he called them. "Oh." Delighted, she turned to him with a plastic container of fresh spinach in her hand. "You didn't have to get this for me!"

"No problem." He shrugged but inwardly was pleased she'd noticed and thanked him. He certainly hadn't gotten it for himself. Not that he was the type to keep score or anything...

Though she couldn't miss his exasperated

sigh and shake of his head, she didn't know what to do about it. If there was anything to be done about it.

Setting out two clean plates, she built them each their preferred sandwich, then turned to find him watching her with a puzzled expression on his face.

"I'm sorry," she blurted. Apologies were usually safe ground when she was confused. "Did you want to make it yourself?"

At that precise moment, he wanted nothing so badly as he wanted to kiss her until he forgot all the questions and decisions. Including about pizza. Instead, he took the plate she'd been about to offer him.

"Let's eat in the front room," he suggested, dodging her question for the time being. "We can watch an episode of something while we eat."

As this was the second time he'd brought the conversation around to a show, she mustered up a smile and a nod.

"Great." He handed his plate back to her. "I'll get the chips and soda." Luckily, he kept bags of single-serve chips and some canned soda on hand.

He was running low, though. They'd had enough sandwiches over the last few days for him to know she liked three kinds of chips, but baked sour cream and cheddar were her favorite. Likewise, while she'd drink nearly any flavor of soda, she consistently reached for the root beer first. He was on his way in to the front room when he belatedly remembered that she preferred her soda flat and at room temperature. Gross, but hey, he didn't have to drink it.

Returning to the kitchen, he got a can from his pantry and poured it into a glass for her. A weird wave of nostalgia hit him as he was opening the recycling bin to drop the empty can inside.

He'd been what…nine? Sandwiches were his first love and almost the entire extent of his cooking repertoire at the time. Mom had come home late from something, maybe a girls' night out? Yeah, she loved those. He'd stayed up late since it was a Friday and made her a sandwich in case she hadn't gotten enough to eat. He'd even sacrificed a can of his special grape flavored soda.

What did he know? As a juvenile boy, starving was a perpetual state with him.

Filled with love for her and pride in himself, he'd watched for her at the front window until a strange yellow car pulled up. Really strange, with a number on its side like that one car in the movies.

His dad had rushed out to get her, half-carrying her into the house and… Long story short, from that day to this, he couldn't get even a whiff of liquor without it making his stomach churn.

The pain in his hand brought him back to his own kitchen and he looked down to find that he was gripping a crushed soda can. With an effort, he forced himself to drop it and was stunned to find he'd managed to cut his palm on a jagged edge formed under the pressure of his grip.

Noella appeared at his side. Took the bin lid from his hand and set it in place. Led him to the first aid kit he kept prominently displayed on the kitchen wall, where she cleaned and bandaged the cut.

Then, without a word, she cradled his head in her arms.

He rested there, breathing in her clean, sweet scent while his mind connected the dots. His nine-year-old self had only been doing what he'd seen his dad do—go out of his way to make his mom's life easier. Nineteen years later, he was still following in his dad's footsteps.

He couldn't complain, exactly; in truth, he'd be thrilled to be half the man his dad was. Except he was a grown man, and it was time to make his own tracks.

His hands settled on her waist and he drew back, ready to tell her he loved her.

Her palms flattened against his cheeks, holding him still as she pressed her lips to his.

Chapter 13

Noella blushed every time she thought of that kiss for the next two days. She couldn't help it, if only because she simultaneously remembered Danny's husky voice whispering, "I love you."

He'd known her less than three weeks, and already he believed he was in love with her.

Parking in front of Cadmia's community center, she reflected that it was probably a good thing she'd needed to come back early this week for the auditions. Lifting the pile of scripts from her passenger seat, she carefully picked her way across the parking lot and let herself into the building.

Getting a key to the community center was, so far, the easiest thing she'd had to do in connection with this play.

Enough light came in through the skylights for her to find her way to the auditorium, where she found a light switch and deliberately blew a puff of air out her mouth. Shivered as she watched her breath crystallize.

"It really *is* colder inside than it is out!" she muttered to herself as she hunted for the thermostat.

Rubbing her hands together, she began setting up chairs while she waited for the room to defrost a little. She'd been planning this day for weeks and knew exactly how it would happen.

The hopeful candidates would enter through the large door on her left. Sign in at the little table and pick up a script, which they could review while they waited their turn. She could read any of the parts to help with the auditions, and still make notes on their efforts.

By the time auditions closed, she would have the entire cast picked out and they could set up rehearsals.

Placing the last chair, she looked around the eerily quiet room and reminded herself that she'd come early on purpose. To meet with Merry, her set designer.

As if on cue, she heard distant sounds of someone stomping, then rapid footfalls approaching the room where she stood.

"Hey." Merry blew into her cupped hands to warm them as she entered the auditorium. "Nice igloo you've got here."

Noella giggled at the joke and hugged her. "Thank you so much for coming."

"Yeah, sure." Merry patted her back before straightening away. Her own boss, she didn't mind coming out on a Thursday to help a friend. "I have some general set ideas, but I thought I'd start by taking some measurements. Then I can sketch things out and get a feel for what works the best."

"The stage is yours." Noella mock-bowed and was delighted when Merry returned the gesture. As often as not, Merry was too solemn for her own good, and Noella loved seeing her smile.

Seating herself at the small table she'd positioned in front of the stage, Noella checked the time and…sat. She tried watching Merry, but quickly lost interest. How many different ways could one measure a rectangle, after all?

Left to itself, her mind wandered right back to Danny's declaration of love.

Danny, we hardly know each other. She hadn't laughed, hadn't dared. He was so obviously in earnest.

I like what I know. He'd answered so quietly, so firmly, that she'd been quite dumbfounded.

"Okay." Merry plopped into the chair next to her. "Give me a minute to work through this…" Producing a ruler from somewhere, she set about sketching the stage on a pad of paper, larger than the tiny one Noella could see in one corner of the page.

"If we put this here," Merry muttered. Paused to consult the short list of props. "And that there…um, no." She scratched her cheek. "It's just one couch, right?"

Noella didn't bother answering Merry's rhetorical question. She'd spent most of Tuesday evening on Danny's couch, coming back into the front room to work after they'd finished eating, just to be near him while he read. Perhaps…perhaps she loved him, too. How exactly did one know they were in love? Really, permanently in love?

She doodled on the back of her copy of the script while she pondered. She'd attended dozens of wedding receptions in her life, some of which had already died early, painful deaths by divorce. On the other hand, she'd watched her siblings' relationships with their spouses mature. And how she envied her parents their affable relationship. They made it look easy, but she wasn't naïve enough to believe that. Not quite.

So, where did that leave her? She very definitely had feelings for Danny. They were growing, too. Was it enough for eternity? She rubbed her eyes and remembered how once, as a child, she'd pulled a plant up by its roots because she wanted to see how deep they were.

Hmm. Her parents. More specifically, her mother. Noella made a note to call her mother, then did a double-take at her friend. She was holding very still.

"Merry." She'd been watching the quietly developing romance between her friend and the handsome Tyrel with increasing interest. It was so sweet. Except that Merry had been staring off into space for…too long. Even for Merry. "My friend, are you well?" Noella tapped her pencil on the table by Merry's hand.

Merry recoiled from the noise and motion near her hand. "Noella!" she protested. "You scared me half to death!"

"Oh, yes?" Noella sat back in her chair, lips

quirking up in mildly sardonic humor. "I should have sent you a text message, perhaps?" Had Merry been thinking of Tyrel, the way she had been thinking about Danny?

Merry laughed a bit sheepishly. "Sorry, I…I guess I did get a little distracted."

Noella clucked softly, her curls bouncing as she shook her head. "I have seen you distracted, my friend. This, it is different."

Merry puffed out her cheeks and exhaled through her mouth. "I was thinking about Tyrel."

"What?" Noella teased. She'd guessed correctly! "Instead of the most interesting stage designs?" She gestured at the bare stage before them, saw what she'd written on the back of the script and hastily covered it with her other hand. *Noella Fitzsimmons.* "This will be your masterpiece!" she blurted, waving expansively.

"I sure hope not," Merry retorted. "But, I've read the play and I've measured the stage. All you really need is a couch for the kids to slouch on; a desk for the dad to do too much work at; and a kitchen counter for the mom."

"Also, a Christmas tree."

"Huh?" Merry scribbled something on her list. "Yeah, of course."

They discussed the designs briefly, though too vaguely for Noella's comfort. Of course, it wasn't even Thanksgiving yet. She bit back questions about the props, assuring herself that

Merry would find someone to loan them a couch, a desk—and if they absolutely had to, they could use the decrepit old Christmas tree that belonged to the community center.

Noella winked, then touched her lightly on the wrist. "You do not wish to tell me what is troubling you?"

"It's nothing much." Merry shrugged. Nothing she wanted to talk about. With anyone.

"It does not go well with Tyrel?" Noella probed.

"No, things are fine." Merry shifted a little in her chair, signaling that she wasn't telling the whole truth.

"Good." Noella knew better than to try to pry the information out of her, so she opted for an optimistic response. "You two, you go well together."

Merry smiled shyly and checked her phone. "Hey, I better get going. It's nearly time for auditions to start." Pausing, she looked around the empty room. "Um… Where did you say you put those signs up?"

"Over all the town." Noella's beam brightened still further. "Every store window, every board." Two at the library.

Merry's eyebrows drew in as she nodded slowly. "I'll get out of your way." Impulsively, she hugged the younger woman. "Pace yourself. You've still got five weeks of rehearsal, programs to design, tickets to sell…" Her shoulders slumped as if just thinking about it exhausted her.

"Go, go," Noella laughed. "Before you talk me out of all this fame and glory."

Alone again, she opened her laptop and checked her email. Nothing new, not even in her spam folder. She'd emailed the invitations days ago. Three separate invitations. Wait. Had she used the right contact emails? She'd been awfully tired that night.

Meticulously, she re-located each email and each artist's page to compare the contact information she'd used against what was listed. Perfect matches. No errors. And no way to tell if the emails landed in their inboxes or not, let alone got read.

Sighing, she asked the room at large, "Couldn't they at least respond?" The silence seemed to glower at her for interrupting it and she curled her knees up to her chest, resting her feet on the chair's crossbar.

The heat being pumped into the room couldn't touch the cold settling into her soul.

There would be no big name.

It would seem that there weren't even going to be auditions.

Rubbing her arms, she wondered idly if she should put the chairs away or leave them out for Mrs. Arnold to use when she had *her* auditions.

Sighing, she bowed her head and began a whispered prayer. "I thank Thee, Heavenly Father, for this opportunity. For blessing me to have fun trying." She smiled as she remembered Jane's enthusiasm. "For everyone's help. In the name of Jesus Christ, amen."

Rising, she closed her laptop and took a deep breath. And nearly jumped out of her skin when a door slammed somewhere in the building.

"C'mon, c'mon," insisted a woman's voice.

Eyes wide, Noella watched in shock as a woman and a boy practically skidded to a stop inside the door to the auditorium.

"Don't say it!" The woman held up a hand as if prepared to forcibly stop Noella from speaking. "Don't say the auditions are over." Mistaking Noella's silence for having achieved her desired effect, the woman marched over, towing her slightly miserable-looking son. "We just found out they were happening today and it wouldn't be fair for you to not at least hear Josh read."

Noella blinked. Put one arm behind herself and pinched the back of her other arm. *Ouch!* Alright, she was officially awake.

Numbly, she pointed at the table by the door. "Sign in, please."

The woman, whom she later learned was named Judy—and a dear friend of Merry's, by funny coincidence—hadn't finished setting the pen down when the door slammed again.

"I think it's here," said someone uncertainly.

"Look! There's a light on down the hall!"

Noella sank into her chair, goosebumps of gratitude prickling along her arms as an entire troop of mothers and children stormed the auditorium, chasing away the silence like an army defeating an ogre.

Judy took command of the situation with ease, pointing out the sign-in sheet and the scripts, then grabbing her son's hand and taking him to one side to rehearse.

With another prayer of gratitude in her heart, Noella spent the next hour and a half working with them. She soothed frightened children. Thanked everyone for coming. Asked a special few to wait.

When it was just herself, three excited mothers, and three rather bored teens and tweens, she wrapped it up as quickly as she could. They should practice every day. Rehearsals would be for one hour every Saturday afternoon. Dress rehearsal the Saturday before the play.

"If we do this right, we will have a lot of fun!" she promised.

The mothers beamed and the children squirmed.

"I'll see you next Saturday. Be sure to take a script home with you and start memorizing your lines."

The older boy, Josh, hesitated. Glanced at the two dozen chairs now scattered randomly across the floor.

"Want some help?"

"That would be most wonderful." Her heart glowing with appreciation, Noella smiled at him.

"Let's all help," suggested Fran, a tall woman who hunched her shoulders as though she wished she were shorter.

"You bet." Heather expertly stomped on the back of her folding chair. "Freddy, hold this." She handed her chair to her young son and reached for another.

"We're practically done already," laughed Judy.

What would've taken Noella fifteen minutes by herself was accomplished in two—and with a lot more laughter.

"You children are much too wonderful to play these blasé characters." The blank stares she got in return had her fumbling for a different word. "I mean, such indifferent characters."

She smiled as she packed up her things and walked out into the cold. Her happiness burst out in hymns on the drive home.

"There is sunshine in my soul today! A carol to my king."

At home, she broke out the ginger, cinnamon, and molasses. She never baked as well as she did when she was happy, and right now she was flying!

As soon as she shut off the beater, she called her mother. She shared all her news while she rolled out and cut gingerbread cookies.

"Oh, you'd love Caesar, Mama. He's a very good boy who has worked hard and now we're teaching him how to play." She told her about the snowball fight next, mostly because she didn't want to be the one to bring up Danny as a potential sweetheart.

"Hmm, sounds like you are having a lot of fun with this man, Danny."

And just like that, all of her carefully planned casual remarks scattered to the four winds.

"Noella." Her mother's tone changed, and Noella wished they were in the same room so they could sit on the couch together as they used to. "Exactly how much fun are you having?"

The stove timer went off and Noella slipped on her oven mitts. "Be right back, Mama. I have to take the tray out."

It only took a few seconds to trade one tray for the other and she was right back at her phone.

"He says he loves me, Mama."

The faint whirring sound of her mother's exercise bike slowed, then stopped. "Do you love him?"

"Maybe?" Ugh. She wanted to go hide. What a ridiculous thing to say. She opened her mouth to say something else—who knew what?—but her mother spoke first.

"Tell me what you like about him."

She swallowed. Picked at the gingerbread dough that had gotten stuck around her fingernails.

"I like the way his eyes crinkle when he smiles, like Papa's do." She especially liked it when he smiled at her.

"What else?" her mother prompted.

She got up and walked in a small circle so she would still be near her phone. "He is smart. And kind. With all the dogs he is kind, but firm. I think he will make a good father."

"That is good."

Noella leaned on the counter next to her phone, imagining the twinkle in her mother's eyes right then. How her mother loved being a grandma.

"But he is here. In the Ozarks." She exhaled slowly. "And my home is…"

"Your home is where you make it," her mother gently interrupted. "This man, does he read his scriptures? Have you heard him pray?"

"Yes, to both questions." She'd come out just the other morning to find him in his recliner, marking his scriptures as he studied for the day. "We take turns blessing the food, and this last week we started having morning and evening prayer together."

"Très bien." Mama grunted a little, probably swinging her leg over the bike to get off. "Tell me, ma chérie, what it is you called to talk about today?"

"How do I know," the words came, but haltingly, "when I am in love?"

"Ooh là là." Her mother's laugh was kind. "I think you must like him more than you know, ma chérie."

"Yes, I…I probably do." Noella felt a heat

rising in her cheeks that had nothing to do with her baking.

"But you have never before asked me this. I remember you have told me, not often, but a few times that you thought you were in love. And…"

"Oui, that's it. I fell into love, I fell out of love." She spread her hands as though her mother could see them. "How do I know this is a 'for time and all eternity' love?"

The answering silence was not reassuring.

"Noella. That kind of love, it is not made only once and forgotten. It is made every day." Warmth rushed through Noella, confirming the truth of her mother's words. "I love your father for time and all eternity. And I tell myself this as I cook. As I clean. As I help him. As I thank Heavenly Father each day for blessing me with such a good husband."

By small and simple things are great things brought to pass… Words from Alma, a Book of Mormon prophet, sprang to mind, followed immediately by a flood of memories. A thousand, a million things she'd seen her parents do for each other. Insignificant things by themselves, but taken as a whole, they added up to over forty years of happily married life.

"Thank you, Mama."

"My pleasure, ma petite."

They talked a little more, then her mother had to go get ready for supper at her brother's.

Noella felt a pang of homesickness as she

thought of her family gathered around the table, then filling her brother's front room after supper. Everyone who wanted to perform would get a turn, until it got so late that even the adults were nodding in their chairs.

With a slight sniffle, she dabbed at her eyes and shut off the timer. As she set her kitchen to rights, she tried to imagine Danny at one of those events. Then, a little more boldly, she tried to imagine a future where they gathered in his—no, *their* living room—and their children sang or played or danced for each other. For the sheer joy of it.

A smile tugged at her lips as she caught herself stroking a towel as though it were Caesar.

She certainly had a vivid imagination. But, she told herself firmly, she couldn't just imagine they'd gotten a big name to come to the play.

Her phone buzzed and lit up, alerting her that a text had arrived from Judy. Odd. She'd traded phone numbers with all three of the mothers after the auditions, but hadn't expected to hear from any of them so soon. Her gut clenched. Had Josh changed his mind?

One way to find out.

[Hey, girl! If you don't have someone for the music, I'd love to volunteer. I have a huge collection of Christmas music. I even have Helen Montgomery. She's really popular right now!]

Hmm. Noella tapped her lip. Maybe she was thinking too big. She hadn't tried for a Broadway star or a movie celebrity or anything like that. However, this was just a small town play.

She sent Judy a thank you, then sat down at her laptop and listened to some samples of Helen Montgomery's music.

She liked what she heard so much that she bought some of Helen's original songs in the morning and listened to them while she updated and redesigned several websites. The singer's throaty alto was pleasant to listen to. Her lyrics were clean and thought-provoking.

Yes. Yes, she would do nicely. *If* Noella could persuade her to come.

Chapter 14

It was her turn to host that evening, so naturally Noella took the opportunity to test her newest creation.

"This is so good!" Harmony closed her eyes in the bliss of savoring her third gingerbread man. "Is this an old family recipe or something?"

Noella laughed and shook her head. "I found it in a book at the library."

"No way!" Harmony's eyes popped open. "In that case, maybe I could get a picture of it? I'm taking treats to my clients next week and this beats anything else I've got."

"Of course!" Beckoning for Harmony to follow her the few steps into the kitchen, Noella pulled out her 'in process' loose leaf. "I keep all the recipes at first," she explained. "Until I have it just the way I want it."

"This is great." Harmony took the neatly written, numbered index cards from her. The adjustments were all noted in red ink. It reminded her of the experiments she'd done in high school chemistry, though better organized. "This one's your favorite?" She held up number five.

"Yes." Taking the cards back, Noella spread them all out on the counter. "I adjusted the ginger first, and it was better," she touched the third card. "But it had to balance with the cinnamon, so..." She shrugged and laughed. "Two more tries."

"Worth every pound you gained test-tasting them," Harmony teased, snapping a picture and getting a friendly slap on the shoulder for her joke. Truthfully, she was impressed. Most of Noella's desserts were a little overly spiced for her taste, but this was perfect. "What else have you got in there?" She pointed at the loose leaf.

Noella happily showed her the recipes she was working on, including a stubborn yogurt curry that she had over a dozen cards for.

Harmony's phone, which she'd placed on the counter, buzzed and a name flashed on the screen—Grant. Frowning, Harmony flipped the phone over.

"Harmony?" Noella touched her arm lightly. "Is everything alright?" A strange sense of déjà vu struck her and she realized she'd asked Merry almost the same question just the day before.

"Fine." Harmony shrugged dismissively and shuffled through the curry cards, pretending they were more important than her growing feelings for a man she couldn't have. And hadn't so much as bumped into lately, doggone it.

Noella gave her a moment to elaborate on her answer. When she didn't, Noella cleared he throat.

"I have a favor to ask."

"Sure." Harmony moved a card to the back of the stack, apparently absorbed in studying them. "What do you need?"

"I held auditions for the play yesterday. And I have most of the cast for *No Time Like the Present.*"

"Okay." Harmony looked up. "And?" A note of suspicion had entered her voice.

"All three of the children's roles are taken, but we have no one to play the parents." She paused just in case Harmony decided to volunteer.

"Why don't you do it?" She bumped Noella's shoulder with her own. "I'm sure Danny would agree if you asked him." She was also sure that wasn't what Noella wanted to hear.

Well, I didn't see that coming!

"I will have a hundred things to do during the play." Shaking her head, Noella went for it. "I was hoping that you and Grant would play the parents."

"Play the—!" Even though that was exactly what she thought Noella was working up to, Harmony still had to work to control her voice. A glance at the others showed they still had their heads together, discussing their own secrets or whatever. "You want me to act like I'm married to Grant?" Her eyes narrowed. "We'd kiss on stage, wouldn't we?" She could tell from Noella's half-shrug and raised eyebrows that she'd guessed right.

Noella winced at the sight of her carefully kept cards being crumpled in Harmony's strong hands. To keep herself from snatching them away, she opened the cupboard by her head and brought down four plates.

"It would be very helpful to me to have the roles filled."

"Well, I'm sorry, but that's not going to happen. Not by Grant and me, anyway."

"I understand you cannot accept without first discussing it with him." Noella got out the milk and some glasses. She was absolutely intrigued by the vehemence in Harmony's tone. Something was definitely going on there, but unlike with Merry and Tyrel, it wasn't something good.

"Ah, but we must get the movie started." Scooping up the cards, she preempted Harmony's reiteration of her refusal by nodding at the stack of plates. "Will you put some gingerbread on those, please?" Once her loose leaf was back in order, she used the microwave to warm the gingerbread a bit and sent Harmony out to the others with the first installment.

"Let me ask her," Grace suggested as Harmony approached. "I'll ask her the next time I see her."

"Ask who what?" Harmony asked, handing them each a plate. Now that she was standing right next to them, her guilt jumped into overdrive. She still hadn't told anyone she might be leaving before Christmas. Had they been talking about her?

"I was telling Grace about our stage crew problem." Merry nodded at Noella to include her in the conversation. "She knows someone she can ask to help out." She shrugged diffidently as she spoke, not wanting to get Noella's hopes up too high.

"Magnificent!" Noella tried to clap her hands for joy and nearly spilled milk everywhere. "We have the theater. Most of the cast." She angled a sidelong glance at Harmony, who had eyes only for the serving tray of gingerbread cookies. "And maybe the stage crew. Yes. Very good!"

"Sounds like things are going great." Merry heaved a sigh of relief.

"Oui, but for one thing." Noella paused for a dramatic moment. "We have no draw." She'd found that word through an online translation system and now anxiously watched her friends' faces to see if she'd used it correctly.

"Draw? Like, a big name to draw in the crowds?" Grace clarified, eyes narrowing quizzically.

"Exactly." Noella handed over the glasses of milk and plopped into her seat. "I hear the talk. Because Mrs. Arnold's children did not make the cast, the people will not come." Not that Mrs. Arnold had bothered to bring them to the auditions. Still, that was exactly what Miss Birdie said earlier that day.

"Of all the two-faced, double-dealing monsters," Merry growled.

They all looked at her, stunned.

"Mrs. Arnold is the committee chairwoman

who sandbagged Noella at that meeting. Now she's upset that her 'little starlets,'" as the woman had often been heard to call her offspring, "didn't get three out of the five roles in the whole show?"

Grace rolled her eyes. "Sounds like her." Her flat tone left no doubt that the words came from personal experience.

"I'll say," Harmony huffed. "Cadmia's queen bee strikes again." She hadn't been there as long as the others, but she'd heard plenty. It was thanks to Mrs. Arnold's vendetta against this play, or rather Noella, that no adults had auditioned. Ugh. Now she felt even more guilty, though this time it was for refusing to perform.

"It was one thing for her to turn the town against the idea of rezoning Fleischer's pasture for a mall," Grace remarked quietly. "But the proceeds from the charity play go to paying for food, fuel, clothes, and even Christmas presents for some of the families around here."

"Maybe we need to remind people of that," Merry grumbled.

"How?" Noella stuck out her bottom lip. "The merchants, they have agreed to set up tables to sell tickets, but nobody buys them. I went to the newspaper to beg them to write a story and they say it is old news. The churches, well, they buy a few tickets." She hesitated, her fingers fluttering. "That is where I hear about Mrs. Arnold."

"The play's only a couple of weeks away." Harmony bit her lip as her guilt poked her again.

"But what draw is there that would counteract Mrs. Arnold?" Merry asked. "It's not like there's room in the play for," she waved vaguely.

"Helen Montgomery."

Merry jerked, nearly dumping her entire plate of gingerbread. "What?"

"Helen Montgomery." Grace repeated uncertainly. "From what I can tell, she's all the rage right now."

"Yeah, she's popular." Harmony frowned. "But do you really think an indie singer is, well, spectacular enough to overcome the bee?"

"If we can get her to come, the teenagers will spend their own money to buy these tickets." At least, Grace knew a few of them who would.

"This may be true." Noella's fingers fluttered descriptively as she added, "Everywhere I go, I hear the voice of this singer." She just hadn't realized it until yesterday.

"The grocery store, the beauty salon, even the family-run restaurants are all playing her," Harmony agreed thoughtfully. "If you could get her, and that's a pretty big 'if,' she might put the play over."

"Wonder how much she'd charge?" Grace mused.

"Who says she'll charge anything?" Merry asked, her tone suspiciously close to sulky.

"Oh, I dunno." Grace shrugged. "She's a performer. I just assumed she would want some kind of compensation."

"We can always ask," Harmony pointed out. "Tell her it's a charity play, sort of a last minute emergency, and see what she says."

"Last minute is right." Merry rearranged her gingerbread men. "She probably has big plans with family by now." Her eyes fastened on Harmony, who was typing on her phone. "What're you doing?"

"Asking Helen Montgomery to sing in our play." Harmony hit send. She didn't want to play the mom in this show any more than she wanted to eat liver and onions, a personal hate of hers, but she could send an email.

They all looked up in surprise when Merry's phone dinged almost the same instant.

"What?" she squeaked.

"Nothing…" Harmony frowned uncertainly. "That was some weird timing, though."

Noella clapped her hands. "This is wonderful! Helen will say yes. The play, it will be a success. And everyone will have a merry Christmas." She hit play on the remote before anyone could contradict her.

For the first time, she noticed that the movie *D Flat Aria* didn't have any dogs in it. She liked cats alright, but the more she thought about it, the happier she was that she'd soon be sharing her apartment with a big, tough dog.

"Okay." Harmony mock-swooned as the end credits rolled. "*That* was a kiss." Her quip was rewarded with a round of laughter.

Merry hopped up and started collecting dishes like her life depended on it, then ducked into the kitchen.

Noella might have gone in to check on her, but Grace gave her a wink as she followed Merry, a couple of glasses in her hands.

So, instead, Noella helped Harmony re-enact the auction scene from the movie.

Harmony cracked up. "Poor Molly," she gasped. "Can you imagine how embarrassing it would be to have two guys take their rivalry for you public like that?"

"Thankfully, no!" Noella's concern for her friend grew as Harmony laughed even harder at that, eventually coming over for a high five.

"So." Harmony plopped onto the couch near her. "I haven't read the script or anything, but how in the world are you going to work in a sixth role?"

"What sixth role?"

"Um, Helen Montgomery?" Harmony quirked an eyebrow. "Or is she just coming to watch from the front row?"

"No, don't be silly." Noella glared at nothing in particular.

Looking over her shoulder at where Merry and Grace were whispering again, Harmony was tactless enough to holler, "Hey, what do you two think?"

"What do we think about what?" Grace laughed as they rejoined them.

"We were talking about working Helen into the story," Harmony explained. "There's no room for another character, so I think she should play the mom." That sounded plausible, right? She'd already tried and failed to convince Noella to do it. Opposite Danny, of course.

"Ridiculous." Noella flapped a hand at her. "You wish only to avoid the role for yourself."

"Which means you have a different plan," Grace surmised.

"Helen will sing the Christmas music." Noella beamed at them, terribly pleased with herself. "The mother listens to music while she works. They all listen to music at the end. Voila. It is perfect."

"I don't know." Merry spread her hands. "It's a two hour-long play. You want her to, what, stand stock still on stage all that time?"

Noella's brows knit together. "No, that would not do. We will have to give her a chair. She can stand each time she is to sing. With a spotlight."

"Then fade into the background again when the spotlight switches to the others." Grace shrugged. "That might work."

"Yeah," Merry agreed halfheartedly.

"Alright, enough plotting for one night." Grace wrapped Noella in a hug. "Thanks for having us over."

"Yes." Merry followed suit, hugging first Noella, then Harmony, who'd risen to hug Grace. "And the delicious gingerbread."

"I better go, too." Harmony collected a hug from Noella. "My place for a musical next time!" They skipped movie nights on weeks with major holidays, so that meant she was free until December sixth. *Hmm.* Maybe it was time for another getaway?

"Can't wait," Grace assured her.

In an instant, they were gone, leaving Noella with silence ringing in her ears. She never used to mind silence. On the contrary, she secretly adored it.

She put on general conference to keep her company while she prepared for bed, where she dreamed about feeding Caesar at the table. She thought he used a knife and fork amazingly well for not having opposable thumbs, and that the whole thing was weird.

A buzzing sound disturbed her in the morning. Opening one eye a slit, she glared at her phone. Who in their right minds would call her at this...well, this early on a Saturday?

Sitting up, she turned her phone over and gasped at the time. Ten o'clock?! She never slept that late.

Just as she was about to answer the call, her phone stopped buzzing. And as she started to set her phone back on her nightstand, it resumed buzzing.

"Morning, sunshine!" At the sound of Danny's voice, her eyes popped open and she smiled.

"Bonjour!"

His deep chuckle came through as clearly it was as if he was in the same room.

"Something tells me I'm going to have to learn some French," he teased.

Blushing, she pushed her blankets back and went into the kitchen to pace.

"I try to speak in English, but it is more difficult at some times than others."

"That's a fact and I grew up speaking it. Some words." She could picture the corners of his eyes crinkling as he smiled. "Let's take the word 'sit' as an example. You can say sit, sat, and seated, but not sot, because that means something completely different."

"I'm sure you're right." Closing her eyes, she kneaded the back of her neck with her fingertips.

"I'm sorry, sweetheart." She leaned against the wall, her stomach fluttering at his endearment. "Chuck told me I was acting weird today and I guess he was right."

"Tell Chuck he's crazy."

"Maybe I will. But first, let me tell you why I called. I've been so busy that I forgot all about Thanksgiving until Toni ambushed me yesterday with the question of how many were coming to supper this year."

Her heart rate picked up and she straightened

away from the wall. Thanksgiving was an important holiday. Families traveled long distances to be together. Including…fathers. She'd met Alec Fitzsimmons casually over the months. She'd even sat next to him at church after her first date with Danny, but this would be totally different.

"I know we're technically scheduled to train that day." His pause nearly drove her mad. Was he about to invite her for Thanksgiving or not? "And if you've got other plans, I'll understand. But, um, since you hadn't mentioned anything, I was hoping you'd join us out here."

She paced from the wall of her kitchen to her front door and started back again. This would be her first year away from home for Thanksgiving. She'd considered making some of the traditional dishes for herself—squash soup, pouding chômeur, and of course, turkey—but no matter where she spent the day, she was going to miss her family.

Spending the day with Danny, and Chuck, and Toni, and…and Alec, that would be nice, no?

"I'd love to."

"Great!" His exhale sounded full of relief. "We probably wouldn't do much formal training that day anyway. Of course, it'll be a great chance to see how Caesar handles being in a small crowd."

"Small crowd?" She *really* wanted to know if his dad was going to be there. She could probably ask Grace about it if she absolutely had to…

"Yeah. You, me, Toni, Chuck," he was speaking more slowly with each name, "and my dad."

There it is.

"Ah, a very small crowd." She didn't want to make a big deal out of it any more than he did.

"Right. It, um… Perfect opportunity to test Caesar's people skills."

Her lips twitched. "You just said that."

"I did? Oh. Yeah, I guess I did." In her mind's eye she could see him shoving his fingers through his hair, rumpling it temptingly. "If you'd rather, I could drive up to Cadmia for Thanksgiving. My dad's trailer isn't really big enough for three people, but we could make it work."

Her mouth opened and closed. She paced more quickly. "But that is not necessary. I will already be there in Fireclay."

"Okay. Oh! I talked it over with Toni and she agrees that you should have a few nights with Caesar to yourself before we turn you guys loose next month."

"To myself? Ah, you mean in a cabin."

"Yes." He was starting to sound flustered. "So she's going to stay with you Tuesday night. You'll still have full access to the house and all for your work or whatever you need." The words came in a rush. "Then when she thinks you and

Caesar are both ready for it, she'll let you have the place, that is, the *cabin* to yourselves."

"Wonderful!" She laughed lightly. Conveniently timed, also, since his father would probably need the guest room.

Chapter 15

"Welcome home!" Toni greeted her in Danny's garage on Tuesday. The twinkle in her eyes suggested she was only half joking.

Noella hugged her back and decided to ignore the bait. "Where's Caesar?" Usually he was with her by now.

"Don't worry, your boyfriends are close by." Mischief danced in Toni's eyes as she put a faint stress on the plurality of the word.

"Great." Noella pulled her bag out of the back of her car and slammed the trunk shut. "Can we stop at the cabin first?" Toni had started to show, ever so slightly, and Noella thought it was a nice look for her. It was understandable, too, that the woman hadn't chosen to share her condition. So many babies were lost to miscarriage in the first trimester.

"You bet." Toni slung an arm around Noella's shoulder and told her everything she'd missed over the last couple of days, a huge transformation from the disapproving woman who'd met Noella by the office the first time. "And tonight we'll be in here, just the three of us."

Noella reached for the door knob, but it opened before she could turn it.

"What's the matter with you, knucklehead?" Danny asked a happily barking Caesar. "It's almost like you think someone important is here or something.”

Noella’s heart soared under the light of Danny’s broad, welcoming smile. If not for Toni, she would most certainly have expected him to kiss her. Instead, she left her bag by the door and bent to rub Caesar’s tummy, one of his favorite things. When she straightened, Toni and her bag were gone.

“Hello.” Danny stole a quick kiss, his eyes never leaving the bedroom door. Toni would find out about them soon enough and he didn’t want to give her any more ammunition before then.

“Hi.” She tried to rub away the goosebumps he’d given her.

“Cold?” Toni leaned against the doorjamb, grinning like she’d knew exactly what Noella was doing.

“Today is not so bad.” Noella hung her things in the tiny closet and signaled for Caesar to follow her the few feet into the next room. The cabin’s open floor plan meant the entirety of the common areas were visible from everywhere except the bedrooms. “Good boy. Sit.”

Ears pricked, Caesar eagerly obeyed each of her commands until it was time for his reward— another tummy rub.

“We’ve been working on playtime with him.” Danny showed her a small bin of toys by the front door. “He doesn’t seem to have a favorite yet.”

"Is that important?"

"No, not really." Danny chuckled as Caesar lightly head-butted her hand. "He's doing a hundred percent better now that he's found you."

"The other dogs. Like Caesar." He woofed a little when she said his name and they laughed. "They have homes now, too?"

"All but one." Toni's smile dimmed. "She's handling her separation from her handler better than Caesar did, though."

"Why is that?"

"Could be any of a dozen things." Danny leaned on the counter, a thoughtful expression on his face. "In her case, for example, she wasn't injured. She's just reached retirement age."

"So not nearly as traumatic as what happened to Caesar," Toni chimed in.

"What *did* happen to him?" She'd asked before but never really gotten an answer.

"You know they were ambushed." Toni began blinking rapidly. "Caesar took five bullets."

Danny put his hand lightly on Toni's wrist and took over the story. "He was the only survivor out of the entire squad." He omitted the fact that the ambushers had made sure of their other victims. "It took four hours for anyone to reach the spot. And they found him curled up next to what was left of his handler."

Noella stroked Caesar's head and tickled his ear. "No wonder you have nightmares, my friend," she whispered in French.

The sounds of someone stomping their feet outside broke the somber mood in time for Chuck to walk in.

"Whoa." He glanced at each of them. "Is this the Tillman wake?"

Toni punched him. Hugged him.

Chuck shot Danny a worried look even as he hugged her back, and Danny gave him a shrug-head shake.

"I just came by to welcome our girl." Chuck nodded at Noella. "And to tell you we got a call back for Autumn." Toni surreptitiously dabbed at her eyes as she stepped away from Chuck, who made a point of keeping one arm around her waist.

"Fantastic. In fact, that gives me an idea. Let's work Autumn and Caesar together today." Danny handed Toni the toy bin. "Will you guys bring her out, please?"

"Sure thing, boss." Chuck spoke before his wife could and led her outside, still keeping her close to him.

Once the door had closed behind them, Danny drummed his fingers on the counter. "I probably should let her tell you this, but…"

Noella rose gracefully. "Toni is going to be a mother? Yes, I noticed."

He blinked. "You…did?"

"Oui." This time she didn't apologize, even to herself, for the French word. "I know the signs."

"Oh." Relieved that he hadn't broken Toni's confidence, he puffed out his chest. "They're making me an honorary uncle."

Coming closer, Noella put her hands on his chest and observed softly, "You will make the most wonderful uncle."

His eyes roved her face, but he kept his hands at his sides. "Of course, someday I hope to be a dad, too."

"I'm glad to hear that."

He had to lean closer to hear her this time, so close that his face was only a few inches from hers. It definitely gave a man ideas.

"Hey."

Startled, he jerked back, but Noella calmly looked Toni in the eyes.

"I, um…" Toni suddenly looked sheepish. "We're ready out here when you are."

"We'll be right out." Noella had something to say first. She'd been doing a lot of praying and thinking about it, and it felt right. Not that her heart wasn't pounding like a bodhrán drum.

Danny quirked an eyebrow at her as Toni closed the door she'd burst through mere seconds ago.

Rather than answering, Noella came up on her toes enough to put her arms around his neck.

A little rattled by Toni's jack-in-the-box appearance, he nevertheless inched closer. Touched her cheek. Cupped one hand at the back of her neck and lowered his lips to hers.

"We better get out there," he murmured huskily. "Before Chuck comes in after us."

"He is more intimidating than Toni?" She raised an eyebrow in disbelief.

"I wouldn't go that far." He tenderly smoothed her hair.

"Mon cher, j'taime." Peace settled over her, calming her racing heart.

"I like the sound of that." He smiled as he rested his forehead against hers. "What does it mean?"

"It means," she answered breathlessly, "I love you."

"Noella." He cupped her face in his hands. "You love me? Are you sure?"

"Yes," she laughed and cried a little at the same time. "I am sure."

He picked her up and whirled her around in the small kitchen, then held her close, savoring the moment.

Noella looked down when someone—who turned out to be Caesar—pawed at her leg and barked. He must've come in through the doggie door. Or been sent, perhaps?

"Smooth, Toni, smooth." Chuckling, Danny kissed Noella lightly and opened the door for her.

They tromped outside together and he introduced Noella to a gorgeous boxer named Autumn. For the next few hours, they alternately ran obedience drills and played with the dogs.

Toni and Chuck used the rest of the lawn to

work with the one-year-olds, which made it interesting for everyone.

Danny looked up as the security lights clicked on. "Ten more minutes," he announced. "Then we'll call it a day." These early sunsets were a big reason he chose not to do intense training during the winter.

They had Search and Rescue dogs and their handlers scheduled for training in January and February, when the snow would most likely be the worst. Working in the dark was actually part of their training, so that worked well, too. He'd spend most of the next couple of months cooped up in the office, catching up on paperwork, preparing taxes…

"What?" Noella cocked her head at him.

"Huh?" Confused, he stopped mid-throw, much to Autumn's dismay. "Sorry, girl." He finished the motion and she raced after the Frisbee, barking happily.

"You sighed." Noella let Caesar get a sniff of the foot-long, bone-shaped toy she'd just found in the toy bin, then threw it as hard as she could.

"I did?" Danny dropped to one knee and wrestled softly with Autumn. She'd been pretty aggressive when she arrived and had come a long way.

"You definitely did." She let Caesar start a tug-of-war with the toy, then let go before it got too involved. "Drop it." Automatically, she gave the hand command at the same time. "Good boy." She rewarded his prompt obedience with a scratch behind the ears.

"I'll be along in a minute," Danny promised her, scooping up the toy bin. Chuck and Toni had already finished with the younger dogs and taken them back inside.

Noella hesitated, unsure if that meant he'd come to the cabin or if she was wait for him at his home. Come to think of it, she hadn't checked her cabin for food. Hadn't even opened the fridge. Of course, she'd been a little busy.

Her lips twitching, she motioned for Caesar to follow her and headed to Danny's kitchen. Once she'd gotten Caesar reasonably dried off, she washed her hands and started heating some canned soup. She was in the middle of frying some cheese sandwiches to go with it when Danny got back from the kennel.

"You know." He hung up his coat and came over to the sink for a squirt of soap. "I missed you." Hands rinsed and dried, he slipped his arms around her waist. "Have I mentioned that I could get used to coming home to you?"

"I believe so." It wasn't easy to act nonchalant when her heart was racing, but she managed.

"And you?" He asked as she slipped the second sandwich onto a plate.

She stepped out of his arms and set the plates on the table. Pretended to weigh her answer.

"Yes, I think I could get used to this."

"That makes me very happy." Danny joined her by the table, where he kissed her forehead and pulled out a chair for her. Taking her proffered right hand in his, he suggested, "Would you like a turn?"

She nodded and bowed her head. As she opened her mouth, a wave of warmth broke over her, filling her to the point that she couldn't speak. Not even to say a simple blessing on the food.

Hearing her start to sniffle, Danny opened his eyes to check on her. Her left hand was covering her mouth; perhaps to muffle the sounds?

Sliding out of his chair, he slid to his knees beside her. Brushed away her tears with his fingers and prayed silently to know what to do.

"Marry me?" Even the newest tear slipping down her cheek seemed to freeze in place as she stared down at him, eyes wide.

Her mind raced, keeping time with her heart, as she tried to comprehend what had just happened. What he was offering.

"Oui," she whispered. It felt like her lungs were released from a vice and she inhaled deeply. "Yes!"

He wrapped his arms around her as he got to his feet, and whirled her around the kitchen. Returned her gently to her chair and smoothed her hair out of her face before stealing a soft kiss.

They were much too excited to eat, but as the food was already prepared, they did what they could with it, then hurried over to her cabin to talk.

"Let's go out tomorrow and pick a ring," Danny suggested as they sat down on the couch.

"With Caesar?"

He eyed the dog, whose ears pricked up on hearing his name, then shook his head. "He won't be able to come in the store and leaving him in the car by himself is something I'd rather not do."

"Oh, yes." She sighed and stroked his head. "But what will we do with him?"

"He'll be alright with the other dogs for a few hours." Danny patted Caesar as well. He'd given up hope of figuring out what had triggered the dog to snarl at him that Sunday. They were on good terms now, as far as he could tell. "I actually think it's been good practice for him to have you go and come back these last couple of weeks."

"Mmm." She put her head against his shoulder. "Yes. I hadn't thought of that."

He rested his cheek against her hair. "What kind of a ring do you want?"

"Simple." His answering chuckle rumbled through his chest, making her smile.

"You don't have to answer right away," he teased. "Sleep on it. Let me know in the morning if you need to."

She poked him in the ribs and he caught her hand, shifting away. "Okay, let's get back to the ring." Lifting her hand to his lips, he kissed each fingertip. "Simple, eh?"

Retrieving her hand, she snuggled closer. "I knew a girl in college who had a ring with a diamond big enough to use for a headlight." He whistled softly and she nodded. "Such trouble. It caught on everything and soon fell out."

He flinched. "I think I understand. It would be hard to bake while worrying about a ring."

"Exactly."

Toni walked in the front door without knocking and paused to smirk at them. "Getting late," she remarked as she walked into the bathroom.

"She's right." Danny winked and stole a quick kiss, then got to his feet. "We'll leave right after breakfast." He spoke loudly enough that Toni came out to squint at them.

"You're going somewhere?" Toni glanced at Caesar then quirked an eyebrow at Danny.

"If you'd be kind enough to watch Caesar." Noella whispered something in Caesar's ears and he trotted over to sit at Toni's feet. Offered her his paw.

Toni's lips twitched. "Alright, alright." Toni threw up her hands in mock surrender. "I yield." Halfway back into the bathroom, she paused. "Going on a date?"

"Yep."

Noella bit her lip and tried not to giggle. Toni spent the rest of the evening trying to tease information out of her, but didn't seem to mind too much when she failed.

Danny woke up to the mouth-watering smell of bacon cooking. And the oddest sensation that he was being watched.

Rolling over slowly, he came face to face with Caesar. Closing his eyes, he exhaled in relief. Since Noella was in the cabin last night, he'd left his bedroom door partially open.

"If I have nightmares tonight," he told the dog as he swung his legs to the floor, "it's your fault."

Caesar sneezed and shook his head as if in disagreement, making Danny laugh.

"I'll be out in ten, okay buddy?" He tossed his shirt in the hamper on his way into the bathroom, where he quickly showered and brushed his teeth.

Halfway out the door, he paused. Dropped to his knees in prayer and apologized for being so rushed that morning.

Noella found him, still praying, when she came hesitantly to knock on his door a few minutes later. Love for him—the man she was going to marry!—flooded through her.

Upon closing his prayer, Danny looked up to find Noella starting to tiptoe away. On his feet in an instant, he stole up beside her and threaded his fingers through hers.

The same, reverent feeling persisted as they decided to have family scripture study and prayer together before they left.

It was almost a disappointment to hear the *ding* of the store's doorbell when they walked in.

"Good morning and welcome to Southern Charm!" A brunette in a modest pantsuit and jacket greeted them with a smile. "How may I help you today?"

Reading her name tag, Danny responded, "Jen, hi. Would you show us the engagement rings, please?"

Jen's smile brightened considerably. "With pleasure." Stepping back, she gestured for them to precede her.

"Something simple," Noella requested.

"Absolutely." Jen produced three trays of rings, ranging from plain to splashy, and answered questions as they discussed their choices.

Danny felt a twinge of irritation as Jen, undeterred by Noella's polite declinations, persisted in pushing the larger settings.

"How about one of these?" He brashly intervened, picking a plain band and one with a single line of tiny diamonds all the way around it.

Noella oohed and aahed as she took them from him. "Do you have more like these?" she asked Jen.

"Let me check." Jen's smile stiffened as she saw her hopes of a large commission fading.

"Thank you, darling," Noella whispered once Jen was far enough away. Replacing the rings in the tray, she selected one that Jen hadn't given her a chance to really look at.

"Anytime." Danny squeezed her shoulders affectionately. "Is that the one?"

"I do like it." Her tone suggested that it wasn't quite what she wanted and after trying it on, she returned it to the tray.

Jen returned, carrying a tray that she hadn't managed to wipe all the dust off of. "I had to hunt for this," she told them in a cheery tone, her professional way of reminding them of how hard she was working for them.

"See anything?" Danny was suddenly tired of the whole store. He'd chosen Southern Charm because of its fine reputation, but by now he had the feeling they were wasting their time.

She shook her head unhappily. "Perhaps we could look at men's engagement rings?" Jen's startled expression sent Noella reaching for Danny's hand.

Surprised as well, Danny asked, "Do men wear engagement rings?" Most of the men he knew didn't even wear their wedding rings. Even Chuck worried about losing his in the grass or having it get caught on something unexpectedly.

"Of course!" Jen chimed in quickly. They both looked at her expectantly. She started to turn, to go get something, then hesitated. Her veneer slipped and she drummed her fingertips on the countertop. She'd gone to the company trainings and sure, most of the time the strategies worked. On the other hand, she'd been born in the area and it was slowly dawning on her what these two were really after.

"May I see your hands?" Jen had already gotten a pretty good look at Noella's while double-checking her ring size, but this time she turned their hands over and examined their palms. The callouses on Noella's hands weren't as pronounced as those on Danny's, but she'd gotten her answer.

"It seems clear to me that you both work with your hands." Jen efficiently restored the ring trays to order and set them in their places below the glass counter. "Because of that, I'd like to suggest something a little outside of the box for you two."

Chapter 16

"Okay." Danny was intrigued, if only because she was actually talking *to* them, instead of rattling off facts and figures disguised as admiration.

"Over here, please." Stepping around the counter, Jen showed them over to a section of hand-carved jewelry.

Danny heard Noella's soft intake of breath and knew that they were on the right track.

"I don't usually suggest these for wedding jewelry. However." Jen placed a velvet-lined tray before them. "I think in this case, these might be just the thing." She waited for him to remark on the price tags, but even though she was sure she saw him check, he didn't say a word.

"They are so beautiful." Noella's hand hovered over first one, then another of the pendants. Jade stones of every naturally available color fairly glowed against the red velvet.

"May I see that one?" Taking her hesitation to mean that she couldn't decide, Danny pointed at a round, white pendant.

"An excellent choice." Jen lifted it out and offered it to him. "This jade pendant features the exquisite carving of a phoenix. For marriage gifts, it was anciently paired with the dragon." She handed Noella a round, black pendant with a dragon carving that the artist had embellished with gold inlay.

Noella studied it. "May I?" She pointed at a handful of satin necklace cords.

Smiling, Jen threaded the cord through the pendant's loop and handed it back.

Danny bent close enough for Noella to fasten it around his neck. The cord length was perfect, dropping the pendant just below the collar of his tee, so he could wear it in or out as he chose.

"Your turn." Taking special care not to get tangled in her hair, Danny accepted the white pendant from Jen and put it around Noella's neck. Smoothed her hair. "Perfect."

"Excellent." Jen didn't rush as she put away the remaining items. "Will you be wanting wedding bands as well?"

"Yes, thank you."

He selected a white gold band for her and asked Jen to have the reference of Proverbs 31:10 engraved on it.

Noella blushed. That was one of her mother's favorite teaching verses—"Who can find a virtuous woman? for her price *is* far above rubies."

Deliberately, Noella returned her attention back to the tray of plain bands. Selecting a yellow gold band, she asked Jen to have it engraved with the reference of Alma 57:21—"Yea, and they did obey and observe to perform every word of command with exactness; yea, and even according to their faith it was done unto them;

and I did remember the words which they said unto me that their mothers had taught them."

It wasn't until Jen began the checkout process that Danny realized something.

"Wait." He held up his hand. "This is all one purchase."

Noella promptly protested, "It is traditional for each to buy the other's items, as a gift."

He rubbed the back of his neck and shot her a sideways glance. If he'd realized that, he definitely would've gone elsewhere. They hadn't discussed money and he had no idea whether or not she could afford this. She had to have seen the price tags, right? Nevertheless...

"Would you excuse me for a moment? I seem to have only brought one insurance form." Jen discreetly took herself off.

Danny didn't fail to notice the other clerk moving to place themselves a little more securely between them and the door. Okay, fine, that made sense. He was more worried about...

"Danny?" She frowned at him. "Is everything alright?"

"Not...exactly, no." Taking her hands in his, he explained, "I thought buying the ring was my job. And, I guess it would've been if we hadn't gotten the necklaces instead, but." He paused and inhaled slowly. "Sweetheart, I just need to know." He lowered his voice a notch, embarrassed. There were certain disadvantages to spontaneously getting engaged. "Can you afford this? I mean, this isn't something we've planned and saved for, so I'd totally understand if we needed to come back."

"You are very thoughtful, Danny Fitzsimmons." She leaned forward just enough to touch her lips to his. "I promise, I would not have agreed to the purchase if I was not prepared to pay for it."

Relieved, he reluctantly straightened away from her tempting lips. Jen must've taken that as her cue to return, because there she was, forms in hand.

The other clerk beamed at them and shook Danny's hand as they left, carrying their duplicates and receipts and bags with the boxes holding their wedding bands.

"I never realized there was so much paperwork involved in getting engaged." Danny started his truck with a laugh.

"And this is just the beginning!" Noella's hand flew up to cover her mouth. "Danny!"

"What?" He froze. Was there a spider on the seat with him? A snake on the floorboard? Wait. What kind of self-respecting snake would be out and about at the tail-end of November in the Ozarks?

"I am Canadian!"

His blood pressure slowly went down as he accepted that there was no imminent threat to his life.

"You're right." He gave her a goofy grin. "I

guess we'll have a little more paperwork than the average couple, won't we?"

"Mais oui!" She didn't have a clue where to begin, either. She hadn't come expecting to marry a U.S. citizen.

"So. We haven't talked about this." He shifted to face her more directly. "I mean, where we'll live after we get married. Do you want to stay in Fireclay?"

"Yes, I do."

"Then…" He drummed his fingers on his steering wheel. "Let's go see my attorney, Mr. Anderson."

Her jaw dropped. "You have an attorney?"

He grinned and explained that he'd needed help setting up his business years ago.

"We go over the paperwork every couple of years," he shrugged, "so yeah, I sort of have an attorney."

While it wasn't the most romantic way to celebrate their engagement, it turned out to be the best thing they could've done.

"Now, I'm not an immigration attorney," Mr. Anderson cautioned them for the second or third time as they rose to leave. "I'll have to do some checking up on the process and all, but don't worry, we'll get it squared away for you."

"And you'll keep it confidential, of course?" Danny half-asked, half-reminded.

"Absolutively," Mr. Anderson promised solemnly. He shook both of their hands and saw them to the front door.

"Oh my." Dazed, Noella fell back against her seat in the truck afterward. "We were so lucky he could see us right away!"

"That's a fact," Danny agreed as he started the engine once more. "I think I need something to eat."

"And then we should go home." She was hungry too, but felt guilty that they'd left Caesar with Toni for so long.

"Yeah." Leaving the truck in park, he pressed a leisurely kiss to her soft lips. "We'll go home."

It truly felt like a homecoming to her as she slid out of the truck and into his arms. Caesar interrupted, which would be a part of her new life as well.

"Thank you, Toni!" She waved at the woman, who wriggled her eyebrows in response.

"Think she knows something is up?" Danny joked. He still wasn't used to having an audience when he kissed her. Well. Besides Caesar.

"Hey, you!" She hugged her dog and made a face. "Eww, you smell like a dog."

Danny cracked up, but helped her give him a bath anyway.

"We want you to make a good first impression on my dad," he told a mildly annoyed Caesar as he finished towel-drying him.

"Speaking of parents." She gathered the dirty towels and carried them over to the washer like

Toni had taught her. "We should probably tell ours."

"Yeah." He frowned thoughtfully as he cleaned up the tub area. "Who should we tell first?"

She bit her lip. "I don't know."

He ran his fingers through already rumpled hair. "You've met my dad casually, right? I mean, you'd wave at each other if you saw him in the store?"

Chuckling, she nodded. "Yes, that's about it."

"I haven't even talked with your parents." His eyes widened in alarm. "Hey, I didn't ask your dad!"

"Ask my dad?" she echoed, pressing the final button on the washer.

"For your hand."

Confused, she got as far as looking at her hands before his meaning struck her. "Danny." She rested her palms on his chest and could feel his heart pounding away like a heavy surf against the docks.

"Yeah?"

"Come. Let's go call my parents." She tucked her arm through his. "Then we will call your dad. Then Grace."

"Grace?" He snapped out of his panic about asking her dad.

"Oui, she, um," Noella swallowed the assumption that there was a marriage in the offing there as well. "And then Harmony and Merry…" She hastily changed the subject.

"And Chuck and Toni," he laughed.

Caesar bounded ahead of them into the clearing, barking ecstatically. Neither of them realized that they'd left the bag with their wedding bands sitting on the counter in the kennel.

Danny fidgeted while Noella booted up her laptop. He agreed that a video chat would be the best way to do this, he just couldn't stop thinking of ways things could go wrong.

"You're sure I look alright?" he asked for the third time.

"Darling." She straightened away from where she'd been about to start the call. "I am the wrong person to ask, no? To me, you are always handsome." Coming up on her toes she smoothed his hair and collar. As her heels slowly settled to the ground, she asked, "You're sure you want to do this?"

"I have to." He ran his fingers through her hair, not sure if he was helping or not. "How can I raise sons to be respectful young men if I don't actually do what I believe is respectful?" He marveled at how easily he spoke of their future children. A few weeks ago, he'd thought of himself as 'too young' to be a parent.

Her cheeks pinked at his words, but she leaned into his palm. "And our daughters?"

"I'm hoping they take after you." The thought

of little Noella's running around conquering the world made him dizzy with elation.

For a long moment, they held each other, basking in the future glow.

Danny took a deep breath. Reached down and hit the button.

"Danny!" Hastily, she stepped out of his arms and seated him on the couch. Was casually adjusting the monitor on her laptop for the best angle when her mother's face appeared on the screen.

"Bonjour, ma fille! Je… Oh." Abigail peered at her device, apparently having noticed something out of the ordinary. "I can hardly see you, the room is so dark."

"I'll get it." Danny hopped up and switched the light on, blissfully unaware of the raised eyebrows and excited nods the women were exchanging.

Noella smoothed her expression in time to smile at him as he returned.

"Um. Did we lose the connection?" He didn't think so. The laptop was still showing a cozy-looking kitchen, but her mother… He jumped when not one, but two faces appeared on the screen.

"Papa!" Noella blew kisses and greeted her father happily. She squeezed Danny's hand apologetically as they rambled briefly in French, then dove in headfirst. "Papa. Mama. I want you to meet Danny Fitzsimmons," she stumbled here, not having planned her words in advance, "my boyf—um, fiancé."

"Well, well." Bernold squinted at the screen. "Stand up, boy. Let's have a look at you."

Startled, Danny looked sideways at Noella to see if he was joking.

"I'll have to move the laptop back." She hadn't really known what to expect and was nearly as surprised as Danny.

"Okay." Danny got up and…and what? Was he supposed to flex? No, probably not. A short list of things he could possibly do ran through his mind, each more bizarre than the last.

"Turn around," Bernold prompted.

Danny complied unhappily.

"I don't know." Bernold frowned. "He's pretty skinny."

Noella opened her mouth to object, but her mother beat her to it, slapping his arm and whispering furiously in French.

"My name is Danny, Brother Cormier." Danny did his best to meet the man's eyes, though it wasn't easy via imperfect tech. "I'm twenty-three years old, I have my own business, and we're currently standing in my home. I'm sorry that I didn't reach out to you sooner, sir. A man has a right to meet the man his daughter's thinking of marrying."

Bernold straightened slowly. "Danny, if you know my Noella at all, you know she has made up her own mind."

"Yes, sir." Danny looked past the laptop to the woman he loved. "She does everything with her whole heart."

A slow smile spread across her father's broad, weathered face. "Yes. Yes, you do know her."

"I've asked her to marry me, Brother Cormier."

"Call me Bernie." Papa rested his forearms on the table before him. "And where will you marry her?"

"In the temple, Bernie, though we haven't decided which one yet."

"Good." He nodded his approval. "You pick one close by us, eh? Then Mama and me, we come, too."

A warmth started in Danny's heart and spread to his limbs as the older man's implicit approval sank in.

"We will, Papa." Noella came to stand by Danny and rested her head against his shoulder. "We will."

Caesar barked then, and stole the show. Bernie wanted to know everything about the big dog, especially when he learned Caesar was ex-military.

Noella put her laptop back on the table and they settled on the couch for a long chat, complete with Caesar's teddy bear.

They might've gone on talking the day away if a doorbell hadn't sounded.

Bernie frowned as he looked around. "Who would ring our bell?"

"That isn't ours," laughed Abigail. "At least, I don't think it is." Grinning at the camera, she explained, "It's been so long since anyone has used it, we've forgotten what it sounds like!"

"I'm afraid it's mine." Danny wasn't expecting anyone, but obviously someone had arrived. "I better get it." He swept her hand up for a kiss. "It was good to meet you two. I can't wait to do it in person."

Noella wrangled her parents for another minute, trying and failing to field their barrage of questions, then laughed as she waved goodbye.

"I'll call tomorrow," she promised. Finally closing her laptop, she slumped back onto the couch, exhausted from the experience.

A man's voice, not Danny's, floated around the corner to her and she frowned. Pizza? On Thanksgiving eve? But no, there was no delivery car in the driveway. Also, this voice was sort of familiar. Like she'd heard it before and often enough to remember it. Almost.

Furrowing her brow, she listened intently. One word suddenly stood out from the rest. *Dad.*

Leaping to her feet, Noella tugged her shirt down smooth, then touched her hair, wishing she'd thought to style it that morning. It hadn't seemed important at the time. Danny liked it no matter how she wore it, but…

Alec Fitzsimmons entered the room a step ahead of his son. "Noella!"

She felt about nine years old as his right hand engulfed hers for a firm handshake.

"I didn't expect to find you here."

She didn't have to guess at the meaning of the look he shot Danny, who tugged at his collar in response.

"Dad." Danny cleared his throat. "We have something to tell you."

Alec looked from Danny to Noella and back again, his eyes lingering on their matching necklace cords. They felt oddly significant. His throat tightened until he couldn't speak, so he gestured for Danny to continue.

"I've asked Noella to marry me."

She slipped her hand into Danny's. "And I have agreed."

Alec wiped at a tear, then grabbed them both in a bear hug that lifted them off their feet.

"Congratulations!"

"Whoa!" Chuck, who'd only come over to return the bag he'd found Toni snooping into, nearly fell backward into the hallway in surprise.

"Congratulations?" Toni peeked around Chuck. "For what?"

Chuck rolled his eyes. "Honey," he modulated his tone to hide his exasperation, "if it's any of our business, they'll us when they're ready." Holding up the bag, he mouthed *sorry* and set it on the nearest flat surface.

"I'm ready." Danny quirked an eyebrow at Noella, who was struggling to get her breath back. She gave him a smile and a nod. "We're engaged!"

Toni squealed and ducked around Chuck to seize Noella's hand. "Wow, Danny." She bumped him with her shoulder when she found a bare ring finger. "I gotta hand it to you. You really know how to pick out a ring!"

Noella burst out laughing at Chuck's chagrined expression. "This is why we drove into town today!"

Toni's jaw dropped. "Wait. He seriously asked you without a ring?" Remembering the bag she'd found with jeweler's boxes inside, she was mystified by Noella's bare ring finger.

"I didn't exactly plan it." Danny began to defend himself, but Noella squeezed his arm.

"Alec, are you hungry?" She sweetly commandeered the conversation.

"Yes, a little." Alec absent-mindedly patted Caesar's head. "Danny and I usually order a pizza."

Noella paled. "But not tonight, the night before Thanksgiving!" Catching Toni's hand, she backed toward the kitchen. "I will prepare something."

Danny saw her wink at Toni as they left and wondered if he should be worried.

"She's a great cook," was all he could think to say.

Toni peppered her with questions while she rounded up what she needed for a hasty sit-down meal. They kept coming even when Noella set her to work buttering bread.

"What did he mean when he said he didn't plan to propose? Did you leave your ring in town to get sized? Do your parents know? You *didn't* get a ring? Then why did you go into town?"

Noella fielded the questions as graciously as she could, but finally gave in with a laugh. "We got engagement necklaces. Now, go get the others so I only have to explain it once tonight."

For all Noella knew, Danny had already explained it to Chuck and his father, but she needed a minute to breathe.

She basked in Alec's praise of the simple meal and sent Chuck grateful looks when he distracted Toni, who was being uncharacteristically gregarious.

Danny, seeing what was happening, waited until they were cleaning up then casually asked, "How did things go in the cabin last night?"

"Slept like a baby." Toni froze. Blushed.

Ignoring her slip, Danny turned to Noella. "Would you feel alright staying there alone with him tonight?"

Her eyes lit up. "Yes, I am sure we would be fine."

"Okay, we'll give that a try." Turning on the dishwasher, he smiled at Chuck, who nodded back surreptitiously. "He's done great with all the company."

"Sounds good." Chuck had his jacket on in an instant. "Hate to eat and run, but we have to get to be early tonight." Wrapping Toni in her coat, he whisked her out the door.

Watching Danny and Noella exchange relieved looks, Alec decided they wanted to be alone. Which was understandable.

"Guess I'll get ready for bed," he announced as he got up from the table.

"Are you sure?" Danny frowned, suddenly worried. They usually stayed up and talked until the wee hours. Which for them was nine or ten at night.

The question caught Alec in the middle of a fake yawn.

Noella, guessing what had happened, tried to untangle the situation. "Goodness! I almost forgot my laptop! I have so much work to do tonight if I'm going to help tomorrow." A slight exaggeration since the meal was more or less taken care of. Danny apparently always roasted the turkey and Toni was bringing fresh rolls.

"Don't stay up too late," Danny cautioned, holding her coat for her when she returned. "We should do a few drills in the morning with Caesar. Too much variation in his routine could make him anxious."

She smiled at Alec. "Good night!"

Chapter 17

"Flour. Sugar." Danny carried the containers over and set them on the table by the other things Noella was asking for. "The spices are in that cupboard over there. And you already know where the measuring cups and things are."

"Yes, perfect." She rewarded him with a peck on the cheek, then shooed him out of the kitchen.

"Hang on, now." Catching her around the waist, he eased closer. "Won't you need my expert assistance?"

Tapping him on the nose, she teased, "The dog trainer is also a baker?"

"Mmm…" Honesty compelled him to answer, "No, not exactly. But I am a fantastic taste tester."

"Go." She ducked away from a kiss with a laugh and shooed him out of the kitchen. "Take Caesar for a walk or something."

"I suppose I could check on the kennels," he offered reluctantly.

"Perfect. Have fun!"

Finally alone in her element, Noella rolled up her sleeves and rolled out the pie dough. She didn't want to overdo it, so she settled for a pumpkin pie, a pecan pie, and lemon meringue. Next year, when they'd all had a little more warning, she'd work in some traditional Acadian dishes.

Caesar followed her around, whining worriedly, until she stopped what she was doing to give him a big hug and a short pep talk in French. His ears pricked up when she asked him where his teddy bear was, and he promptly trotted off to get it.

Whispering a prayer of thanks for doggie doors, Noella washed her hands and resumed baking. Much to her amusement, Caesar returned a few minutes later and curled up with his teddy bear in a corner of the kitchen, where he fell fast asleep.

She smiled a little every time her necklace bumped against her skin as she straightened up. She didn't know everything about her future, but she knew she'd made the right decision.

The feast itself was almost as good as being at home on Prince Edward Island for Sunday dinner, though the group was much smaller. And, of course, there was no seafood. She made a mental note to add some next year.

At her coaxing, they retired to the front room between courses for an impromptu talent show. Since it was her idea, Noella went first, playing a simple jig on her violin. Chuck bravely performed second, juggling tennis balls. Toni sang a Christmas carol, and Danny and Alec performed a ridiculous skit called 'Who's on First?'

"Alright." Danny tugged Noella up out of the recliner. "Now that we've all sung for our supper, so to speak, how about some dessert?"

The compliments flowed freely, making Noella blush despite herself. After that it was five very full people trying not to fall asleep while they watched a Christmas movie at Toni's request.

Noella picked a spot on the floor next to Caesar, who had started chewing on his teddy bear. She made a point of rubbing his tummy and whispering to him until he relaxed.

It was late by the time the movie ended, and she got caught yawning when they turned the lights back on.

"Second the motion." Alec grinned at her.

"Third!" Toni piped up.

They all laughed and exchanged hugs before Toni and Chuck headed home.

"You two make yourselves scarce for a while," Alec admonished, pulling a box of plastic wrap out of a cupboard. "I'll tidy up what's left, which isn't much, then I'm going to go to bed."

"See you in the morning?" Danny clarified, accepting the coat Noella handed him.

"I'll be here," Alec promised.

In the end, Alec outstayed Noella, who had to head back to Cadmia on Friday for the rehearsal.

"You're sure you have to be there?" Danny asked as he carried Noella's bag to her car Saturday morning.

"It is bad luck for the director to be absent at the first rehearsal," she improvised.

"Yeah." He scratched his head. "I guess I can

see that."

"And I will see *you* on Tuesday?" She rested her hands on his chest and waited for him to put his arms around her. She loved the feeling of security she found in his embrace.

"I'll be on your doorstep with Caesar and his gear." Trailing kisses down her cheek, he observed, "Usually I recommend people have their backyard fenced before bringing their dog home, but since you'll be here permanently soon…" They hadn't actually decided on a date and this was his way of prompting her.

Chuckling, she touched her lips to his. "How soon?"

"Break it up, you two." Toni came out of the office, nose more or less buried in papers. "Danny, you're going to have to bite the bullet and call this guy."

Noella's moment slipped away when Danny groaned and rubbed a hand over his face.

"Don't tell me he's done it again?" He hugged Noella close, then stepped away with a grimace. "Duty calls." Halfway to Toni, he stopped and looked back. "Tuesday."

Her heart light again, she nodded and waved. "Go with him," she prompted Caesar, pointing at Danny.

The dog obediently sat beside Danny, though he, too, looked sadly after Noella when she drove away.

Her phone rang just as she crossed the county

line.

"Hello?" Not for the first time, Noella felt grateful that her phone could channel the call through her car stereo.

"I got an email from Helen Montgomery," Harmony announced without preamble. "She said yes."

Noella squealed in delight. "Perfect! We have our draw!" Squinting at the road ahead, she casually begged, "And our parents?"

"Oh, good grief." Harmony's exasperation came through loud and clear. "In a town of two thousand people you can't find someone else to play those roles?"

"It is short notice!" Noella squirmed. "Sort of."

"Yeah, I'll sort of..." Harmony broke off mid-threat to sigh. "Does it have to be Grant?"

Noella smirked at her near-whine. "There is someone else you would prefer to kiss in front of an audience?"

Harmony hung up without answering and Noella laughed the rest of the way to the community center. Hopefully, the day's warmer weather would mean a warmer building.

"Eww." She covered her nose with her scarf as she opened the door. "What is that smell?"

Leaving her things in the auditorium, she tracked the odor to the classrooms that lined the outer wall. Specifically, the odor was coming from the hanging fluorescent lights. In *every one* of the classrooms. As she left the last room, she spotted something on the dark carpet. A shrimp? Not just any shrimp. A professionally prepared shrimp, such as one might get from the store. From Stock's, even.

"What in the world?" A woman's voice echoed down the hallway as Noella retraced her steps to the auditorium.

"Did something die in here?" asked a younger, male voice.

Noella grabbed her things and marched past Judy and Josh. "Come with me. We cannot rehearse here today."

Bewildered, they followed her to the door, which she locked behind them. Leaning against the building, she sucked in several lungfuls of clean, fresh air.

Fran and Heather pulled up at the same moment and got out, worried expressions on their faces.

"Is everything alright?" Fran asked, hurrying up.

"Not exactly." Judy scrubbed her nose and wished she hadn't been five minutes early.

"I have an idea." Noella pasted on a professional smile. "Excuse me a moment?"

Walking a few steps away, she pulled out her phone and called Father Tom. As she waited for him to answer, she heard an engine start. Reflexively glancing toward the sound, she stared in shock at none other than Tammy Arnold, driving away from the scene of the crime.

The mental image stayed with Noella all through the rehearsal and came up later over supper at Blinky's.

"The way you describe it," Harmony interrupted her retelling of the moment, "I'm surprised she didn't wave at you on her way past."

"Perhaps she will next time." Noella massaged her temples. The noise level at Blinky's on a Saturday guaranteed they wouldn't be overheard, but did nothing to ease her headache.

"*Next* time?" Harmony scowled as she dunked one of Noella's fries in ketchup and ate it.

"Oui." Shoving her half-eaten burger aside, Noella put her elbows on the table. Ticked off the events on her fingers. "First, I get committee approval with no help from the committee. Next, someone mysteriously takes down all my flyers." She hesitated. She only knew that because Miss Birdie told her. "Just as mysteriously, they go back up, which I do not understand. But third, people go out of their way to tell me how sorry they are Mrs. Arnold's children will not be in the play."

"Maybe if they'd showed up at the audition," Harmony muttered.

"And now, this! This…rotten shrimp." She felt a sudden kinship with the cartoon characters who got so frustrated that smoke came out their ears.

"With her conveniently on hand to watch the

results of her sabotage." Harmony twisted the straw of her shake. "Yeah. She probably will try again if she figures it's the only way to stop you."

"Wait. This is an idea." Noella sat up. "Yes, I think it will work." Her forehead creased as she thought it through. "Father Tom will let us keep using the kitchen, I am sure of that."

"Hello?" Harmony waved a hand in front of Noella's face. "*What* will work?"

Noella grinned and filled her in.

"I like it." Harmony shoved the plate with Noella's burger back where it belonged. "Now eat. Tomorrow's fast Sunday."

Noella delicately lifted the top bun and rearranged the remaining pickles while Harmony's eyes narrowed.

"You have asked Grant about the play?" The expected explosion didn't come and Noella peeked at Harmony through her lashes.

"Actually." Harmony wiped her mouth, then her fingers, stalling. "I did." Her eyes flicked toward Noella. Returned to studying her food. "And he said yes."

Noella's headache vanished in a surge of elation. "Magnifique!" She squealed.

Harmony glared at everyone who turned to look. Next, she glared at Noella. "We are not kissing at rehearsals," she hissed.

"No problem." She took a bite of her burger and winked. "I'm sure you get enough practice as it is."

Harmony crumpled her napkin savagely. It was none of Noella's business, but Grant had never kissed her. Not even when she wanted him to.

"When are you going to clean out the building?"

Noella swallowed her food and shuddered. "Monday. *Very* early." While the building was still an oversized ice box.

"I'll help you." Harmony shrugged off Noella's thanks. "I guess I'm just a glutton for punishment, that's all."

They got to the community center at sunup on Monday. Unloaded their cleaning supplies and relocated Harmony's car to the far side of the park in case Mrs. Arnold chanced by.

Two hours later, Harmony finished cleaning a light fixture and dropped the soiled paper towel into the trash bag.

"Mine's full." She slid down and tied off the bag. "Want me to take yours out, too?"

"Yes, please! Oh, another bag, please?"

Harmony tossed one up to her. "Leave it to the queen bee to pick such a ridiculously expensive sabotage." Harmony hefted the bags full of rotten shrimp.

Noella shoved damp hair out of her face. "The price, it is nothing." She leaned against her ladder wearily. "What I find most difficult to believe is that she climbed up and down ladders this many times."

Harmony snickered as she left, but it was a valid point. They'd gotten lucky in the sense that the community center had two ladders tall enough to reach the hanging light fixtures, so they only had half as much climbing to do. On the flip side, they had to check *every* light or risk missing a shrimp. They'd discovered quickly that there was just enough of a lip on top to hide the tiny shrimp from a distance.

Noella's back screamed at her when she tried to touch her toes, but a careful stretch had her up to hobbling speed.

"Just five more rooms," she promised herself. "If we leave even one room, even one shrimp behind, it will continue smelling." Thank goodness Father Tom had agreed to let her volunteer at the food kitchen tomorrow night! She couldn't have possibly done it tonight.

Two exhausted, bedraggled women limped out of the building as the sun was setting.

"You poor thing." Harmony patted her car apologetically. "We are so sorry."

Despite the chill, they rolled all four windows down partway on the drive back to Noella's.

A long, hot shower later, Noella collapsed on her couch. Despite wearing gloves while she cleaned, her fingers still reeked of shrimp. Her stomach growled weakly, but was outvoted by a jaw-popping yawn.

The sound of ecstatic barking roused her the next day. Also, the doorbell. And the knocking.

"Noella?" Danny's voice called.

"Coming!" she croaked. Stumbling over to the door, she opened it and yawned into her hand.

Caesar bounded right in, but Danny stood as if he was rooted to the spot. They'd had plenty of early morning at his training center and she'd never looked this…um…disheveled. He'd come over as early as he thought he could get away with, though, so maybe he'd taken her by surprise.

One corner of his mouth quirked up. Doggone it if she wasn't kinda cute.

"Come in, come in." Thinking she was blocking the door—he did have an enormous bag of dog food over one shoulder and had a dog bed under the other arm—she stepped aside and waved him along. *Oooh, the floor was cold!*

Shivering, she closed the door behind him. Reaching up to smooth her hair out of her face, her fingers got tangled in a knot. Suddenly, she was wide awake. Looking down at herself, she saw her bare feet and the comfy clothes she'd fallen asleep in.

Danny, who'd been trying to think of something to say, was startled by her suddenly darting past him into the back.

"Make yourself comfortable," she called before closing the bathroom door. Caesar scratched at it. Whined. Then turned in a circle and plopped himself down beside it to wait for her.

Running a finger around his collar to loosen it, Danny put the bag of dog food down by the end of the couch. Tried to piece together what little information he had. It wasn't much. Unless he was wrong, though, the droopy-eyed Noella and messy couch added up to her having slept out here instead of in her own room.

Why she would do that was anybody's guess.

A discreet check of the kitchen yielded no evidence of a recent breakfast. *Hmm.*

The bathroom door was still closed, so he took off his coat and opened the fridge. He couldn't make a fancy breakfast like she did, but maybe this once she wouldn't mind fried eggs and toast.

Emerging from the bathroom a little while later, Noella took a minute to welcome Caesar, who showed her his teddy bear as enthusiastically as if he'd just gotten it.

"Yes, it's a lovely bear, sweetheart." She kissed his head and tickled his chin. She couldn't quite bring herself to look at the man puttering in her kitchen, making something that smelled delicious.

"Shall we put your bed away? Hmm?" Climbing to her feet, she grabbed his bed and showed him where it would go in her bedroom. "Here, try it out." Kneeling by the dog bed, she patted it invitingly.

For once, he ignored her, his nose glued to the floor as he swept the bedroom, overwhelmed by all the unfamiliar smells and things to see.

"Caesar." She called him sternly. "Come." She squelched her feelings of guilt as his ears drooped. Held the hand signal until he obeyed. "If I let you get away with this now, what will you do next time?" She paraphrased Danny. "Sit. Shake." She ran him through a handful of simple commands, then told him to stay. Getting to her feet, she sauntered over to the door.

She could feel his eyes boring into her back, but she forced herself to stay strong for ten more seconds.

"Go ahead."

Dismissed from duty, the dog gleefully resumed inspecting his new home.

"Good job."

Danny's voice in her ear made her jump, which in turn made him jump.

Hands over their hearts, they stared at each other and laughed.

"C'mon." He took her by the arm and seated her at the table. "Breakfast is served."

"And such a wonderful breakfast, too!"

Danny stifled his desire for a kiss when he heard her stomach rumble. Taking his seat instead, he offered a blessing on the food, then did his best to wait patiently.

"This is so good!" Noella paused to guzzle half a glass of milk.

"Rough night?" Out of habit, he kept one eye on Caesar as the dog toured her home.

She sighed. "Yes, sort of. Harmony and I spent hours cleaning the community center yesterday."

Noticing her wince when she reached for the milk jug, he frowned. "Let me." Removing the lid, he filled her glass for her.

"Yes, please." Finishing her breakfast, she gave a contented sigh. "Thank you. That was perfect." She tilted her head back hopefully, then grimaced when her shoulder muscles started cramping.

"I think I can massage some of that pain away," Danny offered.

Her eyes widened. "That would be wonderful!"

They settled on the couch, where he worked over her shoulders and neck until she leaned back against his chest.

"I feel much better now." She tilted her head, offering a kiss that he gladly accepted.

"Me, too," he grinned, and stole another kiss. Nuzzling her hair, he reluctantly released her. "I should get the rest of Caesar's things."

"There's more?" Surprised, she got up, too.

"Not much. A few toys, things he can chew on besides your furniture. That sort of thing." He was already at the door. "We should probably take him for a walk, too."

Caesar expressed his opinion of that idea with a joyful bark and wagging tail, making Noella laugh.

She hurried into socks and shoes, only thinking of Caesar's leash as she shrugged into her coat.

"Danny," she called as she closed her door behind her. "Did you bring a leash?" She did a double-take when she spotted Hailey watching them from her driveway. "Hello! Are you ready for more gingerbread?"

Hailey shook her head.

"Yep, here's his leash." Danny turned to toss it to her, but realized she wasn't looking at him. Twisting further around, he followed her gaze to a young woman who stood nearby, her pretty face marred by a deep crease in her forehead.

"Thanks, Danny." Taking the leash, Noella walked over to Hailey, who shoved her hands deeper into her pockets as she approached. "Hailey? Is something wrong?"

The teenager shook her head more vehemently this time. Looked past her to where Danny was carrying a bundle into Noella's house.

"Your boyfriend's cute."

Noella chuckled. "Thank you, Hailey. But he's my fiancé."

Hailey gulped. "Does that mean he's moving in?"

Shocked, Noella didn't answer at once. "No," she said slowly. "It means we're getting married." Hailey's shoulders relaxed marginally. "Then, after we are married, I will move in with him."

"Oh." She scratched her nose. "He's your fee-say?"

Noella politely kept a straight face while she coached her young friend on the correct pronunciation of 'fiancé.'

Hailey's eyes widened. "Is that your dog?"

"Yes." She smiled and beckoned to Danny, who'd kept Caesar by him. "Caesar, this is my good friend, Hailey. Will you shake her hand, please?"

Danny smothered a smile as Caesar plopped his seat on the ground and offered Hailey his paw. He'd known Caesar was smart, but was genuinely impressed that the dog had picked the correct command out of an entire sentence.

"Wow!" Hailey solemnly shook the proffered paw. "Good boy!"

"And I'm Danny." He winked at Noella over Hailey's head as he offered his own 'paw' for Hailey to shake.

"Pleased to meet you." Hailey giggled, then asked Noella, "Can I bring Brit out to meet your dog?"

"We have to take Caesar for a walk now," Danny inserted quickly.

"But when we get back, we'll knock on your door and she can meet him then. Alright?" Noella compromised.

Hailey nodded excitedly and dashed off to her house.

"Sorry." Danny ran his fingers through his hair. "We had a long ride and he needs to run off some energy before he gets trapped in another new house.”

“That makes sense.” Tucking her arm through his, she started them down the street, telling him about the houses as they passed them.

Danny listened in growing wonder as she drew back the curtains and painted word pictures of the lives of the houses’ occupants. An older woman who loved her flowers lived there. A young couple with four cats was staying here. And so on through the neighborhood until they arrived back at her home.

“Ah, very good. Kirsten’s car is here.” Hailey and Brit’s mom had worked late most of last week and Noella was glad her neighbor was home already.

By the time they returned to Noella’s house to warm up, Caesar *and* Danny had been introduced to all three of her neighbors.

“Wait here, Caesar.” Noella made a mental note to get a welcome mat for him to sit on while she rubbed him down with an old towel.

“You’re sure you don’t want me to stay tonight?” Danny eyed her entertainment center and kitchen chairs. They looked better without gnaw marks on them. “He’s going to be a little overanxious.”

“I think we will be alright.” Noella tossed a rubber bone that bounced weirdly across the floor and Caesar chased it eagerly. “I will take him for another walk after we finish at the food kitchen.” Besides, she didn’t want to give Hailey the wrong impression all over again.

Chapter 18

In the end, Danny convinced her to let him stay with Caesar while she went to the food kitchen, just in case.

"I wish I could take you with me." She scratched under Caesar's chin. "But they will not let you in with the food."

Danny was ready with her jacket and she pointed at the fridge. "Help yourself to whatever looks good. The plates are in the cupboard above…" She gasped as he spun her to face him.

"We'll be fine." Danny gave her a kiss to keep her warm, then watched her until she was safely away. Rubbing his hands together, he addressed Caesar, who had already claimed a patch of carpet as his unofficial bed. "Okay, buddy. What shall we do first?"

Father Tom greeted her at the door as usual, and she was a little embarrassed to be empty-handed, but he waved it off.

"I'm just glad you're here." He hung her coat for her while she washed her hands. "Sterling has been asking after you."

"He has?" Smiling, Noella slipped on an apron. The food kitchen was only open four nights a week due to limited resources, and Sterling was a Tuesday regular. She sometimes wondered where he ate the other nights of the week, but nobody seemed to know.

"Yes, I think he was pretty distressed at first." Father Tom handed her a potato and a paring knife, then got one of each for himself. "I told him you were getting ready to adopt a dog and I think that made him feel better."

They talked briefly about Caesar before the topic shifted to the kitchen's plans for Christmas.

"We rely pretty heavily on proceeds from the charity play," he admitted. "And frankly, I'm worried."

"Worried? Why?" Rising, she started washing and chopping the potatoes. She hadn't heard anything new since, well, since spending all of yesterday sanitizing the community center.

Her breath caught. He'd insisted on being allowed to attend their rehearsal. Surely that wasn't the cause of his concern? It was a *first* rehearsal, after all, and bound to be chaotic.

"Just some things I've heard around town." Father Tom finished peeling the last potato, then gathered the peelings that had escaped. He had a small greenhouse behind his church and used whatever scraps he could as compost. "Is there anything I can do to help you with it?"

"You can tell me what you've heard." Relief loosened her tongue a bit more than she'd intended.

He chuckled. "I guess you could say it's the same old song. People complained that they were bored after having the same play five years running. Now," he joined her at the cutting boards, "they're grousing because they don't know what to expect from the new play."

She rolled her eyes. "If that is the worst you have heard, we are doing well. Besides," she started water running into a pitcher, "you can tell everyone the play is good."

"I'll do my best," he promised.

A handful of new helpers arrived and he was called away to oversee their introduction to the kitchen, leaving Noella with her mind racing.

He'd accidentally given her a great idea. Why not have others at the rehearsals? It wouldn't just help with their publicity. It would help her amateur cast, give them some experience with an audience. Yes, of course! They were rehearsing at the kitchen, so why not have their dress rehearsal for the entire kitchen group? That would give people nearly a week to purchase tickets. And with Helen Montgomery coming, even the people who came to the final rehearsal would still want to purchase tickets for the official performances.

Ohhh, she'd forgotten about Helen! She needed to post flyers announcing their big name. And maybe she should list some of the organizations that would benefit from the charity play. If only as a reminder that the play was about more than merely being entertained.

"Are we ready?" Father Tom smiled encouragingly at his nervous, temporary staff and rolled up the metal curtain at the serving area.

"Let's make people smile."

Noella worked hard until Sterling came through the line. Then, with Father Tom's nod of approval, she took a plate and joined him. They traded stories about his cat, Found, and Caesar, and were both laughing by the end of the meal.

"It was good to see ya," Sterling murmured, ducking his head shyly as he prepared to leave.

"Sterling?" From her pocket, she produced a small package. "This is for Found."

He stood there awkwardly, eyes darting around the room, before accepting the gift and tearing away the wrapping paper to reveal a cat-sized sweater.

"You made this fer Found?" His voice roughened with unshed tears.

"Yes." She cleared her throat, unprepared for his response. "I was worried that she might be too cold." Getting to her feet, she tried to laugh. "Let me know when she outgrows it and I'll make her another one."

Sterling sniffled. Wiped his nose on a napkin.

"Oh!" She held her breath as Sterling hugged her. Hugged him back. And then he was gone, his odor and a muffled 'Thanks' trailing after him.

She sniffled a little herself as she told Father Tom goodbye. His approving nod did nothing for her composure and she had to blink back tears before she trusted herself to drive.

Opening the door to her home, she found Danny lounging comfortably on her couch,

Caesar at his feet and clean dishes in her drying rack.

"Hey." He grinned and lifted his arm invitingly. "Did you have a good night?"

"Better than good." Tossing her coat over the back of the couch, she joined him, snuggling close.

"Yeah?" He kissed the top of her head and watched her pet Caesar, who'd come to put his chin on her knee.

They sat there in silence, enjoying the feeling of home inherent in each other's company.

"I better go."

"Mmm." She stayed where she was.

"It's getting late." Gently, he shifted her into a seated position. Tucked her hair behind her ear. "Going to be awfully lonely at the center this week."

Leaning into his touch, she sighed. "You…better go."

"Yeah." Getting to his feet, he stepped over Caesar and shrugged into his coat. Finding Noella at his elbow, he engulfed her in a hug.

She shivered slightly as his breath stirred her hair.

"Don't forget to walk Caesar before bed." He flinched when she slapped his chest. "Hey! I was going to offer to go with you…"

"What a wonderful idea." Going up on her tiptoes, she pressed a kiss to his cheek.

"I'm not so sure I want to now." He waited

for her to try coaxing him, but she just threw on her coat and tucked her arm through his.

"Yes, you do."

He held out for about five seconds before admitting, "Yeah, I do."

Laughing, they put Caesar on his leash and took him for a long walk on a different route than before.

"Do you know where you'll take him to play?" Danny was not impressed at the size—or lack thereof—of the backyards in this area.

"Yes, I have a friend with some property on the edge of town. She has agreed to let us play there."

Their steps slowed as they neared her home and his arm tightened around her waist.

"We're here," she observed unnecessarily.

Stopping at her front door, he bid her a tender farewell. Opened the door, pushed her and Caesar inside, then marched himself back to his truck.

Moving in something of a fog, Noella double-checked Caesar's things, then got herself ready for bed.

"Here, boy." She called Caesar over to his bed, where she surprised him with a second teddy bear. "This is Peggy. She will keep you company since I have to sleep way over there." She pointed at her own bed, an entire twelve inches away.

Caesar put Peggy by Ted and whined at Noella.

"Yes, I know." Giving his head a final pat, she crawled into bed, where she dreamt about Danny.

After tripping on an over-solicitous Caesar in the dark during the night, she put 'night light' on her shopping list.

His 'short' pre-breakfast bathroom walk wound up taking half an hour. Starving and freezing, she barely had time to make some toast before Peter's call came in.

Caesar was only mildly distracting while she worked, but demanded play time immediately afterward.

By lunch, her feet ached and her shoulders drooped.

"You, sir," she tossed a ball for him to chase in her tiny backyard, "are a lot less trouble when you have enough room to play by yourself." She finally wore him out enough that she was able to spend a few hours working on her transcription, then packed him along for the shortest shopping trip in history.

The rest of the week passed in essentially the same manner, though the night light prevented future mid-night mishaps. And, she started taking a snack along on their morning walks so that, by Friday, she felt more or less like she had things figured out.

Which was fortunate, since Grace's friend, Eddie Brooke, had agreed to oversee the stage crew and wanted to meet on Thursday. Not to mention movie night at Merry's. Caesar was the darling of the group and behaved beautifully.

She was still telling him what a good boy he was the next morning, when she looked up and saw a familiar truck in her driveway.

"Danny!" Dropping Caesar's leash, she dashed into his arms and kissed him enthusiastically.

"Wow." Holding her tightly, he spread feather-soft kisses across her face. "That kiss almost makes up for not seeing you for four days straight."

"Almost?" she asked breathlessly. A car drove by and she suddenly felt as though they were on display. "Let's go inside."

Caesar pranced over to his mat and sat patiently while she checked him over a towel.

"Not so bad today." She tossed a treat into the air and he caught it, then trotted over to his favorite corner.

"Looks like you two are getting along." Danny dropped his coat on the couch.

"It is a learning process." Laughing, she began pulling things out of her fridge. "Join me for breakfast?"

"Don't have to ask me twice." He finished setting the table and peeling an apple right as she started serving a feast of scrambled eggs with cheese, bacon, grapes, yogurt, and toast.

"Will you get the milk?"

"Huh?" He tore his eyes off her. "One cow,

coming up!"

They laughed through breakfast, then had a wonderful scripture study together. He volunteered to take Caesar for a long walk while she finished her morning business. By the time she was ready to go to rehearsal, man and dog were fast asleep in her front room.

"Danny?" She shook his shoulder. "Danny, wake up. It's time to go."

"Hmm? Go where?" He blinked up at her, still asleep enough to wonder if she was part of his dream. "Noella?"

"Yes." She tapped him lightly on the nose. "Wake up, endormi."

"End…what?"

Straightening, she picked up his jacket. "I think you would say 'sleepyhead'."

"Oh." He chuckled as he sat up and stretched. "That's me, alright." He was still yawning as he followed her outside. "My dad says I used to fall asleep tying my shoes in the mornings."

She opened the back door of her car for Caesar, who leapt in and got comfortable like he'd been a dog of leisure all his life.

"Is that seat cover washable?" he asked as he buckled himself in.

"Absolutely. And I bought *two*."

"Smart." He nodded approvingly. From what he'd seen, she was doing a good job with her new charge. Caesar certainly seemed happy.

She filled him in on the play as she drove, specifically on her plans for the updated flyers, which she stopped long enough to pick up on her way to the food kitchen.

Slipping one out of the box she'd given him to hold, he whistled admiringly. "Full color, very nice." Skimming over it, he whistled again. "Helen Mont...*the* Helen Montgomery?"

"You know her?" She parked by the food kitchen.

"It's impossible to avoid knowing about her." Getting out, he clipped the leash on Caesar's collar while she collected her copy of the script and so forth. "The teenagers in Fireclay are all her biggest fans."

"Oooh, do not let the Cadmia teens hear you say that," she warned with a wink. Secretly, she hoped that would ensure the success of this year's play. As a teen, she would have driven forty minutes to see her favorite singer without giving it a second thought.

Judy and the other mothers were already inside with Father Tom, who welcomed Danny and Caesar into the common area.

"Are you helping with the play, too, Danny?" Father Tom asked as they shook hands.

"That is brilliant!" Turning to Danny, Noella explained, "Grant and Harmony, who are playing the parents in the play, are out of town today. I was going to play both roles, but perhaps you would play the father?"

"You want me to play the workaholic dad?" Danny laughed. "I mean, if it'll help, sure, but I'll need a script to read from."

"Of course!" Noella produced a spare from her bag.

"The things I do for the woman I love." Danny chuckled as he accepted it.

Father Tom's eyebrows went up. "So that would make you Noella's boyfriend, then?"

"I'm her fiancé," Danny corrected politely.

All the women in the group suddenly swarmed them.

"Engaged?"

"When did this happen?"

"Let me see the ring!"

Danny watched, bemused, as Noella answered them each in turn. When she finished explaining about their necklaces, which they then had to display, the women were all gushing like emotional rivers.

"So unique."

"Such a story!"

"I've got to tell my niece about this. *Her* boyfriend is always saying he's saving up for a ring, but this is just as good."

Amused, Noella left them to chat.

"Hi, Josh. Freddy." She smiled at each of the junior cast members in turn. "Sarah."

"Hi." They chorused.

"How are you all doing today? Have you been practicing?"

Danny sat next to Father Tom and talked about their respective interests until Noella called everyone to attention. A few other staff members had arrived as well and they pulled their chairs into a semi-circle in preparation for the performance.

Noella pointed at Josh, who cleared his throat.

"Mom, we're home!" he yelled too loudly.

"I'm starving!" yelled Freddy at exactly the same volume.

Sarah stood there, twisting her hands and looking everywhere but at the ring of chairs in front of her.

Noella caught Josh's eye and gave a slight shake of her head when it seemed he was about to say something. Sarah knew her lines, she'd demonstrated that at their first rehearsal. This was something else.

"You boys," Sarah stumbled over the words, "are so messy."

Noella gave her a thumbs-up, then launched into her portrayal of a harried mother of three. Danny did a great job for an emergency stand-in, giving them all a better feeling for how the play would actually go.

They stopped to review things as necessary, and Noella did her best to encourage Sarah, who was struggling with stage fright.

"Think she'll get the hang of her role?" Danny asked later, tearing off another piece of tape for the flyer Noella was putting up.

"Yes, of course." She dropped a stack of the old flyers into a public trash can as they passed it. "She is just nervous. Her mother has promised me they will practice her lines each night in front of the rest of their family."

"Will it be enough?" They paused to let Caesar thoroughly investigate a park bench.

"We have another rehearsal on Saturday. A *dress* rehearsal." She shuddered for effect. "Thank goodness their costumes are just their regular clothes."

"That should help," he agreed, slipping an arm around her waist. Casually glanced around to see if they were alone enough for him to steal a kiss. "The city's really gone all out on the Christmas decorations this year."

"Yes, it is so pretty." She stopped when he did. "I think I like the clear giant, icicles better than the silver ones. They're more realistic, don't you think?"

He stole a kiss. Another. Rested his forehead against hers.

"I love clear, giant icicles."

"Do you." Unconvinced, she stole a kiss of her own.

"Uh-oh." Danny straightened as naturally as he could. "Heads up. The bee's heading straight for us."

Noella stifled a groan. Pasted on a smile and took the offense.

"Mrs. Arnold!" Walking toward the woman, Noella ignored the curl that marred the curve of the other woman's lips, and thrust a flyer at her. Good thing she'd made extra. "I'm so glad to see you. We haven't had a chance to coordinate since the last committee meeting."

"Miss Cormier." Tammy took the flyer and stuffed it into her purse without looking at it. "I've been hearing things about your efforts. None of them good, I fear."

"Oh?" Catching herself starting to worry about what Mrs. Arnold could've heard, Noella gave herself a mental shake. "Well, let me tell you some positive things. Our first two rehearsals have gone well. The stage crew and props are well in hand. Ticket sales are up."

She allowed herself a smile at that last. A group of teenage girls just happened to be bored enough to watch her put up a flyer at Stock's, and went squealing to purchase tickets as soon as they saw Helen Montgomery's name. Probably the first tickets they'd sold, but definitely not the last. She'd seen two or more of the girls on the phone with friends, demanding that they come buy tickets *now.*

"Wonderful." Mrs. Arnold's lips thinned until they were barely visible. "But I understand you have been rehearsing at the food kitchen. Not the community center."

That brought Noella up short. She'd almost forgotten her plan to out-subtle the bee. With an effort, she got her shoulders to droop slightly.

"Well, that is true."

"There's nowhere else in town that would do for a play with an audience of the size we usually have." Mrs. Arnold brightened as she spoke. "And you know how young, amateur actors are." Her tone made it clear that *she* knew. "So prone to nerves the first time they get up on the big stage. Not like my little starlets, who've been performing almost since they could walk."

Noella tried not to cringe away from the woman. Bit her lips to keep from pointing out that this created a situation where no one else got a chance to learn how to act. No. The direct approach was not for the bee. At least, not yet.

"You make a good point."

"Yes, well, you just enjoy yourself, dear. And don't worry." Mrs. Arnold patted her arm solicitously. "A show will go on." Wriggling her fingers at Danny, Mrs. Arnold turned on her heel and walked away, head held high.

"Of all the unmitigated gall," muttered Danny as he came up beside Noella. "What do you suppose she's up to?"

Noella slowly tilted her head to the side, listening to her feelings as she watched Mrs. Arnold stop to lecture a teenage boy on posture.

"It will be alright."

She spoke with such quiet conviction that Danny believed her.

Chapter 19

Noella arrived early at Harmony's next Friday. There was only one more week until the play and she was sort of relieved that she and Peter had failed to breach Netherland Transport's security that afternoon. She enjoyed the challenge, she just needed to focus on the play right now.

"Hello?" A young woman opened Harmony's door, taking Noella completely by surprise. Intelligent blue eyes, not quite as dark as Harmony's, assessed Noella. Eyed Caesar with a mix of apprehension and appreciation. A smile blossomed on her already pretty face, making it even more lovely. "You must be Noella."

"And you must be Harmony's sister." Noella fairly prickled with excitement. She was finally meeting some of Harmony's family!

"Right the first time." She stepped back. "Won't you come in, please?"

Charmed, Noella did exactly that. Her coat was off and hung in the closet before she realized...

"You haven't told me your name."

"Lydia." A firm, friendly handshake accompanied the brief introduction. "I've just finished school and have come to stay with Harmony."

"But that is wonderful!" Noella refrained from hugging her, though only just.

"I'm back here, if anyone was wondering." Harmony's sardonic voice came from the kitchen.

"She's been looking forward to this evening all day," Lydia laughed. A knock sounded at the door and she gestured for Noella to go on in. "I'll be along momentarily."

Noella rushed into the kitchen, where she verbally pounced on Harmony. "You have a sister?!" A much younger sister, come to think of it, but she kept that to herself. Caesar tugged on his leash and she signaled for him to sit. He'd have to explore later.

"The one and only." Harmony lifted a tray of tinfoil pouches out of the oven. "Hope you're hungry."

"Harmony!" Noella at once pleaded and snapped in frustration. "You never told me you had a sister."

"She never told anyone." Lydia led their next guest into the room. "Which we'll explain once we're all here."

Grace and Noella exchanged exasperated glances. Merry was never late, but how could they wait when Lydia was being so mysterious?

"I'll get that," Lydia announced as the doorbell rang.

Harmony shook her head. "Have to give the girl credit for dramatics." She held up both hands when Grace and Noella started to talk at the same time. "Bear with us, please. We've… we've earned the right to a little recreational drama."

Recreational drama? Noella turned the words over in her mind, trying to see them from Harmony's point of view. The implication was that she dealt with a great deal of real-life drama. Yet, as far as Noella knew, Harmony lived modestly, running her own business delivering allergen-free products to families in the area.

She did have her own plane, though. Who had their own plane?

"Merry, thank goodness you're here!" Grace grabbed her friend's hand and hauled the startled woman over to the kitchen table. "They refused to tell us anything until you came."

"A whole three minutes." Harmony's lips twitched. "Gather round, folks. We'll talk while we eat."

"Is it alright," Noella caught her arm, "if I let Caesar off the leash?"

"Sure, go ahead." Harmony scratched Caesar's ears, remembering how well he'd behaved at Merry's last week. "He's a good boy."

Lydia brought over some drinks from the fridge and Harmony passed out the tinfoil pouches. Lydia offered a heartfelt prayer of gratitude that settled some of the impatience the others were feeling, then looked meaningfully at Harmony.

They all looked at Harmony and it struck Noella as funny to realize that their hostess was sitting a little lower than the rest of them because she was in a camping chair. But of course. There were five of them tonight and her apartment only had four chairs.

Harmony used her fork to open her pouch, revealing a single-serve tinfoil dinner.

"Fifteen years ago, our mother died." She painted a picture of their life after that, including a parade of unsavory women that her father brought to their very large, very expensive home. "The servants did what they could to shield us, but things kept getting worse. When it got to the point where Dad was drunk more often than he was sober," she shrugged, "I petitioned the courts for custody of my little sister."

"*Younger* sister," Lydia corrected, grinning slightly.

"You were little at the time." Harmony rolled her eyes. "Anyway, it turned into a spectacular mess. Exactly the kind of thing that earns promotions for people who make a living peddling other people's trouble in print or picture."

Noella grimaced sympathetically.

"We tried everything. Unlisted numbers. Bodyguards. Restraining orders." Harmony shuddered at a bad memory. "It was like a flea infestation. Just when we thought we'd won, they'd be all over us again."

Grace twitched perceptibly. The local vet, she had an ingrained loathing for the tiny little parasites.

"And, thanks to certain restrictions in my mom's will, my dad had to have one or both of us at home to continue sponging off the family estate." She shrugged, reluctant to go into sordid details. "He's not poor without it, but it made his life a lot easier. Naturally, when our lawyers evicted him, it was just fuel on the fire as far as the tabloids were concerned."

"You have lawyers?" Merry interrupted to ask.

"Yeah, well." Harmony squirmed. "They're sort of a necessary evil when your parents are wealthy."

"Anyway." Lydia filled the subsequent silence. "Rather than live under a microscope, we snuck out of the country and into Canada, where I stayed with friends of a friend," Lydia deliberately went light on detail, mostly out of habit, "for a few years."

"When I couldn't take the separation any longer, I arranged for her to stay with a family in New England and attend a private high school." They'd only risked in-person contact once a year, but it had been an improvement.

The sisters' eyes met across the length of the table and suddenly everyone in the room had a lump in their throats the size of a duck egg.

"Is that why you moved so much?" Merry set her fork down and wiped her mouth. "You told me once that you'd live in Portland. And I got the impression you'd spent quite a bit of time abroad, too."

"Yes, that's why." Harmony crumpled her empty tinfoil pouch. "I'd stay somewhere a while, get comfortable, and then someone would recognize me. I usually made it out of town ahead of the swarm, though there were always at least a handful of people willing to give 'tell all' interviews about me." She'd sued for libel a time or two, but didn't want to get into that.

"So… How long before you leave?" Merry asked flatly.

Noella gasped. Merry was right! If they were determined to stay ahead of the tabloids, they couldn't risk staying somewhere they might be traced to.

Harmony took a deep breath. Cocked an eyebrow at Lydia, who made a 'go ahead' gesture with her fingers.

"We've decided to stay right here for a while." She let the others protest briefly, then explained. "It turns out that out Dad is sick, ironically as the result of his degenerate lifestyle. The reporters have left him alone the last little while, now that he's relatively boring." She shifted in her chair, bringing both forearms to rest on the table and leaning on them. "Anyway, he's sick enough that the doctors aren't making any promises. We've agreed to see him tomorrow." For the first time in ten years.

Shocked, Noella stared.

All their heads swiveled toward Lydia when she spoke.

"We won't make any long-term decisions until after we've met with him." Her smile brightened. "At the moment, we really hope you're in the mood for a silly movie."

"You got it." Merry meant it, too. She'd act amused to the best of her introverted ability if it would help her friends.

"I second the motion to adjourn to the living room." Grace picked up Merry and Harmony's paper plates, stacking them on top of her own.

"Motion carried!" Noella snagged Lydia's plate with a wink. "Let's go watch a movie."

Nobody had to fake laughing at Danny Kaye's antics in *The Court Jester*. Merry and Grace even sang along, hamming it up at the ending.

There were hugs galore when it came time to leave, all three friends hugging both sisters at least twice.

"We'll all pray for you tonight," Grace promised.

"Yes, of course!" Noella agreed from where she was clipping the leash back on Caesar's collar.

"And tomorrow." Merry gripped Harmony's hand.

"Thank you."

Noella was reluctant to leave, but could tell the sisters were ready for time to themselves. Besides, Caesar's urgent tugging on the leash meant he'd had enough inactivity for now. Thank goodness the sidewalks were dry. A long walk home was just what he needed.

It might even wear her out enough to sleep, for now that she was back in the cold, crisp air, thoughts of tomorrow's dress rehearsal were racing through her mind.

Aside from tending Caesar, Noella spent the following morning finishing two important transcription projects and overhauling a small business' website so that it was cleaner, more modern, and easier to navigate. Then, for both their sakes, she took Caesar on a long run.

A cold shower dulled what was left of her nerves, leaving her calmly efficient as she helped direct her cast at the food kitchen.

"You're doing fine, Josh. Lydia." She patted the teenagers' shoulders as she passed them and sent Grant a grateful smile. Who knew that a retired doctor would be an expert potato peeler, too?

"Try again." Grant handed Josh another potato. Lydia was actually pretty good at this. "Use a shallower tilt on your knife, like this."

Noella caught Harmony watching Grant, too, a wistful expression on her face that took a little of the joy out of the proceedings for her. Now that she had a better understanding of everything Harmony had gone through, she wished even more fervently that the two of them could have their own, quiet happily ever after.

Rubbing her pendant between her fingers, Noella walked over to where Father Tom and a handful of regular volunteers were overseeing the main course—lasagna.

"Thank you so much for letting us practice here."

"That's the third time you've thanked me." He chuckled and patted her shoulder. "Really, I should be the one thanking you."

"But why?"

"Ever since you suggested I put the word out about tonight's dress rehearsal, donations have doubled. Look." He opened one of the wall freezers to reveal trays of food. "And the pantry is the same way. Not to mention the number of volunteers we've had every night for the last week." He blinked suddenly watery eyes. "We may never see any of them here again, but now they know we're here. They *know* Cadmia has people who are hungry and that, if they want to, they can do something about it."

He surprised her with a quick hug. "Honestly, I hope having the dress rehearsal here becomes a new tradition."

"Father Tom?" Sarah spoke from where she was helping her mother make rolls. "Do you really mean it? There'll be lots of people here tonight who wouldn't be here if we weren't?"

Father Tom answered her question as seriously as she'd asked it. "That's exactly what I mean, my dear."

Noella remembered that poignant moment later when Sarah appeared on stage and delivered her lines with superb confidence. She took notes throughout the performance on little things that could be improved, questions to ask Eddie, and so on.

Each child's mother took on the job of prompting them from the wings of their makeshift stage, though Fran had a bit of trouble mastering the art of whispering. Thankfully, the audience was in a jovial mood, and let that pass with kind chuckles.

The play ended with Harmony and Grant's 'make up' kiss, which was met with whistles and clapping that didn't seem to bother the couple in the least.

"I think the children should mingle a little, yes?" she asked their parents as the cast took their final bows. "Let them meet some fans?"

"They might as well practice that, too," Fran agreed pragmatically.

"Does anyone have a pen I can borrow?" Judy asked quickly.

"What do you need a pen for?" Heather was already digging in her oversized purse.

"In case someone wants Josh's autograph!"

Fran and Heather both scoffed at that, but Noella was pleased to see that the children were already out talking to the new friends they'd made at supper.

"Miss Co-mee-eh?"

She turned, barely recognizing the butchering of her last name. A middle-aged man stood a few feet away from her, tugging at his tie like it was choking him.

"Miss," he wisely refrained from a second attempt at her name, "I'm…"

"Ralph Dixon." She nodded slowly. "I remember you." She wasn't likely to forget the newspaper editor who'd dismissed her so casually.

"Yeah, well." He coughed into his hand, then stuffed both hands into his pockets. Puffing out his chest, he tried to sound magnanimous. "I've decided to do a story on your play after all, Miss Cormier. That is, if you can confirm that Helen Montgomery will be part of it." He'd seen the flyers and heard the buzz, but it bait-and-switch was an old trick. He wanted to hear the words from her own lips.

"Oui, Miss Montgomery has graciously agreed to come. Wherever we would have used a radio for the Christmas music, she will sing for us."

"How much is that gonna cost?" He asked even as he scribbled down her first response. "You know the proceeds of this play are supposed to…"

"The proceeds of this play *will* go to charity, Mr. Dixon." If her voice had gone any colder, she would've frosted the glasses he squinted at her through. "Miss Montgomery understands this and has not asked for any recompense whatsoever."

"You mean she's gonna perform for free?" His voice squeaked uncharacteristically.

"Oui, exactly. Now, you will have to pardon me, monsieur. The play is in less than a week and there are still many details I must review tonight."

"Hold on there," he protested. "I have a lot more questions for you."

She gave him a patient smile. "The play is not for or about me, Mr. Dixon. It is for the citizens of Cadmia, to give them an opportunity to help their fellow-men in this, the Christmas season."

"Uh…yeah." He frowned, apparently having trouble wrapping his mind around her answer. Was she refusing to be interviewed?

"However, if you would like to talk to our cast, with their parents," she hastily stipulated, "or interview Father Tom, who has made available to us this place to rehearse, I am sure you will find a story worth telling."

"Yeah." For a writer, Mr. Dixon was surprisingly short of words tonight. "Thanks, I'll do that."

He was long on ideas, though. He already had a story! A new play the town had never seen before. A celebrity coming to take part. *And*, a director who didn't grab the spotlight with both hands to keep it trained on herself. Yup, he was going to have to get out a late edition. Of course, what she said made sense. There was a lot more he could do with this. Follow-ups, maybe even a feature story on each of the three kids. Definitely one on the food kitchen, people lapped that stuff up this time of year. His mind spinning with the possibilities, Mr. Dixon hustled off to catch the cast.

"Never play hardball with a reporter!" Harmony's voice hissed in Noella's ear.

"Never sneak up on a play director," Noella hissed back, one hand over her nervously jumping heart. "You almost scared me to death!"

"Sorry." The twinkle in her eyes belied the apology.

Something about Harmony's awkward stance caught Noella's attention.

"Why are you hiding your hands?" Noella folded her arms across her chest to keep from trying to pull her friend's hands out where she could see them.

Harmony's face flooded with pink and she backed up several steps, with Noella following, until they were hidden behind one of the makeshift curtains.

Noella clapped both hands over her mouth as Harmony brought her hands forward, revealing a huge sparkler on her left ring finger.

"It's a lot ostentatious," Harmony half-apologized.

"You said yes!" Noella skipped straight to the point and grabbed her friend for a hug.

Harmony pulled back, her eyes narrowing. "Did you know he was planning to propose?" She hadn't even known he was going to kiss her! Right up until he cupped her face in his hands and smiled at her, she thought they were just going through the motions for practice. And *what* a kiss. She'd required prompting for her final line: "Merry Christmas to us all."

"No, of course not!" Noella looked up from where she was studying the light playing on the ring. "But if you said no, you would not be wearing a ring."

They both giggled at that.

"Danny and I are engaged as well." Noella lifted her necklace out for Harmony to see.

"What?!" Harmony burst out. "When? Why didn't you tell me?!" She turned Noella so the necklace was in better light and examined it. "Noella, that is so beautiful."

"Oui, I know." She sighed. "I only wish we did not have to wait."

"Wait? What do you mean?" Harmony hadn't even started to think about picking a date, but she was pretty sure she'd need every second in the interim to fully grasp that she was really going to marry the man she'd come to love.

"My parents want to come for the wedding and that means applying for the necessary documents, which takes time." Noella wrinkled her nose. "I am starting to see red tape everywhere!" She'd picked up that term from the lawyer and congratulated herself on finding a conversation to use it in.

"Wow, I didn't even think about that." Harmony thought for a moment. "You'll be getting married in the U.S., then?"

"That is the plan." She giggled. "I think Danny wants to get married the same day that

Alec and Grace do." At least, that was what he'd begun hinting at after Alec and Grace privately announced their engagement.

"That's sweet of him." Harmony cocked her head to one side. She thought she knew Noella enough to offer... "I'd be happy to arrange transportation for your family. If that's alright."

"You would?" Noella hugged her friend. "That would be the best wedding present ever!"

Chapter 20

"Caesar?" She frowned as he whined and put his head back on his pillow. "You don't want to go for a walk? Are you ill?"

"You took him for two walks today already," Hailey reminded her from the kitchen, where she was piping decorations on her gingerbread Christmas tree. "Are you nervous about the play tomorrow, Miss Noella?"

Noella rubbed Caesar's side and belly. "Yes, Hailey, I think I am."

"You done all your homework?"

Her forehead wrinkled as she got to her feet and faced her teenage neighbor. "I have tried to."

"It'll be alright, then." Hailey surveyed her artistry and reached for a different color frosting. "My mom says that if you do your homework and say your prayers, you'll be ready for the test."

Noella's heart lifted considerably at the tidbit of wisdom. "You know, I think she is right." Putting Caesar's leash away, she came over and washed her hands. "What do you think of the gingerbread, Brittany?"

Hailey's little sister had a mouth full of it, so she answered with two thumbs-up, making them laugh.

"I am very glad to hear that." Taking up the nearly empty bag of white frosting, she opened it to refill it.

"How many more of these are we going to make?" Hailey asked, setting the one she'd just finished aside so the frosting could dry. Trays of gingerbread were scattered and stacked around the kitchen.

"Oh, not too many." Noella winked as she picked up a gingerbread candy cane and took a bite. "I just want there to be enough for both nights."

"We sure do appreciate you getting us in." Kristen, the girls' mother, smiled as she shut off the bathroom light behind her. "We wanted to go, but those ticket prices are a little steep."

"I thought so, too." Noella shook her head. Mrs. Arnold had snuck into the stores while she wasn't looking and changed the prices with the merchants so that anybody who'd waited to buy tickets had to pay nearly twice the original cost. "But I am not 'getting you in.' No one who volunteers to help has to buy a ticket." She almost had more volunteers than she needed now, thanks to the softening of some of the committee members.

They sang Christmas carols as they bagged up the gingerbread to sell at the play, then it was time for Kristen to take her girls home for supper.

After waving goodbye to them, Noella finished cleaning her kitchen and turned on a jig to step dance to. As tired as she was, she still couldn't relax.

Picking up her phone, she called Jane for a chat.

"I'm so sorry that I haven't been able to come by lately," she apologized. "I promise, after the play, was can have a wonderful supper and catch up."

"That sounds lovely, dear, and don't you worry about me. My son and his wife have come by for a surprise visit!"

"Oh, Jane, I'm so happy to hear that!" Noella wiped away a happy tear and whispered a prayer of thanks. She'd been praying that Jane would have time with her family over the holidays.

"I'm happy, too. This visit, it's an answer to my prayers." Jane sniffled quietly, then announced, "We've even got tickets to that play of yours. Front and center on opening night."

"You do?" Noella put her hand over her mouth. "I will be so glad to see you there!"

They talked a while longer, until Jane's family came in from building a snowman, then said goodnight.

As soon as she turned off her phone, her mind began racing again. It blew through her memorized list of everything she had to do tomorrow, but that wasn't the problem. Everything was ready. Except Mrs. Arnold.

Her temperature rose as she thought of the woman and she put on another jig. She danced faster and faster until Caesar ducked past her to hide in the bedroom.

Once the song finished, she took a hot shower,

then curled up on the couch in front of a classic TV Christmas DVD she'd purchased from Stock's on a whim. She laughed a little. Cried a little. Forgot about tomorrow for a while. Caesar came in to lie on the floor and she stroked his soft fur until she fell asleep.

She didn't try to eat a solid breakfast the next day, opting instead for a rare protein smoothie. They were ordering pizzas for the cast and crew, thanks to a very generous offer from Arlene Garello, the co-owner of Stock's, but she knew her own stomach well enough to pack small snacks so she could nibble as needed.

The community center was open when she arrived around noon—apparently the entire town knew where Mr. Tuttle 'hid' the keys by the sign—and she found Eddie's crew hard at work. The tables and signs for their 'concession stand' were positioned in the hallway near the double doors that led to the auditorium. Inside the room itself, rows and rows of chairs were arranged in three sections, a center and two wings, and she took a moment to make sure that there was a decent view from each of the back seats before hunting for Eddie.

"How's it going?" she asked the younger woman, bracing herself.

"Better than I expected." Eddie tugged on her short braid. "Merry and I finished setting up the kitchen counter," she pointed at the erstwhile refrigerator box on one side of the stage, "and I think we've finally got the Christmas tree running smoothly."

"Très bon." Noella nodded as if she'd never had a doubt. "The cast will be arriving soon. Show me the moving parts, please."

Eddie turned away to hide a pleased grin and whistled loudly. "Heads up! Let's do a dry run!"

Giving her small cooler of snacks to Caesar to 'guard,' Noella instructed him to sit beside her while she watched. They hadn't bothered with a prop door, just sound effects, so that was easy enough. The cardboard 'kitchen counter' was raised and lowered twice, with Eddie shouting reminders to the crew when one of the winches hung up.

"This is old equipment, people!" Eddie paced back and forth on the stage. "You have to baby it or it will have a meltdown that'll make a toddler look like a mannequin."

"She's good at this," Noella whispered to Caesar, who cocked his head to one side.

The rest of the exercise went smoothly enough that Eddie called a halt and turned to Noella for approval.

"Very good." She checked her watch. "Reset the stage, please, and show me the lights."

Eyeing the corner of the stage that was set up with a microphone and a chair for Miss Montgomery, Noella shivered with anticipation. She hoped the woman was a nice person, as well as a good vocalist.

"We're here!" Judy hustled into the auditorium. "Are we late?"

"No, not at all." Noella kept an eye on Caesar as she welcomed her cast, then looked around. "If I could have everyone's attention, please?"

Eddie whistled again, two short blasts this time, and the stage crew promptly straggled out.

"I'm not going to make a speech about tonight." She folded her hands in front of her. "This play is a tradition in Cadmia, so what can I tell you that you don't already know?" There were a few answering smiles. "We know our lines. We know our cues. Let's practice the play once more so we can have pizza." She winked at Josh, who shyly grinned back.

As planned, she declined the pizza when it came and took Caesar to the park with his tennis ball. He romped through the snow for twenty minutes, hunting for his ball in the drifts, rolling with his feet kicking wildly, and just generally making her laugh.

"What do you think, huh?" She flopped his ears lightly. "Does it look like Christmas yet?"

Every pole in sight had lights or ribbons or a hanging decoration of some sort. Storefront windows were done in red, green, and Santa. She even saw a car go by with plush antlers on its roof.

But what warmed her heart the most was witnessing a teenage boy hop off his skateboard to help a woman struggling with her packages. Hearing a family on the far side of the park laugh while they built a snowman.

"Well." Mrs. Arnold loomed up in front of her, startling her. "Resting on our laurels already, I see." She jerked back when Caesar growled at her. "Control your animal, Miss Cormier!"

"Control your tone, Mrs. Arnold." Noella motioned for Caesar to lay down, which he did, though he hadn't finished growling. "Let him see that we are friends." She held out her hand, but the other woman turned up her nose.

"I just came by to tell you that I'm ready."

"Ready? For what?" Noella didn't bother trying to hide her confusion.

"For tonight. When your celebrity doesn't show up, when your amateur play falls apart," Mrs. Arnold smoothed the front of her coat and smiled like she thought there was a photographer lurking somewhere, "I will save the day. For Cadmia."

Noella's mouth hung open as the woman sailed away. Cringed as Mrs. Arnold's elegant exit was spoiled by a driver who dared to honk at her just as if she was some common jaywalker.

"Did you hear that?" she asked Caesar, who…was wagging his tail? Curious, she followed his gaze. "Danny!" And Chuck, *and* Toni!

"It's so wonderful to see you." Noella hugged Toni, and even Chuck, who laughed.

They politely focused on an ecstatic Caesar so that Danny could kiss Noella properly.

"I've missed you," he murmured, emotion making his voice deeper than usual.

"And I, you." She stroked his cheek lovingly.

"So, how can we help?" Toni threw the tennis ball Caesar had brought to her and he chased after it, barking joyfully.

Noella pushed her hands into her coat pockets. "We have only the waiting left to do." Someone called to her from the community center and she turned to wave at Heather. "Come, let's wait inside."

Three more cars pulled up at the side door as they crossed the street, and Chuck and Danny hurried over to help carry baked goods inside.

"I…have some news." A beaming Toni put one hand on her bulging abdomen. "Though I suspect everyone knows by now."

"Congratulations!" Noella laughed and gave her friend a careful squeeze. "You will be an excellent mama."

"Thanks." Toni exhaled nervously.

They paused at the door for Noella to wipe Caesar's paws, then plunged into the chaos. Toni was almost immediately drafted by Chuck to help tape Christmas decorations on the walls between the front doors and the auditorium.

"That looks wonderful, Mrs. Tuttle." Noella gave a big smile to the woman who was overseeing the concession stand. "Can I help?"

"No dear, no, you better not get bogged down in any one little thing." Mrs. Tuttle, a plump older woman, waved her away. "We'll handle this and I'll sing out if any emergencies crop up."

Laughing, Noella obeyed. Checked the kitchen, where Danny winked at her, then stopped by the classrooms they'd turned into 'dressing rooms,' complete with paper stars listing the cast names.

Grant answered the door of the 'men's dressing room,' where Heather was helping Freddy with his shoes, and assured her everything was fine. From behind him Noella could hear Josh rehearsing his lines.

She spent a few minutes in the 'women's dressing room,' enjoying Harmony and Sarah's company.

"So you see," Harmony explained to Sarah, "I'm wearing a genuine engagement ring."

"That's soooo romantic," Sarah sighed.

Grace—who had kindly volunteered to keep track of their simple wardrobes for quick changes—sighed, too. She wouldn't trade Alec's proposal for anything, but as the three friends exchanged looks, it was clear they all agreed that being proposed to in the middle of a Christmas play *was* romantic, even if it was just a dress rehearsal.

Noella excused herself then and went to her 'office,' another repurposed classroom. A handful of spare scripts sat on a chair along with a few props they'd decided not to use. A stack of color photos from their dress rehearsal waited for cast signatures beside a box of fine-tipped markers. And on the far wall, hung her outfit.

Closing the door, Noella changed into the plum-colored shirt dress. She checked it in the mirror hung on the back of the door and buckled the loose belt.

Brushing out her braid, she redid her hair in a low chignon, grateful for hair ties and bobby pins and years of practice.

"You'll have to wait here, alright sweetheart?" She picked up the box she'd dropped off earlier in the week. She'd deliberately withheld toys that he could play with by himself, too, in preparation for this night. "I've got a surprise for you."

From the box she pulled a brand new bone for him. He trotted over and took it daintily from her fingers, then curled up on his dog bed and started to chew.

"Good boy. Stay here, alright?" She left the door open behind her and put up a 'baby' gate to keep inquisitive passersby out. "I'll be back in a while to give you another toy." She blew him a kiss and hurried to the auditorium, smiling at everyone she passed.

There were steps up to the stage for when Helen Montgomery arrived and she climbed them now, realizing she hadn't personally checked the singer's station. She'd barely reached the top step when she heard sharp clapping sounds.

"Alright, everyone. Attention." Mrs. Arnold clapped her hands as she marched into the otherwise silent room. "You two." She pointed at two Rockin' R hands. "Clear away what's on the stage. We won't be needing it."

"You there." She rounded on three perfectly innocent ticket takers. "Open the theater supply closet and start bringing out the sets marked 'Christmas.' I'll be along in a moment to make sure you get the right ones."

"Mrs. Arnold." Noella smiled from where she stood, arms folded across her chest. "You are here to help?" Like a rabbit in a canine obedience class, she was there to help!

"What else? And you do need my help rather badly, don't you?"

Noella counted the steps as she descended them, doing her best to overlook the woman's patronizing tone.

"No, thank you." She put her hands in her pockets. "A month ago, we needed your help. Two weeks ago even. But today?" She lifted her shoulders in mock apology. "No." From the corners of her eyes, she saw smiles replacing frowns and took that as encouragement.

"Noella." Her face perfectly blank, Eddie held up her phone. "Can I see you for a minute?" She'd posted someone on lookout in the lobby and a limo had just pulled up.

Noella joined her at the theater door, then

hurried out into the hallway, leaving a perplexed stage and refreshments crew alone with a very determined Mrs. Arnold.

Noella's stomach leapt into the air, tucked, and rolled, making even her last skimpy handful of nuts threaten to embarrass her right there in the lobby.

Taking a deep breath, she went to greet their celebrity guest. And *Adina Cohen?* She'd met a lot professional performers, but this was her first Broadway star. Noella tasted bile and swallowed hard.

Cameras flashed all around her while people shouted for the attention of their guests. Oh, dear. Helen looked like she was going to faint! Noella shoved aside her own nerves and took decisive action.

"You are here!" Noella addressed Helen first, offering her hand. "I am Noella Cormier. Thank you for coming, we are so excited to have you." She naturally shook hands with Adina as well, though she had to bite her tongue to keep from asking for an autograph. Glancing past them at the swelling crowds, she invited, "Will you come with me, please?"

Their footsteps echoed in the nearly empty lobby, where the sound of Mrs. Arnold's unpleasant voice reached Noella's ears all too clearly. Should she ask her guests to wait…somewhere? Ah, but they could already hear what was going on.

She offered up a silent prayer as they entered the theater area and found Mrs. Arnold continuing to harangue the entire crew.

"Enough of this nonsense." Mrs. Arnold's voice was harsh and her shoulders rigid with irritation. "We've got crowds and crowds of people out there, in the cold, waiting for this…this, this *person* who hasn't shown up and simply isn't going to." She clapped her hands sharply, oblivious to the fact that nobody was paying attention to her. "My little starlets have been practicing like mad all month and are ready to perform this evening, but the entire stage will need to be rearranged. Quickly now!"

Noella met the eyes of several of the crew members, who grinned and got back to work. Grace gave her a friendly wink, which she returned. However, when her gaze reached Eddie, she raised her eyebrows.

Eddie responded promptly by walking past Mrs. Arnold to where Noella stood with the others.

"Ms. Montgomery, my name is Eddie Brooke. Welcome to Cadmia." Eddie offered her hand. Turned to Adina, Broadway diva extraordinaire. "Mrs. Cohen. I've had the great pleasure of attending several of your performances. I'm…so honored to meet you."

Noella gave Eddie the slightest of nods, grateful for her own supporting role to take her mind off being nervous.

"My, how sweet of you to say." Adina's sincere smile took in everyone she could see as graciously as if she were a queen returning home.

"We were only expecting one singer," blurted John, Eddie's assistant. He withered when Eddie slowly turned to look at him.

"What he's trying to say," Eddie smoothly translated his words to her own satisfaction, "is that we were about to run a sound check. And though we're not sure if you'll be joining Ms. Montgomery on the stage, Mrs. Cohen, we will be happy to make the necessary arrangements if you'd like to." She hadn't spent her formative years around society's smoothest for nothing.

"We've only got six mics!" protested John in a near panic.

"John." Eddie put her hand on his shoulder and spun him so that he was facing the stage. "I just remembered that I haven't seen the cardboard turkey since this morning. Would you go find it for me, please?"

As Noella faded into the background, she couldn't help feeling a little sorry for Mrs. Arnold, who had collapsed onto a chair like a kite whose string was just cut.

"You didn't tell me you were going to have a *Broadway* star here!" Mr. Dixon hissed as he tried to slip past, intent on capturing some quotes for his article. "This is the biggest thing that's ever happened to Cadmia!" he protested as she blocked his path.

"I'm sorry, no interviews before the play." She politely overrode his insistent objections and herded him into the hall. "We begin seating in a very few minutes, Mr. Dixon." Her no-nonsense tone seemed to finally get through to him because he stopped talking and started sulking.

"I will try to arrange for you to meet her tomorrow night." She rushed on before he could get his mouth all the way open. "For now, I suggest you go interview some of her fans."

"Yeah. Hey, that's a good idea!"

"Well played." Danny slipped his arm around her as the newspaperman rushed off. "How're you holding up?"

"I am fine." He quirked an eyebrow at her and she shrugged. "At least, I will be until after tomorrow night's performance. Then I will be a nervous wreck."

He chuckled and stole a kiss before going over to help with a refreshment cart.

"You ran out of hot chocolate quickly," Noella heard him say as she re-entered the auditorium.

Helen and Adina were singing "I Will Dare," one of Helen's original compositions and Noella stopped to listen to the powerful, soaring words.

The audience started trickling in and she noticed that they were all too busy listening to talk. One father slipped his arm around his son's shoulders and gave him a smile as if to say, 'It's okay to try,' which was one of the song's multifaceted messages.

"Noella!"

Turning, Noella saw Jane immediately. Rushed over to hug her friend.

"It is so good to see you!" Noella shook hands all around with Jane's family members, then showed them to their seats. The teenagers only had eyes for the singers, naturally.

"Now don't let us keep you." This was Jane's first night out in a long time and she was enjoying herself immensely. "You go on ahead and get this show on the road!"

Laughing, Noella kissed her cheek and hurried off to check on things backstage.

Chapter 21

Noella held her breath through most of the first thirty minutes of the play. From her position behind the curtain, she could see approximately half of the audience. None of them walked out, so she allowed herself to breathe after the second major scenery shift.

Grant had just called to say he'd be working late again, and Harmony was center stage in full spotlight, giving a soliloquy on how much she missed him. Then, she decided to turn on the radio while she worked in the kitchen.

Noella heard a faint rustle of skirts on the other side of the curtain, then the sweet, throaty voice of Helen Montgomery filled the room with the cheerful "Home for the Holidays." "Jingle Bells" came next, including Adina's silky smooth soprano.

"Ugh, what is that noise?" Josh's voice cut them off rudely. "Nobody listens to music like *that* anymore, Mom."

Noella winced. She'd had to coach him on using that tone, and they both agreed he'd probably be grounded for a month if he ever tried it on his real mother!

Things got worse and worse for the family until Harmony collapsed on the couch, near tears.

"I just…I just want a *real* Christmas this year. Is that so much to ask?"

Perhaps not, but there was no one on stage to answer her. Between work and extracurricular activities, Harmony's 'family' had scattered to the four winds yet again.

The stage lights dimmed and the house lights came up, signaling intermission.

Confident in her cast and crew, Noella stepped out from behind the curtain. Under the guise of providing pens and offering new water bottles, she supervised the crowd thronging their celebrity guests.

Danny and Chuck were invaluable in that regard, helping establish a straight, mostly single file line, and handing out numbered tickets that they'd gotten from who knew where when intermission was nearly over.

"We'll resume this same line in this same order as soon as the play is over," she heard Danny's voice over the crowd. "Our guests will stay as long as they can, and Helen Montgomery will be returning tomorrow night."

She saw Helen go pale and had the strangest urge to give her a hug. Of course, that wouldn't be appropriate, so instead she looked around for Eddie, who gave her a thumb's up.

Good, everything was on schedule. Her smile drooped slightly. The second half of the play was when Grant would read the Christmas story from Luke 2. She'd very much wanted to have him also read the story from the American continent, as found in 3 Nephi 1. But as the ward mission leader had gently pointed out, unless they worked the Book of Mormon into the entire play, it probably wouldn't be well understood by the audience.

"Five minutes," Noella announced, using Helen's microphone. "The play will resume in five minutes. Please retake your seats."

An audible groan came from the back of the autograph line, but as soon as the house lights started to dim, they scurried off to their seats, precious number tickets clutched in their hands.

Inch by inch, the little family on stage found itself again over the next hour. By their 'Christmas eve,' they were all singing along with Helen and Adina while they decorated a tree and caroled their neighbors. Christmas morning was a delight as they each chose gifts for each other to open. Finally, the stage was covered in crumpled wrapping paper and empty boxes.

"Alright, everyone, you have an hour for sledding before we need to head over to Grandma and Grandpa's!"

Sarah and Freddy's characters gleefully made their final exits, stage right, but Josh lingered, a worried expression on his face.

"Aren't you coming out, Dad?"

"I'll be there in a minute," Grant promised. Looking over his shoulder at Harmony, he stage-whispered, "I need to talk to your mother first."

Josh gave him an understanding smile. "Don't take too long. I want you to show us how to zigzag."

Grant nodded and patted him on the back, then wiped his hands on his trousers as if nervous. He turned back to Harmony.

"You should go with them, darling." Harmony sounded a little breathless. Perhaps because the kiss was coming?

"I will." Grant took a stack of plates from her and set them in the cardboard sink. "I just didn't want to leave you with all of this mess to cleanup." They worked silently for a few minutes, until the stage kitchen was relatively clean.

"I wanted to apologize," he admitted abruptly, setting the broom aside.

"For what?" Harmony smiled up at him sincerely. "For giving me the perfect Christmas?"

He sighed softly and caught her hands in his. "For getting so caught up in trying to *buy* you the perfect Christmas gift that I nearly ruined Christmas for all of us."

Noella heard Helen rise once more. This was it. The big song that none of them had ever heard. That Helen had written *especially for this play*.

Lifting a hand free, Harmony touched Grant's cheek. "I will always remember what you did to make it wonderful."

As the music started, Helen hummed along, raising goosebumps on Noella's arms.

Helen's voice poured through the speakers like sunlight through a window whose curtain has been thrown aside.

"It happens every time. Every time that I remember life before you. My heart cracks a little—till you take me in your arms."

Grant complied, sweeping Harmony into an embrace that brought a gasp from the audience.

"And promise me again your hopes, your fears. Your smiles, your tears. Are all mine. Mine to share."

Grant lowered his head for the happy ending and Noella smiled as Harmony rose ever so slightly to meet him.

Helen sang with increased feeling, "I am yours and I'll be there. Every time. For all time." She continued to the second verse, her volume lowering as the stage lights dimmed. "For," she held the final notes, "all time."

The audience came to their feet to applaud the cast and yes, even the stage crew.

Then the houselights came on and the world erupted into chaos. Autographs. Selfies. Fans. Some for the cast and most for the celebrities.

Noella heaved a sigh of relief when Judy, Heather, and Fran joined their children on stage. Harmony and Grant could fend for themselves—most of the reporters hadn't stuck around for the play—so she went to rescue Helen and Adina.

"It's getting late," Noella called out over the din as the last of the numbered tickets was surrendered. "The community center is closing and I'm sure Ms. Montgomery and Mrs. Cohen need to be going."

There were groans and disappointed protests, but she held firm. The last thing the town needed was to get a bad reputation for how it treated celebrity guests.

"I'll…be here again tomorrow."

Noella couldn't help feeling puzzled. Even as Helen smiled, Noella had the strangest feeling the woman wanted nothing more than to find a hole to crawl into. A shy singing star? Well, why not, come to think of it?

Danny appeared at her side and they blocked the crowd after Helen and Adina disappeared into the wings.

"Thank you so much for coming out tonight, ladies and gentlemen." Grant flashed a mile-wide smile and hopped down off the stage. Harmony was right behind him and they started chatting and waving as they walked a group of guests toward the door.

The mood of the entire audience shifted just like that, and soon everyone was in line to leave.

"Nice move," Danny whispered to Noella, giving her shoulder a one-armed hug. From where they stood on stage, they could better appreciate how Harmony and Grant positioned themselves, one on each side of the double doors that lead into the hall. They signed programs, shook hands, and generally turned on the charm.

"Absolutely amazing." Noella looked around at a hand on her arm and smiled at Mrs. Tuttle.

"You two go on ahead. We'll take care of cleanup."

"That's very sweet of you, but that would not be fair. You've all worked so hard today."

"As have you." Mrs. Tuttle patted her arm. "But you needn't worry. We've decided," she looked over her shoulder at a small knot of people that Noella recognized as the community theater committee, "that Mrs. Arnold is indispensable after all."

Danny's arm tightened around Noella's shoulder.

"We've unanimously voted her in as head of the cleanup crew."

Noella blinked, startled. "Oh." She didn't dare say anything else. Did she? "I, um…"

"Yes. I quite agree." Mrs. Tuttle winked. "Just consider it our apology for letting her talk us into giving you such a bad time."

"All I want is for us to work as a team." The words slipped past Noella's lips.

"We will, I'm thinking, from now on. The queen has been dethroned. Long live the republic!" Mrs. Tuttle gave a determined nod and joined the others.

"How about that?" Danny brushed his lips across her temple. "You really set Cadmia on its ear."

Noella was proud of all she'd done with the play, but that faded quickly as she watched a forlorn Mrs. Arnold delicately sweeping between a row of chairs.

"Darling?" She turned to him and very nearly got kissed properly. "Danny!" Laughing, she turned her face just in time. "Would you get Caesar for me, please?" She told him how to find her 'office.'

"Be right back." He paused, his brow furrowing as she caught his arm.

"Don't hurry, alright?"

He looked past her and saw what she saw. "We'll meet you by the south exit," he promised.

Slowly, Noella descended the steps to the auditorium floor, where she got one of the rolling trash cans and started picking up discarded items.

"I don't need your help," snapped Mrs. Arnold when she saw what she was doing.

Noella raised her eyebrows and picked up another piece of trash.

Mrs. Arnold began blinking rapidly and put one fist on her hip. "Why would you want to help me, anyway? I'm a mean, meddlesome woman who thinks she can run the whole town!"

Noella considered the statement and couldn't decide if that was what someone actually said to her or if the woman was merely being overdramatic.

"Many hands make light work," she said simply.

"That's what my mother always said." Mrs. Brooke, Eddie's mother, set her expensive purse down on a nearby chair. She knew a good deal about Mrs. Arnold's underhanded tactics.

One by one others came to join Noella. Mrs. Arnold's wing of chairs was left largely to her efforts, but the rest of the floor got cleaned in a matter of minutes.

"You did a wonderful job with the play tonight." Mrs. Brooke hugged her lightly. "Thank you so much for including my Eddie."

"We couldn't have done without her." Noella smiled sincerely. She accepted accolades from each person with quiet dignity until it was just her and still-further wilted Mrs. Arnold.

"Can we not be friends?" She held her hands out slightly toward the other woman.

Mrs. Arnold emptied her dustpan into the trash can beside her. "I'm not sure I know how anymore." With an uncharacteristic meekness, she set the broom aside and began lifting out the large trash bag.

"Start with one friend." Noella mirrored her actions, tying off the bag next to her.

"I…I think I'd like that."

"Mom?" A young man entered the auditorium from the hallway. "We got the trash out of the kitchen."

A teen girl came up beside him, her face a mask of disgust. "And the *bathrooms*."

Mrs. Arnold scowled. "No attitude, young lady."

Noella hesitated, not sure what to do under the circumstances. "I have to go, but," she made eye contact with Mrs. Arnold, "call me."

"I can get that for you," volunteered the young man, hold out his hand for the trash bag Noella started to carry toward the door.

"Thank you." She smiled and slanted her eyes in his mother's direction.

"Yours, too, Mom." He hurried over and took the bag from his mother.

"Thank you, Anthony." Mrs. Arnold stared after him as if about to ask, *Who are you?*

"Goodnight." Waving, Noella started for the south exit, where Caesar greeted her happily. "Want to go for a walk?" He bounced on his front feet, making her laugh.

"Here we go." Danny opened the door, letting them out into the crisp, cold air. "Watch out," he cautioned. "Today's slush is probably back to ice at these temps."

"It was a wonderful surprise, seeing you here this evening." She wrapped her hands around his arm.

"We'll be here tomorrow, too." He nodded to answer her raised eyebrows. "Mr. and Mrs. Brooke are letting us sleep at the main house tonight." He blew out a breath. He usually slept at his dad's trailer, but with his two friends along, well… "That's a first." He slowed his steps and used the retractable leash to let Caesar range ahead. He could already see her car and wasn't quite ready to part.

"How very kind of them!" She was about to say something about Eddie and the play when she gasped. "Danny, see?" She held out her hand and showed him the flakes collecting on the palms of her gloves. "It's snowing!"

"How about that?" Smiling boyishly, he caught one on his tongue, and they both laughed. Sobering, he glanced at her. "I had an ulterior motive in coming tonight, you know."

"Oh?" She let him draw her to a stop more or less in his arms.

"Mhmm. I have good news." He smoothed a finger down the bridge of her nose, then kissed the tip of it. "Mr. Anderson called me today."

"Your lawyer?" She rested her cheek against his shoulder and felt him nod.

"He's confirmed that the paperwork for us will start after the wedding, and a friend of his is setting him up with everything we'll need to fill out." That sounded fun. Clearing his throat, he continued, "So we should be able to get married as soon as your parents can get here." Caesar tugged on the leash, which was extended all the way. Sighing, Danny shifted and started them walking again.

"I spoke to Mama about that the other day. They have many plans with family for Christmas, so they are hoping we will wait until after that."

"I don't think that'll be a problem," he chuckled. "When did you say your wedding dress will be ready?"

"Mmm, probably not until February." She frowned thoughtfully. "Isn't that when Grace and…"

"My dad are getting married. Yep." He grinned down at her. "What do you think? Will that be alright?"

"I think…" She hesitated, her mind racing over everything she'd discussed with her parents and sisters. Blessed Harmony for her offer to bring them all out for the wedding. "I think I can be ready by then." She tilted her head back invitingly.

"I was hoping you'd say that." Gently, he pressed his lips to hers.

Thank you for reading <u>Food for Thought</u>, I hope you enjoyed it!

To learn more about Grace, Merry, and Harmony, read the rest of the "Gifts of the Heart" series.

Visit me at
leacarterwrites.wixsite.com/flinch-free-fiction

More titles by Lea Carter: